DATE DUE

In Light of Shadows

In Light of of Shadows

More Gothic Tales by Izumi Kyōka

Translated and with essays by
Charles Shirō Inouye

University of Hawai'i Press
Honolulu

Library of Congress Cataloging-in-Publication Data

Izumi, Kyōka.
    In light of shadows : more gothic tales by Izumi
Kyōka ; translated and with essays by Charles Shirō
Inouye.
      p. cm.
    Contents: "A song by lantern light" — "A quiet
obsession"— "The heartvine."
    ISBN 0-8248-2824-0 (cloth : alk. paper) —
ISBN 0-8248-2894-1 (pbk. : alk. paper)
    1. Izumi, Kyōka, 1873–1939—Translations into
English.   I. Inouye, Charles Shirō. II. Title.

PL809.Z9A23 2005
895.6'342—dc22

                       2004051610

University of Hawai'i Press books are printed on acid-free
paper and meet the guidelines for permanence and durability
of the Council on Library Resources.

Designed by inari information services

Printed by The Maple-Vail Book Manufacturing Group

*For Nagae Teruyo
and Nishimoto Yoichi*

Contents

Translator's Preface

This collection follows an earlier volume of *Japanese Gothic Tales* (University of Hawai'i Press, 1996). I was gratified to see the welcome that first attempt to introduce a body of Kyōka's work to an English-reading audience received. This quixotic though gifted Japanese author, considered retrograde in his own day, is now being read by a number of readers, though in a language very different from his own and about a century after his first publications appeared. I can only hope that this second volume will continue to feed a growing interest.

I have chosen for inclusion here the famous novella *A Song by Lantern Light* (*Uta andon,* 1910) and two well-known short stories, "A Quiet Obsession" (Mayu kakushi no rei, 1924), and "The Heart-vine" (Rukōshinsō, 1939). I considered many other possibilities, works of comparable quality and importance that still await translation. My reasons for picking this particular medley are presented in the introduction and critical essays that are grouped together in a section following the stories. The essays themselves have their own coherence and resisted division. Even though it is true that much in these stories requires explanation, I was concerned that too extensive an introduction to each story might overinfluence their reading. (For this reason, I have also made a point of avoiding notes in the text altogether.) Of course, there is nothing to prevent a reader from reading the essays first, if that seems appropriate.

Those who find pleasure in these pages might take note of Cody Poulton's translations of three Kyōka plays. His *Spirits of Another Sort* (2001) introduces another, in many ways even wilder, aspect of

Kyōka's literary imagination. Given the present thirst for Japanese gothic, we should not be surprised that these plays, for the most part too outrageous to be staged in Kyōka's own day, are now being performed in translation for English-speaking audiences.

I am indebted to many who have helped me prepare the manuscript for this book. Matsumura Tomomi, friend and professor of Japanese literature at Keiō University, deserves special thanks for patiently handling numerous questions about textual difficulties. I also wish to thank Yoshiko Samuel, who carefully compared all three pieces against the originals and made many helpful suggestions, and Haruko Iwasaki, who generously spent three full days answering my lingering questions about *A Song by Lantern Light,* perhaps the most challenging of the three pieces. These texts are maddeningly complicated, delicately nuanced, and rarely annotated. If I have failed to capture their true and full power, it is not for lack of effort, both on their and my part.

Hosea Hirata, my trusted colleague at Tufts, and Howard Hibbett, my lifelong mentor, reviewed the entire manuscript. It is not an exaggeration to say that my work as a translator and critic has been inspired by the examples of both Professors Hirata and Hibbett, whose ability to negotiate between literary pleasure and scholastic precision has served as an unattainable, flowers-in-a-mirror goal for me. My thanks also to the members of the U.S.–Japan Friendship Commission, and especially to Donald Keene, whose tireless and wideranging work as a translator and scholar has established a high standard for those of us who follow.

I have also been helped by the constructive and detailed comments of two anonymous readers for the University of Hawai'i Press, some of whose suggestions I have followed. For the cover illustration, I thank Amano Yoshitaka for generously providing the image at no cost.

Finally, I would like to thank Nagae Teruyo, to whom this book is dedicated. Without her grassroots efforts as a Kanazawa citizen and dedicated internationalist this book would not have happened. If in everyone's life there is an angel or two, I must count her as one of mine. I cannot begin to thank her for the role she has played in many good things that have come my way, including the opportunity to share my love of Japan with my family and my continuing ties to the city of Kanazawa. Nagae-san introduced me to Nishimoto Yoichi, to whom this book is also dedicated. Some of my best memories of Japan are trips I took with Nishimoto to the seas and mountains around Kanazawa—fishing for squid and flounder on the Japan Sea, angling for *ayu* in the mountains of Gifu Prefecture. Suddenly, he is gone; and I miss him.

Introduction

A Literature of Shadows

Izumi Kyōka (1873–1939) was a fragile and fearful man. He had crippling phobias about bacteria, dogs, and thunder. Famously eccentric, he allowed himself to eat only a very limited number of foods that had to be prepared in special, exacting ways. These strange habits notwithstanding, he was saved from becoming a mere oddity because his fear was not simply phobia and horror but reverence and worship as well. Fear in this dual sense allowed him to make weaknesses into strengths. His inordinate and even obsessive drive to maintain an emotional balance for himself enriched his work and ultimately turned petty concerns into mythical truths.

Compelled by both dread and reverence, Kyōka became a dedicated writer of "radiant darkness," to use G. Richard Thompson's description of the gothic imagination and its particular corner of the larger Romantic garden.[1] Thompson defines the gothic spirit in this way.

> The Romantic mind . . . is divided against itself. In its optimistic phase, Romanticism, like tragedy, like Classicism, affirms a world order: but in its pessimistic phase, it agonizes over the inevitable dissociation both between man and the universe he inhabits and between the various aspects of his own psyche. As a mode of Romantic literature, the Gothic shares many Romantic impulses toward transcendent vision; but the vision is incomplete, fragmented, blurred. The Gothic also shares many tragic impulses toward ritual, the awesome, the didactic. But the high Gothic romance rarely affirms an ordered universe of man's place within it. The Gothic evokes pity and fear not to

purge them but to indulge in pain. The Gothic hero rarely comes to recognition of error and acceptance of divine order. Instead, he goes half-comprehendingly to his destruction, paralyzed with fear or raging to the end, perishing not with a prayer but with a curse or in sullen silence. For him, the world is without any apparent meaning. In *Moby-Dick,* the Gothic establishes no hopeful equilibrium, no unambiguous resolution, no affirmation of order, and the Gothic hero meets his end in isolation. In this, the Gothic is the epitome of the radiant darkness within the Romantic mind.

Were we to place Kyōka's work in a worldwide gothic tradition, as Henry J. Hughes has recently attempted to do, we would have to expand upon Thompson's understanding of the subject and reconsider the meaning of pessimism.[2] Certainly, an element of fear is common, as is transcendent vision. While the stories translated here definitely share impulses toward "ritual, the awesome, the didactic," I would hesitate to characterize the idiosyncratic space that Akutagawa Ryūnosuke described as "Kyōka's world" *(Kyōka no sekai)* as "incomplete, fragmented, and blurred" in precisely the way that is meant in Thompson's reference to "order." Those descriptors would apply to many of Kyōka's works; but the cultural context of Kyōka's incompletion is different, and the particular nuances ought to be understood.

Central to Thompson's understanding of the gothic is a higher symbolic realm of completed meaning, a place of equilibrium and order against which the gothic mind supposedly rails. The wholeness of the metaphysical realm renders rebellion isolated, silent, split, and, sometimes even meaningless. But were we carefully to work out the details of a comparative gothic in which Izumi Kyōka might find a place—along with Pu Songling, E. T. A. Hoffman, and Nathaniel Hawthorne—we might question the universality of this notion that the meaningful and the meaningless can be so easily divided, and that a rebellious and even fragmented gothic vision will necessarily close itself off from order. To be sure, Kyōka responded in a binary, romantic fashion to his particular historical moment, positing two great opposing forces—Kannon *ryoku* (the power of Kannon) on the one hand and *kishin ryoku* (the power of evil spirits) on the other. But the actual expression of his response necessarily drew from a cultural milieu in which the higher realm was neither necessarily transcendent nor a place of perfect order.

At play in the Japanese context is a developed and sophisticated appreciation of evanescence, with its attendant epistemological and ontological complexities and nuances. Reality itself is impermanent, always changing, and hard to know with perfect surety. Within this evanescent realm, Kyōka was a writer of shadows. He affirmed impermanence, though not in Poe-like rebellion so much as with Bashō-like acceptance. His stories and plays form a literary adumbration, a *kage no bungaku,* that explores and exploits the inherently *inclusive* meaning of shadows.

The Japanese term *"kage"* has a wide range of meaning. The several Chinese graphs used to write it tend to mask and compartmentalize both its ancient root and its vast reach. On the one hand, *kage* is shadow and shade, as in the shade of a tree, *ki no kage*. By extension, it is that which attends to something else, that which is attached—as a trace. But at the same time *kage* is also light, as in the light of the moon, *tsuki kage*. As both darkness and brightness, as "radiant darkness" in a *normative* sense, *kage* is a duality rather than one pole of a dyad. Thus, darkness is as real as light; and light no more real than darkness.

Kage is the thing behind, the hidden. It is an imitation. It can be a lie, or even something nefarious, as in *kage de yaru,* working in the shadows. The point of Kurosawa Akira's famous film *Kage musha* (The shadow warrior) is that the secondary can become (confused with) the primary; and when we pause to consider this ambiguity, we see that the literary consequences are potentially far-reaching. In terms of representation, the image can be as powerful as the thing itself. An object's *kage* can actually be heightened by being secondary. This is the force of similitude—the enhanced beauty of flowers in a mirror, as Kyōka's pen name expresses. *Kyō* (or *kagami*) and *ka* (or *hana*) together mean "mirror's flower," a term that derives from a Chinese couplet: moon on water, flowers in a mirror. These are images of things indirectly perceived and never obtained. Precisely because of their unavailability, the reflected manifestation can be *more* beautiful than the original. In this way, the unreachable gives a kind of pleasure rather than bitterness and despair.

Introduction

In the Japanese context, the secondary *kage* can have its own aura: the primacy of the trace, or the immediacy of the secondary state. We find a trail of footprints in the snow, and we imagine someone walking. On the wall in the sushi shop, the sumo wrestler's inked handprint provides a sign of the giant who once dined here. To meet the makers of those traces might bring joy. Yet, at times, the traces are more affecting and memorable than the people who make them, just as (according to the play) a Bunraku doll can be more evocative than a kabuki actor, a mask more expressive than a real face.

Of course, the face itself is a kind of mask. One's countenance, or *omokage,* is the appearance *(kage)* of a surface. As a surface, it is meaningful and essential. Thus, *omokage* gives identity as a similarity, as in *chichioya no omokage* (a resemblance to one's father). Or it can be a vestige, a sign of some general condition—*mukashi no omokage* (the way things used to look or be). In essence, *kage* is that which cannot be cleanly separated from something else—whether it be light from darkness, a tree from its shadow, or a child from its parent. By extension, *kage* is someone's aura or force. It is a person's beneficent connection, protection, patronage. I am well because of your *kage*. This is the proper response to the often asked greeting, "Are you well?" Rather than simply saying, "Yes, I am," the fuller elocution is, "Yes. Thanks to you" *(Hai. Okage-sama de).*

Like other formalities, this point of etiquette establishes order and connection in an evanescent world. In the face of constant change, etiquette provides order and system, though in a way that is more grounded in the present (and therefore more specific, situational, and day-to-day) than "Good-bye" (God be with you) or *"Adios"* (to God). Japanese etiquette is very often an ideal order cleansed of (or completely saturated with?) metaphysics—a concrete matter of how to bow, how to eat, how to walk, how to use space in clearly prescribed ways. As a highly stylized form of etiquette, as a recounting of a particular mythical narrative of personal salvation, Kyōka's literature of shadows establishes order amid disorder. Its critique is not of God, nor of the gods, but of this world of human life in its barbarity and lack of etiquette and beauty. By writing stories that dramatically demonstrate proper uses of the highly localized spaces we call Japan—a noodle shop, an inn in a mountain village, a cemetery—Kyōka creates meaning and definition within the ambiguities of constant change. Life is change. And in its momentary fragility there is sadness. Yet by affirming this state of sorrow, we can also find beauty, and even gothic hope and gothic peace.

Tanizaki Jun'ichirō praised Japan's shadows as a source of "immutable tranquility," a profundity that those who favor brightness might not readily understand.[3] With Kyōka, he shared an appreciation of *kage* as we find it repeatedly referenced in the three stories brought together here. In *A Song by Lantern Light* we encounter the unforgettable moonlight of Kuwana. We meet the shadowy masseur Sōzan and understand the dark plight of his faithful daughter Omie. We experience her indebtedness to Kidahachi, who must suffer and atone for his misuse of art's power. In "A Quiet Obsession" we meet Otsuya, a ghostly woman gone mad with envy, and the taciturn Isaku, a cook who obsessively sees her image upon the surface of a fishpond. In this antipsychological tale of mirrors and dimming electric bulbs, Kyōka presents us with the naked logic of the ghost story: as a past that refuses to be contained and breaks into the world of the narrator's present. Finally, in "The Heartvine," we find *kage* in the last story Kyōka wrote. We visit a Buddhist graveyard, where dim memories are recovered as evening shadows lengthen and gather. We consider death and the miraculous protection provided by the compassion of others. We end in the blueness of night, in a darkness punctuated with lantern light.

Along with these various manifestations of *kage*, lanterns figure prominently as an image of radiant darkness. Whether the colorful street lanterns of Kuwana, the swirl-patterned orb of the haunted Tottoriya, or the dragonfly lantern that soars above the temple gates on Mount Utatsu, all share a gothic luminescence. For Kyōka, lanterns mark the porous border between the dead and living. They allow an all-important trespass into the world beyond as they help to connect the living with the dead, and the dead with the living. Within the Japanese tradition, lanterns are associated with religious ritual as well as with the haunted and monstrous. They are a light surrounded by skin, the inner flame of a delicately rounded body. For Kyōka's concerns in particular, they are a wavering yet persistent radiance that invites us to watch for things that might never be, though they have to be, and are.

Notes

1. G. Richard Thompson, *Romantic Gothic Tales 1790–1840* (New York: Perennial Library, 1979), p. 43.

2. Henry J. Hughes, "Familiarity of the Strange: Japan's Gothic Tradition," *Criticism* 42, no. 1, pp. 59–89.

3. Tanizaki's famous contemplation of beautiful darkness, "*In'ei raisan*" (In praise of shadows), has been translated by Thomas J. Harper and Edward G. Seidensticker, and is made available by Leete's Island Books, 1977.

A Song by Lantern Light

A Song by Lantern Light (Uta andon, *1910) is two stories combined into one. The reader must jump back and forth between two narratives, two sets of characters, and two sites of narration until the point, near the end, where all merge. This structurally complex story is further complicated by numerous references to Jippensha Ikku's famous novel, Shank's Mare (Tōkaidō dōchū hizakurige, 1802–1809), and especially to that passage where his heroes become separated while traveling in the Ise area. It also makes great use of a nō play, The Diver, in which the heroine sacrifices herself by diving deep into the sea in order to save her son. Boldly experimental for its time, the novella has been appreciated for its flawless use of these two texts, and for a structure that anticipates the age of cinematic collage.*

1

On a cold night in mid-January, a single muffled voice recited the opening lines from Book Five, Part One, of Jippensha Ikku's famous *Shank's Mare*.

Many were the sights and tastes that delighted our two travelers as they viewed the massive, daikon-shaped pillars of the sacred shrine at Atsuta and partook of the local cuisine—the same daikon radishes topped with miso. Continuing on, they ferried themselves over seven miles of choppy waters until they arrived with thankful hearts at the safe harbor of Kuwana on the Bay of Ise. . . .

The sky was clear. As the two travelers crossed an elevated walkway, their shadows stretched out in an intense moonlight that was bright enough to bathe the stars. Moving toward the Kuwana Station exit, they took in the sight of the town's flickering lanterns and the naked forms of wintering trees that appeared here and there below them.

One man wore a black overcoat, a suitable match for the bright moon, even if cut a bit generously for his frame. On his head rested an umber fedora with two stiff-looking peaks that rose up like mountains. Certainly, its obvious newness was a breach of good style, but perhaps we can forgive this lapse of taste. Even more telling was the way he had pulled the hat down until its brim rested firmly on his ears. Along with the dangling chin strap, a defense against a possible gust of wind, the hat suggested a nod to practical necessity. Bowing to the new age, he had abandoned the straw hat of an earlier era. A few years over sixty yet still young at heart, this one likes to call himself Yajirobei, after Ikku's famous drifter.

This Yajirobei didn't seem to be carrying much in the way of luggage. In one hand was a cheap velvet suitcase with another cloth bag tied to it. In the other hand he held an umbrella that doubled as a walking stick.

Again he quoted from *Shank's Mare* as he walked. "As the text says, 'In celebration of their safe arrival in Kuwana, our two travelers feasted on the town's famous broiled clams and enjoyed numerous cups of wine.' Before we go find our inn, how about a drink near the station? I want to call you Kidahachi, but I'm afraid you're a bit old for the part. On the other hand, we've come to the place in the book where Yajirobei and Kidahachi become separated. I quote, 'Without his companion, a lonely Yajirobei trudges along the road to Ise. Fighting to hold back his tears, he checks at every trellis-fronted inn along the way—all to no avail.' And you? You, sir, are more like the new partner Yaji finds 'on the road lined with pines.' So how about a drink with my new partner? What say ye, Nejibei?"

"Oh, cut it out."

His companion made a sour face. He was four or five years

older, which put him near seventy. On his head was a brimless otter fur cap, pulled down to his white eyebrows. He wore a traditional gray wool traveling coat, baggy trousers, white socks, and leather-soled clogs. Strapped across his back was a bundle, a faded saffron *furoshiki,* fastened with a cord and tied at his chest. He also carried a cloth pouch. And although he favored the walking stick that he held in his other hand, he seemed to be a fit, good-natured fellow.

"Stop calling me Nejibei! It gives people the wrong impression. I don't mind being your partner. But 'on the road lined with pines' has a bad ring to it—like I'm a pickpocket or something." He planted his stick to emphasize the point; and like a goose forming a new formation, he quickly passed the other man and proceeded through the ticket gate.

Making a point of letting the older man pass by, Yajirobei eyed his partner, this older man who seemed to be in such a hurry to give someone a scolding. "See? Spoken like a true Nejibei! My making your acquaintance 'on the road lined with pines' doesn't necessarily mean you're a highway robber. Although I wouldn't be surprised if there was a little of that in your past!"

Yajirobei laughed at his own joke as the station attendant snatched the ticket from his hand. Stunned, he stared blankly at the fellow.

And no wonder. He was the last of the passengers to clear the gate, having dawdled along the way. The train that had brought them to Kuwana was now gleaming through the blue fields in the distance, its white plume floating dreamily toward the moon like the waft of smoke rising from the town's famous broiled clams.

Once on the other side of the ticket gate, Yajirobei resumed his recitation, unabashed. "'He soon sets off. As he walks along, he hears a traveler singing.' Hey, Nejibei-san, here's a good line.

> 'Clams boiled in soy,
> Are better than a toy.
> No gift could be so fine,
> As maidens at the shrine!
> That's dandy for me.
> Good and dandy for me!'"

"Need a ride, sir?"

There in front of the station, from a lonely row of four or five hand-drawn carriages parked in the darkness, a man with arms folded stepped forward.

Hearing his voice, Yajirobei made a crooked smile. "Many thanks, young man. What impeccable timing! Still, if it's all the same to you, why not say, 'How about a ride on my homebound packhorse?'"

"Yes, sir," responded the man. He stood blank faced.

2

Yaji waved the sleeves of his coat and pleaded like a drunk, "Come on, say it! Say 'How about a ride on my homebound packhorse?' Be a good sport and play along!"

"Sure. You want me to say 'How about a ride on my homebound packhorse?' All right. How about a ride on my homebound packhorse?" The rickshaw man rattled off the line, and seemed earnest enough as he did.

Laughing, Yaji teased him. "My friend, if you don't care for the long set phrase, then how about if I make it a bit fancier? If he gets mad when you call him Former Senior Regent Currently Priest of the Hōjō Temple, then call him Honorable Former Senior Regent Currently Priest of the Hōjō Temple. Makes all the difference, you know."

"So, please get in." Considering the deal closed, the rickshaw man ignored the rest and turned his carriage toward them.

Yajirobei glared. "What now, a carriage? That's good and dandy for me!"

"Stop joking around." Standing in the bright moonlight like a withered chrysanthemum clinging to its bamboo support, the older gentleman chided his partner. The moonlit sky seemed to make him feel the sadness of travel. "Hire the man, for heaven's sake! We have this luggage, and we have no business wandering around at night in a strange town." He half mumbled these scolding words.

"But first, we must have a 'That's good and dandy for me' or we won't be in agreement with the text. This is where Kidahachi speaks

A Song by Lantern Light

up. 'Can we ride for four *mon?*' To which the horseman replies, 'That's not so dandy for me.' And the horse neighs twice."

"Young man, don't pay attention to that fellow. Let's just get going. We'd like to you to take us to an inn called the Minatoya, near the mouth of the river."

"You'll need two rides, right?"

"I suppose. We're in a hurry." Yajirobei's partner looked back, grabbed hold of the side of the rickshaw, and climbed in. His sandaled feet pressed tiptoe against the footboards as he straddled his bag. Without bothering to take the bundle from around his neck, he simply let it bounce around on his lap.

"My fate is yours. If we die, we die together. Wait up, Nejibei!" Still giggling, Yajirobei climbed into a second carriage.

"To the Minatoya!"

"Got it."

As the two rickshaw men raced off to the edge of the square, the pale lanterns of their carriages wavered in the moonlight. Rattling over the rocky street, they sped down a narrow alley lined by wooden fences, then turned at an intersection of earthen walls. They seemed to be taking a shortcut, passing through many lonely neighborhoods. By and by, they came to a row of two-story buildings, the road between them as narrow as a thread and shadowed from the moon by overhanging eaves. Tucked into the darkness on each side were a few lanterns, glowing white; and above their heads, stars were sprayed upon the naked tendrils of willow trees, and walls were illuminated by the blue moonlight that appeared here and there in the night. At the end of a long road, a fire tower rose to pierce the mist of the distant mountains, casting the sharp silhouette of a fire bell that seemed as if it were alive, while the clapping of night guards' sticks—Beware! Beware!—sounded in the deepening night. Even though business is usually slow in January, the moonlight was still shining on the latticed windows. And yet, the girls of Kuwana seemed to be keeping early hours, for the pleasure quarter seemed quiet and desolate.

Beneath the spokes of the rickshaws the street turned into a narrow river of quicksilver. Hanging from the eaves of black-pillared houses, rows of plain and patterned lanterns looked like river otters crossing a bridge on festival night. Suddenly, the rickshaw in the lead, the one in which the older gentleman rode, came to a stop.

Listen to that! Falling over the hushed, one-street entertainment district of this small town, in the silence of the stilled wheels, came a voice that sparkled among the stars and echoed upon the crest tiles and over the moonlit waters that stretched to far-off Chikuzen, drawing its moonlight over a thousand miles of ocean, up the lapping river, pulled hand over hand like a silver thread.

> The clasp that holds his sash in place,
> Clothes softer than a pillow,
> Hardly seems a country boy,
> Smooth walking like a willow—

The sound of a Hakata ballad flowed out from the shadows of the eaves; and right there before the old man's eyes stood a street musician with his head covered with a white towel, his gaunt silhouette standing before a sign on which was written in red the word "Noodles." He was looking down and to the side, lingering like a shadow.

With his scarf-covered bundle still tied around his neck, the older traveler looked back from where he sat in his rickshaw and said something . . . just as the second rickshaw came to a sudden stop and surrounded the song, capturing it between them and the walls of the buildings that lined the street. Before Nejibei had a chance to make himself understood, his rickshaw started ahead; and the one in the rear followed in pursuit. The two carriages pulled up neck and neck for a moment, then one fell back into line behind the other; and together they continued their journey through the moonlit night.

> The rising moon, the shadows of the pines,
> *Ara, dokkoisho!*

Standing there on the corner in front of the noodle shop, the street musician suddenly ended his song with one last, frost-cutting note, as if throwing his plectrum into the cold moonlit waters of the ocean. He lifted the head of his samisen slightly and, freeing his hands, turned the plectrum around and used its handle to gently push open the faded red door of the noodle shop. It slid open easily.

A Song by Lantern Light

"Anyone home?"

The proprietor seemed to be caught off guard by the sight of the musician's clear eyes suddenly peering at him from beneath the towel on his head and through the cloud of steam that rose from the shop's boiling kettle. The owner was dressed in a striped apron, a cotton kimono with its skirts tucked up, and a pair of green pantaloons. He had been sitting next to the register, listening intently to the musician's song. It's a bit much when he jumps to his feet and shoots back, "Sorry. No solicitors!"

This is obviously his way of dealing with all itinerant musicians—to enjoy their music first, then brush them off at the crucial moment with a "No solicitors!" The problem this time is that the towel-wearing singer entered the shop so suddenly that he caught the owner completely off guard. Luckily, no customers were there to witness his behavior.

Unaffected by the comment, the one who had come in from the street simply closed the door behind him. He lifted the neck of his samisen and stepped into the shop. "No offense, my friend. I'm the customer here. Isn't that right, ma'am?" The singer chuckled as he said this.

Also enraptured by the street singer's Hakata ballad, the shop-owner's wife was standing amid the steamy haze of the hearth, with one fair-skinned arm resting atop the lid of a large pot of boiling water. She was a middle-aged woman, dressed in a teal-colored kimono with its sleeves tied up. Her hair was done up on top of her head and a bit disheveled. Her teeth were dyed black. She had a fair complexion, and blushed at the musician's comment. Quickly, she left her place by the hearth. Her wooden clogs made a dry, scraping sound as she hurried over the hardened dirt floor, past the spot where her husband sat, directly to the register, where she plunged her hand into the till.

"Oh, don't worry about that," the young man said gently. "Don't bother. This isn't extortion. I'm the customer, not you."

On one side of the shop was a narrow area covered with six worn-out tatami mats all in a row. Customers were welcome to take off their shoes and relax there. But the musician chose one of the stools near the hearth. He sat down and stretched his legs.

"Cold weather we're having tonight. Thought I'd come in and have a drink. No need to worry, old man. I'm not going to make trouble."

When he removed the towel from his head, he certainly didn't look like someone who would create an incident. He had a thin face with excellent features. Fatigue showed around his eyes, but they were clear, and his eyebrows thick and dark. He seemed a well-bred young gentleman, about twenty-eight or -nine years old.

"I see." Laughing nervously, the shopowner got off his stool and came forward, rubbing his hands. "Well, let's hope this clear weather holds up." He looked aimlessly at the soot-blackened ceiling, then glanced at the votive altar above the register.

"Young Master," the wife said as she patted her apron. "Shall I warm a flask for you then?" She smiled.

The musician placed his plectrum down on his scarf and moved the samisen around to his back. He sat down with one leg tucked beneath him. Arranging his skirts to keep out the cold, he called out, "How about something good."

"I'll bring you our best." The owner's wife shuffled sideways to the tatami area on her left. With a pair of metal chopsticks, she stirred the coals in the hibachi until they flared red, then quickly pushed them over to where the musician was sitting on his stool. "Here. Warm yourself over these."

"Thanks."

He wasted no time making himself comfortable. He positioned himself around the hibachi and let out a long sigh. "When I realize there's a wonderful fire like this in the world, I think of home. And that thought makes me feel even colder. It's freezing tonight, ma'am. Make that wine boiling hot, won't you? I have this cheap habit of trying to get as drunk as possible on as little as I can—just as you probably guessed about me. Isn't that right, sir?"

The owner chuckled. "Go ahead, Okata. Make it boiling hot."

His wife flashed her dyed teeth at the musician with a beautiful smile, "Coming right up."

4

The musician pointed toward the front door, empty *sake* cup in hand. "By the way. I just saw two rickshaws rush by with their passengers. Went down the street and stopped over on the left—a big building, judging by the roof. I could see them in the blue moonlight. Is that place an inn or something?"

"That would be the Minatoya." The woman turned from the hearth and looked at her husband. "Around here, that's the place to stay. It's been around for generations. It used to be a teahouse, but they've made it into an inn now. All the rooms have been kept just like they were in the old days. The sitting room in the back has a veranda with a railing, and right there is the mouth of the Ibi River. You can watch the white sails pass by. The sea bass leap. The mullet fly. The atmosphere is wonderful! Sometimes, though, the otters scramble up the stone embankments and play tricks. They put out the lights in the hallways and toilets. It's not like they're scary monsters, though. On a moonlit night like this, they perform gourd-drumming rites in the garden. And on rainy nights, they run errands for a few pennies. All that sort of thing amuses the customers and adds to the Minatoya's reputation. You're new to the area, I take it."

"Drifted in last night, as a matter of fact. I'm afraid I still don't know north from south. Even in this moonlight, I'm like a crow lost in the dark." He looked down and took a sip of *sake*. "I guess I should eat these noodles before they get soggy. Wow!" He rubbed his eyes and turned his head. "My, that red pepper's hot! You know, I fell into this same trap just a while ago. Should have known better, I guess. I underestimate this Kamigata pepper. Poured it on thick, since condiments are free. Seconds later, I fell off my stool. Boy, what a kick! And now I've done it again. Sorry. Crying and running at the nose at the same time. Not too sexy, right?" He wiped his nose with the back of his hand.

As she warmed a second flask of *sake,* the woman tested the temperature by touching it with her palm. "Master, you're from the East, aren't you?"

"That's right. Born in the East, but my finances have gone south." He swirled the flask around, then poured the last remaining drops into his cup.

"I guess you'll be staying at the Minatoya too," she said, but her husband thought to himself, "No way. They'll throw him out on his ear." The warmhearted fellow evidently wants to warn the young man of what to expect.

"You have to be joking. I'm afraid my accommodations are as humble as they come. Straw sandals, an umbrella, a straw mat—they're my closest friends. From their holes in the walls, the rats stick their heads out and wait longingly for my return. I'm thinking of staying here in Kuwana for four or five days. If you think I look good enough for the Minatoya, maybe I should request a night's lodging here. How about it, ma'am?"

"If you think this would do. Of course, we'd love to have you," the woman answered as she nimbly fetched more *sake*.

"Heaven forbid!" The shopowner raised his eyebrows in surprise and sat down before the register, as if to block the intruder. Until now, he'd been standing there like a scarecrow, with hands tucked into his sleeves.

"Thank you for your kind offer, ma'am. But who could stay the night at a noodle shop but the King of Soy Sauce caught in a rainstorm, or the Queen of Bonito Flakes on a pilgrimage?" He laughed to himself.

"Then allow me to pour for you, young Master." She sat on the edge of the raised tatami area and held a flask over the dirt floor.

"Please, don't bother. You're busy enough as it is."

"Not really. Most of our business is takeout for the geisha houses, and things are slow tonight, as you can see. You know, Master, you do have a marvelous voice." She glanced over at her husband. "Don't you think so, dear?"

"I guess," grumbled her husband as he puffed hard on his pipe.

"As I was listening to your Hakata ballad, I felt the music come right through my body. It gave me the shivers."

5

"Generous praise dampens the fun. I'm afraid your words might even sober me up, and that is a truly sad thought. I'm nothing but a street singer." He folded his arms and looked embarrassed.

"I'm not trying to flatter you. It's the truth. Your music is, well, chilling. It's like being tied up, or getting loose, or being thrown down. How would you describe it? It's like this. If there were a willow tree growing in the ocean, I'd want to throw myself into its reflection in the moonlight and die. It's a feeling I can't describe." She moved both shoulders and leaned toward him.

"Hey now!" The shopowner cut in, seeming put out for no reason.

"What's wrong with you?" She looked back over her shoulder at her husband. He had already taken his post beneath the votive shelf. Leaning against the register, he flipped through the pages of his account book, and glared at her.

"Didn't the Masuya take care of their bill?" He flicked his abacus noisily.

"Why now? It isn't the end of the month yet." She turned back to the musician and called him "Master."

"Master nothing. I'm talking about the Masuya's bill here!"

"If it bothers you that much, dear, why don't you just go there and get it yourself?" She stuck out her lower lip.

With a defeated look on his face, her husband started doing his bookkeeping, abacus in hand. "Four divided by two is two. Six divided by two is three." Balancing the books requires addition and subtraction, but he was doing division, like cutting a quart of soy sauce with a cup of water.

Just then, through the white steam rising from the hearth, came the piercing sound of a blind man's whistle, cold enough to freeze the stars. With the winter moon at its zenith, the noise whistled through the town like a blast of cold wind.

The street musician grasped his bony shoulders. "It pierces the frosty night!" His voice was clear and sharp, as if he were reading lines from a story. "Ma'am, a blind masseur passes by."

"Yes. Blowing his whistle."

"Damn! That sound goes right through me. So cold I can't bear it."

With his legs still crossed, he drew himself up. He tipped his teacup and emptied it on the floor. "Here, how about pouring me a drink in this. It'll save you some trouble."

"My pleasure."

"I appreciate your kindness. It's like burning twigs beneath a kettle. As soon as this wine starts to cool, it's like ice carving my throat. My whole body's going to crack apart. Fill it up."

As if waving his hand, he downed the entire cup in one gulp.

"My! Very impressive!" She looked at him with admiring eyes. "But you shouldn't overdo it, you know. I'm sure a lot of people would worry."

"Okata. What about the greengrocer's bill?" Her husband blinked and stuck out his chin.

As if toying with her man, she said, "If they come to get it, just pay it, dear." She didn't even bother to turn around and look at him.

"What was that exchange rate?" He flicked his fingers in the air, as if doing more calculations on his abacus.

"Ma'am." The musician's voice had grown subdued.

"Yes. What is it?"

"Could I bother you for another one? And right after that, another one? Do you understand what I'm saying?"

"I do. You're quite the drinker, aren't you?"

"How could I live without *sake*?" He started to speak in a cheerful voice, but he suddenly looked up at the ceiling and widened his eyes. "There it is again. A masseur's whistle. Coming from the crossroads to the north. It's still not that late, but I hear it coming over the rooftops, from the outskirts of town. A block away, maybe more. Well, let's see. Maybe he's still some place beyond the rice paddies." Nervously drawing one knee to his chest, he looked this way and that. "Another one? It's the same whistle, but a different tone. Ma'am, do you know what those masseurs look like?"

Just then, looking pale in the blue moonlight, a white-eyed man peered up at the rooftops and listened. The musician stared sharply.

A Song by Lantern Light

"Sir, you can't judge a blind man by the sound of his whistle. It's not like telling a stag from a doe."

"True." The musician gave a lonely laugh, and stared at the *sake* brimming in his teacup. He mumbled to himself and looked down at the floor. "Then let's toast, Mister Blindman. With the moon in our cups."

Was it a line from a Hakata ballad? Whatever their source, the words seemed dark and lonely, like the cold moonlight that showed through the *shōji* of the noodle shop. The blind man's whistle echoed over the cross-roads, the town, and the waves of the river.

6

"What? A masseur? Barging in on us like that. No thank you. No thanks!"

Down the street from the noodle shop, in an inner room of the Minatoya, Yajirobei sat with his partner. They seemed to be in one of the luxury suites that enjoyed a view of the water—an aging ten-mat room with a six-mat room attached. Beyond the wall of *shōji* was a veranda with a railing and a wall of glass windows; and on the other side of those windows, a cloud of mist rose into a clear sky, and a single star shone above the edge of a long sandbar, sparkling just above the Ibi River as it poured into an ocean of white fog. In the streaming moonlight, rush mats and straw raincoats were hanging out to dry, and, beyond a hedge, the masts of many moored ships.

Yajirobei was seated next to a candle stand, warming his hand over a round wooden brazier. He had a look of puzzlement on his face. "Here we are in our room, settling in for the evening. The head maid greets us, 'You must be tired.' We're all set to have dinner or maybe some wine. Then out of nowhere comes that face. We had just said goodbye to an older woman and were hoping to see a younger girl with bangs come to take her place, when in comes this melon-head from behind the door. 'Care for a massage?'

"He came out from the other side of that candle stand, like a doorman for the snow fairy making her debut at some monster's palace. He leaned forward, and sat with his legs out to the side—the collar of his kimono loose. 'Thank you, no!' I said, and he quietly backed out and disappeared into the darkness of the hallway. Good riddance!"

Yajirobei laughed wryly and looked over at his traveling partner, the bald-headed gentleman now sitting before the alcove, leaning over the warm brazier. "Nejibei, it's no fun getting old. We should be enjoying an evening of samisen music, not getting offers for a pre-dinner massage. What an insult!"

"You know, if you just acted your age a little. When that old woman with the widow's haircut came to the front door to greet us, you stared at her and said, 'Now there's a beauty for the Buddhist altar! Wish I could fall from the ceiling!' You never let up on that *Shank's Mare* business, do you? That's why strange things happen." The one called Nejibei examined the knotted alcove pillar. "Old and spacious. Solidly built. A thousand-year-old mulberry tree. A river unfathomably deep. The lamp dark, the river otters about to make their appearance. Better straighten up or something bad's going to happen."

"As you say. Something to be learned from everything." Yajirobei puffed his cheeks out and folded his arms. He looked up and read the calligraphy that was displayed in a frame above the sliding doors.

> Facing 'to the breezes,
> The sound of oars here pleases.

"Well said."

"White chrysanthemums in the alcove, casually thrown into a vase. A nice touch, I'd say."

"Now you *do* sound like an old man."

"Didn't you just say we ought to act our age? What's that! Look! Out from the sleeve of my overcoat. Behold! The fuzzy brown paw of an Ibi River otter!"

"My goodness." Nejibei glanced at the creature.

"Good heavens!" Yajirobei quickly pulled it back in.

"What was that?"

"I was born with a careless nature," Yajirobei laughed. "Since yours truly was always losing things right and left, my old lady came up with this strategy to tie my mittens together with a string. You thread them through from one sleeve to the other. Pull them out, and

put them on. Frightfully clever, don't you think? Nejibei, out of respect for my wife's thriftiness, I mustn't be extravagant with my tips!
Ah, Praise Buddha!"

"You weasel." Nejibei hunched his shoulders and turned away.
"Here comes that lady. Mum's the word! Quick!" He tucked
the glove back into his sleeve.

One of the serving women entered the room. She kneeled and
bowed, pressing both hands to the tatami. "Shall we proceed, then?"

"No. We've just kicked off our shoes. I think we'll stay. So, no
procedures, thank you." Yajirobei spoke in a serious tone.

The woman's complexion was a bit dark, though she did have
handsome features. A puzzled look formed on her face. "So you'll
be eating dinner?"

"Something to drink first would be nice."

"And what will you have for dinner?"

"Why even ask? As promised. Your famous broiled clams, of
course!"

7

"If you want broiled clams, you'll have to go to one of the roadside
stands just outside of town. They still cook them over pinecones,
which is really the only way to have them. We can only offer you
steamed ones here. We put in a little *sake* to bring out the flavor."

"I see. Those tents along the road, where they cook turbot right
in their shells. I can see them now. In the distance, the road lined
with pines, the flickering flame of burning cones, smoke rising into
the moonlit night. It would be just like feasting in the Dragon Palace,
entertained by the Princess herself, with a scarf tied over her head.
That would be nice, but not nice enough to be sneaking out on a
night like this. I guess we'll just have to make due with your steamed
clams with *sake*." With a look of approval, the old man nodded.

"You'll be having wine with your clams?"

"Come again?" He made a point of leaning over, as if he were
having a hard time hearing her.

"I mean, will you be having clams with your wine?"

"No, no. We'll be eating with chopsticks." Yajirobei laughed at his own joke and produced the fifth volume of Ikku's *Shank's Mare* from his bosom. "I swear by it!" he said and tapped his forehead.

The maid suddenly burst out laughing. "Oh, I get it. You're Yajirobei, right?"

"Precisely. On this visit to the Ise Shrine, we had reason to stay at the Gonikan. But on our way to the Inner Shrine, when we passed in front of the Fujiya in Furuichi, where we stayed before, I peered into the entrance and saw the brass brazier with lion's heads for legs gleaming in the darkness. While it wasn't exactly good manners, I took off my cap and, without getting down from my rickshaw, bowed rather casually to thank them for their earlier hospitality. Unfortunately, the street was narrow, and I showed my bald spot to the young woman standing in front of her tea shop. A most embarrassing situation." As a part of his confession, Yajirobei leaned over and pointed his spot toward the lantern light.

"Oh, my!" The maid giggled, and Nejibei, too, broke into laughter.

Had the others been waiting for this moment? When our two travelers first arrived at the Minatoya, the inn was alive with the sounds of samisen playing and drums beating. In the sitting room next to theirs, separated by a dirt-floored hallway and a zigzagging wooden bridge, a group of a dozen or so men and a few women had been making a great clamor. Around the time the blind masseur appeared, the noise suddenly receded, as if lured off to some distant shore by the river's waning tide. The low rumble of voices suddenly fell silent. But now, from that vast space came the high, piercing voices of geisha, suddenly sounding like monkeys screaming and running about. And then, as if smothering everything, came the indistinguishable, heavy sound of many people's voices suddenly reverberating like wind belching from a sea cave.

Taking advantage of the moment, the maid stood. "It *is* a bit gloomy over on our side, isn't it?"

"Just the way we like it, nice and peaceful." Nejibei hunched over the brazier and looked at the volume of *Shank's Mare,* lying on the tatami. "It just occurred to me. Since I've been having such a hard time getting to sleep, maybe I'll set up a lamp by my bed and read your book tonight."

A Song by Lantern Light

"Don't. You'll be so moved, you'll never get to sleep."

"Nonsense. Nobody cries over *Shank's Mare*. You talk about me, but you're the Nejibei here, always twisting things." Just as he spoke, the older woman came back with a helper. They brought two low serving tables and wine.

"Your clams will be done shortly."

"Great."

"But first, *sake*." Nejibei quickly took up his cup.

"And one for you. Drink up while it's nice and hot." With the slightly trembling hand of a habitual drinker, Yajirobei placed the small cup from which he had already partaken on the tatami, away from his serving table and next to the book where it was still lying on the floor. With a serious look on his face, he said, "Miss, pour a cup for him."

Noticing the blank look on the younger woman's face, the older one who was pouring for Nejibei said, "Kino, go ahead. Pour. This man here is Yajirobei. And now he's going to toast his missing partner, Kidahachi."

How quickly the woman catches on!

8

For some reason, Yajirobei's mood became subdued.

"Well said. Thank you for calling me Yajirobei. This is a comfortable place. The wine's good. If only Kidahachi really were here with us, then this truly would be *Shank's Mare*. We truly would be 'people of the great peace.' But within the fading glow of flickering candles, this seems more like a libation to a dead child in hell. I wonder what that fool's doing now." With one hand on his knee, Yajirobei stared gloomily at the *sake* cup on the tatami.

Nejibei suddenly looked away and folded his arms.

"But, sir. Why haven't you brought this Kidahachi along?" The maid smiled amiably.

Yajirobei's smile was tinged with sadness. "Well, I'll tell you. As it says in the book, Kidahachi got lost on his way to Ise. Yajirobei is old enough to understand the ways of the world, but he still likes to drink and have a good time. Life is a journey, they say. When he gets

separated from his younger companion, this man who was his staff
through heat of summer and cold of winter, he feels like a lost child
at the age of sixty. He becomes weary of constantly searching for the
Fuji-something inn, where he might find Kidahachi again. He's tired
of wandering by himself through the noisy quarters of town after
town, one disappointment after another. He throws his bones down
in front of some stranger's shop and asks for a moment's rest, completely without hope. When I read the passage, it's no joke. Nejibei,
truly, the story makes me cry." The flickering candlelight illuminated the moisture in his eyes.

"Young Lady, how about trimming the wicks for us?"

"Certainly." When she turned the other way, Nejibei, too,
blinked his eyes.

"What a party they're having over there!" Yajirobei stretched to
look at the room across the hallway. "My! They've brought out
everything, right down to the washbasins. The people are flying up
to the ceiling, skirts and all; and the plates and bowls are dancing over
the floor. The samisen is pitted against the drum in a fight to the
finish!"

"Sorry about the noise. It's that time of year when our new
draftees have to report for service. They're having a farewell party.
People are having parties everywhere these days. It's been a total
madhouse. By the time you two gentlemen are ready to retire for the
evening, though, things should have calmed down. If you could
please put up with it . . ."

"No problem at all." Yajirobei reassured both women. "To the
contrary, the livelier the better. If it gets too quiet, that blind masseur might show up again. And we don't want that."

"Masseur?" The maid repeated the word with a puzzled expression on her face.

Trying to avoid the subject, Nejibei forced a cough. "Well, let's
go another round. How about it? Maybe we should get a little com-
pany over here, too. Could we get someone to sing us a local song?
You know. How about that one about the Lord of Kuwana and
clams? Liven things up a bit. Do something wild! They say you can't
have too much fun when you're on the road. You could even
mumble your lines from *Kanjinchō*. I have no beard to dye, but, look,

A Song by Lantern Light

I'll take this towel and put it over your shiny head like this." Nejibei
straightened his back and sat up a little taller. Yajirobei stared with
wide eyes.

"This might be the greatest rebellion since the Heike. Your plan
is long overdue. Never mind the two-person saddle, I'll just jump on
the hump!" Yajirobei was suddenly animated. "Miss, anyone will do.
Rustle up four or five geisha. Bring in a crew!" He threw back his
shoulders and spoke boldly.

The maid withdrew the hand that was serving wine and held the
flask straight up on her knee. "The party over there just requested a
few more girls, too. We put in a call. Kino, were there any geisha left?"

The thick-necked assistant shook her head. "They've all been
called out."

"I'm terribly sorry, sir. Kuwana's a small place, and we don't
have many entertainers. With several parties on the same night, anyone who is anybody gets called out right away. And, of course, for
people from Tokyo like yourselves, we wouldn't want to call just
anyone. She would have to be pretty, or have some special talent."

"Now that we've come this far, if we don't hear the sound of a
samisen, we might just run off in the night without paying the bill! As
long as they're not one-eyed or harelipped, get us someone, anyone,
even if you have to call an antique shop."

"Wait a minute. I wonder if that new girl at the Shimaya is still
available. Go see. Kino, hurry. Run and put in a call."

9

"Bring it on! You pompous fake!" Back at the noodle shop, the street
musician suddenly shouted in a loud, strong voice. Drinking hot *sake*
on a frosty night, the singer of Hakata ballads quickly sobered up in
the bright moonlight. His face was still pale as ever, but after gulping
two or three teacups of wine, one right after another, he showed a
little color around the eyes. "Blow your damned whistles. Beat your
drums. Play your flutes. I'm just a kid. Isn't that right, ma'am? In any
case, you seem to have more than your share of masseurs here in Kuwana." The young man's eyes darted here and there to the high cry
of whistles.

"People say the eyes of the blind look like oysters," she replied. "But it's clams we're famous for. I doubt we have more masseurs than anywhere else. Maybe it's because we have so many brothels and inns here. The blind come to find work."

"I see. The brothels." The young man seemed to realize something. A bit dazed, he propped himself up with one arm.

"Master, why don't you take that voice of yours to one of the geisha houses? Let them hear it there. It's enough to die for." She twirled a lacquered tray in front of her.

"Woman, what a mirror you are! Heaven forbid if someone should die because of my voice! As it turns out, I don't think I could stand in front of a geisha house."

"Why not?

"I might meet up with my enemy." He looked down at the floor.

"They say a good hobby helps a person through hard times. Master, are you here tonight because of some geisha? Is that why you call her your enemy?"

"No. *I'm* the enemy!"

"Oh, go on. Listen to you." As the shop owner's wife spoke these words, from the dark side of the narrow street came the light scrape of a woman's clogs. The sound echoed beneath the shadowed eaves and came into the earthen-floored noodle shop. Immediately, the desolate wail of a blind man's whistle came again, as if tangled around the young woman's feet.

The street musician stared sharply.

"Speak of the devil, I'll bet that was a geisha who passed by just now. Go ahead. Open the door, if you like. Take a look. Careful, though. Your enemy might be waiting to strike you down."

"I'm ready. Any time! Just stop that damned whistling!"

Suddenly, someone else opened the door from the outside.

"Scare me to death!"

"Evening, ma'am. Six bowls of noodles, right away." Dressed in a livery coat and straw sandals, a man from the pleasure quarters had come to put in an order. The moon poured down on his back as he stood in the entrance. His nose was red from the cold.

A Song by Lantern Light

"Coming right up," the shopkeeper cried out. Standing at his place of command next to the counter, he became erect as a stick. "Hurry up, Okata."

Ignoring him, the shopkeeper's wife asked nonchalantly, "We just heard the sound of lovely footsteps. Who was she, anyway?"

"The new girl at the Shimaya. Just got transferred in from Yamada." The young man with the red nose turned around and looked out the door.

The street musician leaned his back against the wall. He straightened himself so he could see into the narrow alley, beyond the shoulders of the man standing in the entrance. The sound of the clogs had faded in the distance but still echoed faintly.

"Did a lot of girls get called out tonight?"

"Not as many as your noodles, I'd say."

"Well, we'll have to get your order done right away because you said that."

"Thanks. That would be great," he said and left.

The shopowner stepped down from the register and fished for his clogs with his toes. He crashed about until he finally pulled out a large carrying tray. It seemed the couple ran the shop by themselves, and the poor man had to double as the delivery man.

"Mind the shop, now. Understand? Got that? I'm going to make a short stop on the way back. You got that, Okata."

The shopkeeper glared about suspiciously. No need for a lantern on a moonlit night such as this. With one hand still tucked into his bosom, he flung the door open with a vengeance. Without bothering to close it behind him, he nimbly pranced away.

The draft tore the plume of steam rising from the boiling kettle, and a shadow fell across the musician's face. The shopkeeper's wife crossed over to him.

"How long are you going to stare out the door like that? Do you really want to meet your enemy that badly?"

"Ma'am. Here in Kuwana, do geisha use blind men as attendants?" The musician hunched his shoulders as if overtaken with chill. When he finally straightened himself and looked over at her, his face was pale and sickly.

10

"We have our names for things, but I've never heard anyone call a blind man a geisha's attendant before. When that young lady passed by just now—where did he say she's from? I forget, but anyway—as I watched her disappear down the street, her lavender gown turned teal in the light of that lantern a few doors down, then blue again in the moonlight. She was hanging her head and moving along as if her feet were in chains. And right behind her was the gray form of someone else. If it had been her shadow, it would have crawled along on the ground beneath her. But it followed her all the way, a yard or two behind, guarding her like Dōroku, god of travelers. It must have been a blind man, judging by the unnatural way it walked—the hips, the shoulders, the strange way it held its unshapely head. Funny that a blind man should be working as an escort, though. He was probably an escort to begin with, then went blind later on."

"What did he look like? I want to see." She began to move toward the door.

"They're gone. They disappeared down the street. Looks like they found the place that called for them. I see, so there's no such thing as a blind attendant, is there? Now I can hear even more of them. Whistles sounding in the moonlight, with shadows following each one. They pile up beneath the cold moonlight, and this town of Kuwana turns into a mountain of needles. I can't take it any longer!" He gulped down another cup of *sake*. "Come, woman! Drink up! Your old man's out. But who cares? See? The door's wide open. And that mountain there above the rooftops is looking in on us like the snow monster."

The musician looked toward the door. "Here he comes! He comes! He comes! Here he is! A masseur! Masseur!" he rattled on without pausing to catch his breath.

Hearing the street singer's "Masseur," a blind man, who happened to be passing by on the street, planted his walking stick and stood still, frozen in the moonlight. His white eyes rolled. His nostrils showed in the moonlight. He held his stick at an angle. Was someone calling for him?

A Song by Lantern Light

"Was it a shadow? Or was it really a masseur? Was it just a silhouette?" The musician asked insistently.

"What if it were a masseur? Are you that crazy about blind men?"

"I am." He let out a deep breath, and looked again. He knitted his brow and laughed in a high voice. "Yes. I'm dying to meet one. And look, here's one now. Hello. Masseur. Mr. Masseur. Won't you come in?"

The musician picked up his plectrum and tapped on his stool to signal the blind man who had appeared at the door. "Please, how about a round? Ma'am, excuse me, but if I could borrow this stool."

"Lie down on the tatami, if you like. Masseur, you've got a customer. Come in. And please close the door behind you."

The blind man entered, tapping his walking stick. "I'm coming. Not much more than a shadow." The man's breath showed whitely in the cold air. He wore a black kimono with a brown coverlet, the lantern light glowing red in the folds of his clothing. Rather than suddenly disappearing and leaving behind only a pair of sandals, he shuffled forward, fishing about with one hand while the other fanned the rich, wine-scented air toward his nose.

"So you heard me calling, did you?" The street singer asked in an arrogant tone. He pushed the serving table aside, now laden with several emptied *sake* flasks.

The blind man sniffled. He took a deep, envious breath of the shop's aroma.

"I've been waiting for you," the musician said. "Even a dog running down the street looks like a masseur tonight. No offense intended, of course. It's just the way you appeared—out of nowhere, just like that. Yes, I am drunk. I thought you might be a ghost."

"Is he happy to see you! At first, I couldn't figure out why the sound of your whistle bothered him so much. Now I get it. All this time, all he wanted was a massage."

"Thank you, ma'am. Business is good, I trust."

"We only have one customer, so take your time. Give him a good massage. If he falls asleep, we'll put him up for the night."

The masseur was unperturbed. "I understand. I'll give him a good one, then. Slow and easy." He clasped his hands together and kneaded his palms. "Well, sir, shall we begin?"

"Don't call me sir. I'm just a beggar." The young man gulped more wine.

The shopkeeper's wife scolded him with her eyes. "That's not true. You shouldn't say that."

11

"Lying down isn't going to work. I'm fine, sitting here like this. This is good enough. If you grabbed my back, I wonder if I could even breathe. Probably not. I might even get dizzy and pass out. Imagine being massaged to death by a blind man." The young musician had a serious look on his face.

"No need to worry, sir. This might be the country, but I've been trained in the Sugiyama method, and I have years of experience behind me. If you asked me to put needles into your solar plexus, I could even do that with no trouble at all." The masseur seemed a little put off. When he widened his eyes, they looked like egg whites.

"I'm not saying you're good or bad. It's just that I've never had a massage before. Not ever. Not even as a joke."

"Oh, come now. The way you were looking forward to it."

"That's right. My shoulders are so stiff that my eyes started to swim with anticipation. Will it be like going into labor for the first time, or maybe that first pang of a healer's flame? I don't know what to expect. Does it hurt? Does it itch? Some say it tickles. I bet it would tickle. Unfortunately, my mother was a chaste woman so I'm no bastard. Still, no one in the world is more ticklish than I am. Feels like you're making rice balls out of me. When I think about those hands squeezing my shoulders, I get so ticklish I can't stand it. Stop!" The musician pulled his elbows to his sides and writhed.

"My. This isn't working." The blind man laughed, not knowing what to do.

The shopkeeper's wife looked into the young man's face again. "How cute."

"Cute? I think the word is 'pitiful.' My whole body, skin and all, is as hard as stone. My back's kinked. My chest feels like it's about to burst. Yes, a massage! Go ahead, do it! Why should I care?" He yelled and lifted a knee to his chest. "Do it like you mean it, like

A Song by Lantern Light

you're going to kill me! I'm ready. Ma'am, you and I must have met in an earlier life. Otherwise, you wouldn't have taken care of a wanderer like me. And now I'm sorry it has to end—now that I'm about to be massaged to death. Sorry to bother you again, but could you pour me one last cup of wine? This might be our farewell toast."

He shook the drops from his cup, then held it out to her. He was acting like a child, surely. And yet, she was struck by how the expression in his eyes had changed. He now stared sharply. Stunned, she watched on in silence.

"So, Masseur."

"Sir."

"Ma'am, could you pour for me?"

"Of course." As she did, her hand trembled slightly.

The young man gulped the wine in his teacup just as the masseur placed his hands on him once again. His body trembled, but his face, fortunately, did show some color. "That hits the spot."

"Perhaps there's something here I don't understand. But I don't think you have anything to worry about." The blind man was also surprised.

"Good enough." The musician relaxed his hand. "I know you won't kill me. Still, that's the way it feels." He dangled his head and his body swayed back and forth. "The moon outside is cold, but your fingers are like flames. They become fire and water, and echo in my bones. My chest is cold, but my ears burn with fever. My flesh is on fire, but my blood is ice cold."

He let both hands drop, and the masseur, startled, drew back. His pouting lips looked like an octopus beak.

The musician sat up straight on his stool.

"No, don't stop. Keep going. Take pity on me. Be gentle. Even if you do, though, my whole body's going to fall apart in your hands. I try to avoid the feeling of annihilation. But when I flee from the premonition, it clings to me. When I pass it by, it draws near. When I run from it, it chases after me. When it has no shape, it has a voice. Those whistles are the sound of its battle drums. When they come as thick and fast as they have tonight, a weakling like me can't take it. Those who lack the courage to stay at the cliff's edge stare into the abyss, they can't stand the tension and jump in headfirst. But I'm past caring now. Blind man, tell me. Are you his cousin? His uncle? A nephew? If you are one of his relatives, then here I am. Take your revenge! I murdered one of you."

12

"It happened exactly three years ago, just a little later in the year. We had an engagement in Nagoya, and our schedule made it convenient —if that's not a disrespectful a way of putting it—to visit the holy shrines at Ise. Anyway, I was more than happy with the way the opportunity came along. We planned to spend a few leisurely days in Furuichi, and then, speaking of convenience, to see the clouds of Mount Asama and hear the wind in the pines at Tsuzumi. We were to see the sunrise over Futami Bay on New Year's Day. Then go from Sakaibashi to Ikenoura. Then on to Okinoshima, where we were to leave the province. From Kamigōri, we planned to enter Shima, where we would see the Hiyori Mountains. We were going to travel by boat, if the weather was good, to Cape Irako to sample the sea slugs there. We planned our trip to take about five or six days. In Yamada, we put up at the Fujiya in Onoe-chō. Don't be surprised. At that time, I wasn't dressed in rags as I am now.

"I was a young gentleman, well-dressed, always ready to change into the formal jacket I carried around with me. I'm sure I sound to you like a palanquin bearer bragging about past exploits—buying grand courtesans at the pleasure quarters, and so on. But I'm not being a poor loser. My success had nothing to do with my own efforts in the first place.

"Listen up. My uncle was also my master, my benefactor. I called him all those things. In Edo, he was considered to be the best of his profession, known throughout Japan as the head of the main school of *nō* actors. He was a slightly balding man with a scowling face.

"His temperament didn't match his looks, though. He was actually a straightforward, fun-loving Edo native. He was sixty years old at the time. But whenever I signed in for him at an inn, he would glare at me and flash three fingers, as if naming the three elements of the universe—heaven, earth, and humanity—or posing some Zen riddle. All those three fingers really meant was that I was

A Song by Lantern Light

to shave three years off his real age and write down fifty-seven. That's just the way he was. Whenever women were serving us, the one thing I was never allowed to do was to call him father. So what was I supposed to call him? 'I'm not Yoichibei, so don't talk like Sadakurō.' He pursed his lips and wouldn't let me call him uncle either. So we agreed that I'd call him *oniisan,* older brother.

"I was this old man's younger companion, and together we enjoyed the pleasures of the road. The wine was good, the scenery great, and the weather couldn't have been better. No matter where we went, we charmed the women. Even in the winter, along the mountain road, the asters were blooming. Some of the blossoms were huge.

"Now, riding on the train that took us along the Ise Road—to Kuwana, Yokkaichi, and Kameyama—were two men who seemed to share our destination. They began gossiping about the performance we had just done in Nagoya. Even if they were exaggerating, it seemed I had a good reputation. My uncle's, of course, was beyond criticism. I can't tell you more than that. It would be a disgrace to our school if I did. If I revealed his name, the whole world would know who we were. Well, listen to this.

"After we reached Ise, I started hearing another name in their conversation about us. It kept coming up. Are you with me? The name was Sōichi, and he was a masseur and acupuncturist who lived in Furuichi in Yamada."

As the name left the young man's mouth, his eyes fixed vacantly on one spot. He no longer paid attention to the masseur, who was standing behind him hunched over his back, nor to the woman who was facing him, sitting with the skirt of her kimono spread near his stool. He stared up at the ceiling and vacantly waved away the steam that drifted around him.

"He was a masseur, but he came from a samurai family that had once served the lord of that area. Listen to this. The fellow was apparently skilled in the same art as our school. Here in Furuichi he reigned supreme. The monster had given himself the name Sōzan, or Grand Master. 'Arrogant, yes. But he has talent. Even those actors who come from Tokyo to see him are intimidated. Such-and-such came and went away humbled. If he had even one good eye, he wouldn't have stayed in Mie Prefecture. The same goes for that group of per-formers who came to Nagoya. I'm not saying they're fakes, but it wouldn't hurt for them to come and take a few lessons from Sōzan. He's the real thing. Eels are tasty, so are bream. They ought to come and taste of what he has to offer before going back to Tokyo.' That's what I heard on the train from the beer-bellied businessman with his mouth of gold-filled teeth, as he talked with a prosperous-looking man from the area.

"My uncle dozed off. Being young and reckless, I let it bother me—these things they were saying. I hid my face behind my muffler and glared at the two men.

"When we reached the Fujiya, I sent my uncle off to bathe by himself while I questioned the maids. I also asked the clerk who greeted us at the front door if he knew such-and-such an artist called Sōzan. Their answers were all the same. His reputation was even bet-ter than I had imagined. Actually, he had recently performed there at the Fujiya for a local retired lord who had called him in. With the performance came great praise, 'Is it because the pines of Mount Tsuzumi are so close by? Such a fine rendition of *The Wind in the Pines* could never be heard in Tokyo.'

"The clerk even mentioned that Master Sōzan had said, 'I wish those other guys could hear me.' 'Those other guys,' he said. Well, that's me, the one telling you this story. I'm one of those other guys.'"

13

"I inquired a bit further, and learned that Sōzan, or the masseur Sō-ichi, was running a small restaurant on the outskirts of Furuichi. He had three concubines and was living the good life. That was the last straw! A blind masseur taking on a name like Sōzan, posing as a mas-ter of the *nō* theater. What nerve!"

The young street singer held a hand to his chest as if it pained him. "Mr. Masseur, I hope you'll forgive me for criticizing one of your kind. After I came to my senses, I realized that farmers in Shin-shū make fun of Tokyo theater because we don't have real boars run-ning across the stage. If Miyashige radishes are the finest in Japan, then the local pickles, too, must be unparalleled in all the empire.

A Song by Lantern Light

And broiled clams the equal of Kuwana's are nowhere to be found in the cities of Tokyo, Osaka, or Kyoto. I should have realized it was nothing but provincialism. But to a twenty-four-year-old, just approaching an 'unlucky year,' it was all very irritating. In the first place, I couldn't stand his name, Sōzan. And his talk about 'those other guys' rubbed me the wrong way. Then there was this business about three concubines. It all made me furious.

"Amid the great changes that followed the Meiji Restoration, the *nō* theater lost its patronage and many among us were barely making ends meet. Even those artists who were earning a daimyō's income were reduced to making toothpicks and selling brittle at roadside stands. Some became delivery boys for noodle shops. My uncle, for example, became a janitor at a government office in the countryside. He got drunk off the lees of cheap *sake* and slept on the dikes of the rice paddies. When his sister was a young woman—this is my mother I'm talking about—one masseur who had managed to save up a little money tried to take advantage of my family's poverty. He relentlessly chased after my mother to make her his concubine, just because he had loaned our family a little money. She sprained an ankle trying to throw herself into the Sumida River, a place she had only seen from inside a palanquin before. So you can see why I dislike masseurs.

"Sōichi, I'll teach you a lesson! I'll make you see yourself for what you really are, blind or not.

"The next day we paid homage at the shrines in Ise. My uncle was so moved by the visit that he only drank a little that evening and went to bed early. I tapped his bed and left a glass of water by his pillow. I told the maids at the inn that I was going out for a little sightseeing, but the truth was, I planned to catch this Sōzan in his own hole. I'd teach him a lesson.

"The wind was blowing hard. I thought the Isuzu River might serve as some sort of boundary and that it would be calm on the other side of the Uji Bridge. But the wind was howling up the long mountain slope—disagreeably warm. The sand in front of my lantern was yellow, and the moon was partially hidden by a covering of clouds. Although the trees of Mount Kamiji were blue, the waves of Futami Bay were white. What a terrific force! The wind nearly blew me over as I stumbled ahead. It would have taken my hat, so I took it off and left it there at the Fujiya. With my jacket puffed up around my back and my sleeves flapping, I set off like a monk sneaking off at night. It was too much trouble to change clothes, so I was still dressed in the formal kimono I had worn to the shrines. I took my jacket off, folded it up, and tucked it away in the bosom of my kimono. Imagine how fashionable I looked when I covered my head with a towel. That was my clever trick, a sign of things to come. Serves me right."

The musician pulled a hand into his sleeve. The other seized his teacup.

"It was still early in the evening in Furuichi, but things were already quiet. The wind roared in the eaves and tossed the hanging lanterns back and forth. I could hear the sounds of samisen playing, but the notes were being blown away like a cat scurrying over the roofs of the great buildings. To put it simply, it was as if I had brought the wind with me that night and hurled it at the desolate pleasure quarters.

"I came to a shallow depression, where a dart and air gun booth stood. It had been set up right against the street gutter and was surrounded by a bamboo railing. The edge of a rug was flapping in the wind, and an island of red light from a sooty oil lamp poured down on the tatami mat in front of it. I spotted a woman with a white, painted face and staggered up to the booth so I could talk with her. I glanced over as I took aim at the dharma doll looking straight at me with its huge enlightened eyes and inquired, 'I'm looking for a blind masseur named Sōzan. Does he live in this neighborhood?' I was trying to get a feel for the situation. It was a surprise visit, and I didn't know my way around.

"'Yes, the Master lives here,' she answered.

"The Master. Can you imagine that? Calling him 'the Master' to one of 'those other guys?'

"'I've come to hear him perform,' I said. 'I wonder if he'd oblige.'

"The booth had a curtain with a good-luck mark on it. Just then, from behind it emerged a middle-aged woman—gaunt, pale, her hair in disarray. 'If you're a stranger, just passing through, I'm not sure he'll do it. But if you like, we can provide you with a guide.'

A Song by Lantern Light

"I tipped her generously and employed her services.

"'Show him the way, then. He looks like a gentleman. But be careful.' The older woman winked. Without further ado, the younger one with the heavy makeup jumped nimbly over the bamboo rail. And we were off.'"

14

"I held both sleeves over my mouth and lowered my head into the wind. I followed the woman, who was now my guide, into a narrow alley just across the street. Everyone's doors were tightly shut against the wind, eerily illuminated by our lantern as we passed by. Among the crowded tenement buildings on either side stood a two-story house. It had a latticed door and wide boards covering the gutter running before it. The signboard read, 'Light snacks and drinks.' Apparently, this was the residence of Master Sōzan.

"'You've got a visitor,' the woman announced and went right in. I saw three women seated around a long brazier. They were strange creatures—one was sitting with her knees propped up, another with her legs to the side, a third leaning over the brazier with an elbow resting on the board that spanned its lip. The restaurant part of the business was slow, it seemed.

"Leading up from the entrance was a narrow staircase. 'So the sitting room is on the second floor?' I asked, quickly removing the towel from my head. I began the ascent. But because of the gusting wind, there were no lanterns in the stairwell. It was pitch-black. While I hesitated at the bottom of the stairs, the place came alive with the sound of people bustling about to find a lantern. As if on cue, a gust of wind blew and the light hanging above the women went out.

"At that moment, I could see two paper-covered doors dimly illuminated by the light of another lantern in the adjacent room. In the middle of the doors was the silhouette of a sitting figure—a shaved head and a face with a protruding forehead and thick lips. So that's Sōzan, I thought. The most vexing thing of all was the distinct shadow of another person—a graceful figure of a young woman with a Shimada coiffure—standing behind him with her hands on his shoulders. She was giving him a massage.

"'Someone get a match,' I heard the women call out. And then came the thick sound of a man clearing his throat. I saw the reflection of a large hand lifting an ashtray, then the outline of a smoking pipe. Suddenly, the shadow increased twofold in size as the man lifted his arms and spread his sleeves. He was dressed in a padded gown.

"Finally, someone lit a lamp. 'Sorry to make you wait. Come this way.'

"I started climbing to the second floor. Halfway up the stairs, I looked for the woman who had accompanied me from the dart stand. She was sitting behind another woman, away from the brazier, with both legs beneath her and her head bowed. When I reached the six-mat room upstairs, my escort said in a low voice, 'Is that one all right? We have other girls.'

"'Ah, so that's their business,' I thought to myself. She asked me in a louder voice. 'What can I get you to drink?'

"'Just a little wine and something to nibble on.' I began to explain that, actually, I had come to hear the voice of the blind masseur.

"'The voice?' she asked, then laughed in a condescending way. 'You want to hear the Master sing? I'll speak to him right away.'

"My usher from hell suddenly straightened her kimono and left the room for the first floor. A few minutes later someone else came up the stairs. This time it was a young woman, maybe sixteen or seventeen years old. This one, as they say, was a dove trooping among the crows. Her sash and kimono were not of the highest quality, but she was as beautiful as the maple leaves in autumn. Her hair was done up high on her head, and tied into it was a pale-blue tie-dyed cloth. Could she be one of Sōzan's three? Such depravity! And so close to the sacred shrines at Ise! It appeared she was the woman with the Shimada coiffure who had been massaging Sōzan's shoulders. What a waste! The cast of her eyes was clearer than the stars above the Isuzu River—only to be muddied by the fins of a catfish. I felt sorry for her. She brought me a ceremonial cup of green tea served on a purple crepe cloth.

"Well, since I had come for an audience with the great Sōzan, he was letting me know that I ought to behave with the utmost respect. This was going to be fun, a real duel with real swords. I took out the formal jacket that I had folded and stashed in the bosom of my kimono, and put it on.

A Song by Lantern Light

"The wine they eventually brought was served on a magnificent red-lacquer stand on which was painted in gold a scene from Futami Bay. Truly amazing.

"'Before I begin, please enjoy your *sake*.' The blind masseur instructed me as he entered the room. His manner seemed to say, 'I expect you to listen in awe to my performance.' What a perfectly arrogant man! He sat himself down. His legs and belly were thick and squat, and his throat was as wide as his torso. A vein meandered like a small snake from his ear to his forehead. His eyebrows were thin, his nose was flat, and his lips grotesquely thick. On top of that, his cheekbones protruded abruptly, and his teeth looked as though they would rattle whenever they came together. His left eye was completely blighted, I could see. His right showed whitely, looking upward. And to top everything off, his face was covered with black pockmarks.

"Clearly, the man was a cripple. His shoulders were rounded and powerless. He was a bald monster with his head hanging forward over his kimono's open collar."

15

"I'm not trying to be mean to you." Back at the Minatoya, one of the maids firmly pressed her hands to the apron that covered her knees and glanced over at the young, twenty-year-old geisha at her side. The latter sat with her head tilted forward as if bending beneath the weight of her full coiffure. The nape of her neck and her legs were white and cold-looking. Her pale-pink undergarment was slipping off her sagging, lonely shoulders, exposing her back all the way to the backbone. Supple and languid, her two-layered lilac kimono was delicately set off with light purple and blue asters.

With condescension in her eyes, the maid spoke sharply, "I'll take care of things here. So go. You're Omie from the Shimaya, right? Well, Mie, go home! I counted on you to come and cheer up our customers, so I left things to that younger girl and went out to help in the kitchen. But what a waste it was to call you! Is it because our guests are old? Or are you looking down on us because you've just come from Yamada? When those men asked you to pour wine for them, you hardly managed a smile. 'Let's hear some music,' they said. But you laughed down your nose at them. Kino was in there with you. She didn't know what to do and finally came and told me what was happening.

"All this time, I've been talking myself silly trying to make you feel better. I asked you, 'How about a song? Please, play your samisen for them, won't you?' Those men are lonely. They want to have some fun. Look. The candles are about to burn out, I've been talking with you so long. Is that all you have to say for yourself—that you don't know how? What's wrong with you? Do you think it'll kill you to touch a samisen? You say you don't know how to play. But who's ever heard of a geisha who can't get through a tune?

"Think about it. You can see they're not just ordinary guests. You can tell they're gentlemen. So what are you going to do for them? I won't put up with it. Come on. Get up. I'll carry your instrument for you." The gentle woman quickly got to her feet, grabbed the samisen case that was lying next to the sliding doors, and stood it upright.

"Oh, please!"

With a start, the young geisha slid the train of her kimono over the floor and gently grabbed the maid by the knees. One hand held the older woman's sleeve, and the other tried to stop the samisen. Omie's figure, as if broken, scattered like the petals of a peony blossom.

"Please, forgive me. Please." Her voice was short of breath and choked with tears. "Why would I insult those two men? Why would I disrespect the Minatoya? I just can't play the samisen, that's all. I really can't." Her words broke off. "I was at another place earlier tonight, at a party for some soldiers, where everybody was having a wonderful time. They told me, 'If you can't do anything, then get out—unless you want to take your clothes off and dance. If that's too much for you, then leave.' So I was sent back alone to my master's house, and when I got there my manager beat me. 'You can't play the samisen? You can't dance? Well, if you won't take your clothes off for them, then do it here!' He stripped me. He took off my sash, everything. He made me lie down on the kitchen floor, and opened the windows in the ceiling to let in the cold air. I was so embarrassed. There in the cold moonlight, he poured ladle after ladle of cold water on me—on my breasts, and on my chest.

A Song by Lantern Light

"So then we got your request for someone to come to the Minatoya, and what do you think happened? The manager made me put on my undergarments, which he warmed by the brazier. He said, 'You have customers from Tokyo,' and got out a special kimono. He told me to go do my best. He even set my clogs out for me himself.

"Do my best? How could I? I could hardly walk, let alone dance. And the samisen? Sister, anyone can make a sound if they hit the strings. But you're asking me to play a song in front of other people. How could I ever do that?

"I wish I were crippled. I'm completely tone-deaf. How does someone like me deserve to play in front of paying customers? When I think about it, I get so scared I can't even talk. What's she pouting about? Why is she so rude? I can understand why you'd think that way, but please. I'll do anything. I'll wash dishes. Please."

The young geisha pressed her sleeves together, and tried to look up through her tears at the maid's face. The maid's expression softened, and the samisen that had been standing straight as a pole began to seem as if it might sway. The young woman immediately looked in the direction of the two customers from Tokyo, and the fluffy bow of her twilled sash pressed ever more tightly against the maid's skirts.

16

Omie formally pressed her hands on the floor and bowed politely to the two old gentlemen. "I know you called for a geisha, but I'm afraid I can't be of use to you. I'm embarrassed to say that. I can't even pour *sake*, my hands tremble so. So please think of me as a maid. Make use of me until you retire for the evening. Perhaps you'd like me to massage your back? Or your shoulders? That's something I could do wholeheartedly." With unsparing passion, she bowed deeply, until her bangs touched the tatami. With her fingers pressed to the floor in the formal manner, she ended her greeting to the two travelers. Even in these distressing circumstances, her elegance was evident.

Nejibei, who had been silently looking at the illustrations in *Shank's Mare,* managed awkwardly to say, "There's something here to be learned for posterity's sake. From now on, we should think twice about calling for a geisha when we're on the road." He reached over and touched the tongs for the brazier.

Gazing with half-opened eyes at the calligraphy hanging in the room—'Facing 'to the breezes/The sound of oars here pleases.'— Yajirobei, indulging in a cigarette, absentmindedly put the lighted end to his lips. He hurled the cigarette into the ashes of the brazier and coughed. "Well, Maid, you'll get your tip afterward. I could hand it to you now, but that would make the girl feel worse. Let her rest in another room somewhere, and you get some noodles or something for everyone. It's on me. Maybe you know an interesting story that will revive her spirits. At the appropriate time, send her back to her house." He reached for his wine cup, now cold, and drained it without pleasure.

Just moments ago, the maid had tried to force the samisen on the girl. But now she pushed it quietly to rest in a dark corner of an adjoining room. She leaned toward Omie, who was snuggling up against her, swaying like water beneath lantern light; and, without saying a word, she rubbed the girl's back. "So the boss of the Shimaya did those terrible things to you, did he? Don't worry. I'll tell the boss's mother just what you told me, and we'll work things out. You're lucky he didn't scar your face." She tenderly stroked the young woman's arm and added, "He probably didn't want to damage saleable goods. That's the only reason he didn't hit you. So thank our customers now. Then go have a chat with the owner's mother, and warm yourself with her foot warmer. She's just covered her head with a scarf and is getting ready to have tea and sweets." The maid took a close look at Omie, turning her eyes from the young woman's angelic neck to her gentle side locks. "My dear girl, what kind of karma is this? Who's ever heard of a geisha who can't play the samisen—not even one note?" She laughed, trying to show her sympathy.

Omie seemed to melt under the woman's compassion. She shed icy jewels of tears as she tried to speak. "I've tried everything. I made a vow and offered prayers. I've even gone without salt. But I just can't learn how to play. I can't even tune a string. I suppose I was just born this way." Her face showed in the candle light like a white plum blossom in a dark winter's night.

"You can't dance either?"

"No."

"Don't cry, young lady," Yajirobei said. "You're such a weakling! Here, have a drink. Cheer up. From now on, whenever you get called out, don't be afraid. Understand? Keep your head, and things will work out. Just hit those strings. Make it up if you have to. Stay away from instruments like the koto. Bang on a gong or a cymbal. Make noise on a flute. No one will know if you're good or bad. Do that, and no one will say you don't have talent. If you can't dance, do calisthenics. Ready, begin. A-one!" Yajirobei puffed out his chest and stretched his arms to the left and right, as if he might snap the ties on his *haori*. "And a-two!" As if playing fox-and-squire, he thrust two fists forward. "See, you can do this. Well, I guess even this would require some courage. Judging from what I see, if you're that shy, you won't be able to do much of anything. That's a shame." His voice became a bit hoarse.

"Perhaps I shouldn't say this about myself, but I can go through the motions of a traditional dance. Just one, though." Omie lowered her head again and timidly pressed her hands to the tatami.

"You dance? You can dance?" The maid's voice was filled with joy. "We've just been talking about the wrong kind of dancing! If you can do the older style, go right ahead. No one in this room is going to be too fussy. But wait. You'll need some accompaniment. Kino, go to the other room. Tell them Sen sent you. Bring back someone who can play."

With a blank expression on her face, Kino got up to go. The one who called herself Sen turned and puckered her lips into a gentle smile, "Wait just a second."

17

"Tonight's different. Once you're a soldier, you can't count on getting time off except on Sundays. We all have to sacrifice for our country. They're having farewell parties for the new soldiers tonight. They have a lot of girls working for them, but they're telling us they can't spare a single one. So we'll make do. This is what they mean by 'Forget your inhibitions while on the road'—except backwards! I'll bang on the samisen in front of our guests. So, Omie, which dance is it? Maybe I shouldn't ask. I hope it's acceptable, whatever it is."

"Oh, please." As Osen got up to fetch the instrument, the charming Omie touched the woman's knee. She seemed embarrassed. "I'm not so sure my dance goes very well with the samisen. The dance I do is from a *nō* play." Before she finished speaking, she buried her head in Osen's lap and faced shyly away from the old man and his partner Nejibei. Although she was a modest girl, the movement of her body caused her kimono to become disheveled; and her undergarment spilled out from her kimono and spread over the tatami, revealing its alluring hue.

"So your dance is a *nō* dance?" Yajirobei asked tersely.

Nejibei put his book down. "Let's drink. I'll pour. I gratefully decline to see your *nō* performance. Maybe you can pound on some Buddhist drums or something." For some reason, the man's hoarse laughter powerfully filled the room.

"Nejibei, Nejibei-san."

"What?" He finally answered lazily.

"This might be the beginning of a good story. I think we ought to take a look."

"Count me out."

"Then perhaps, sir, you could just close your eyes?"

"My god, what a thing to say to an old man. Until I get back to Tokyo tomorrow and see my granddaughter's cute little face, I don't think I'll be closing my eyes, thank you."

"How fond you are of twisting things. But, then, that's Nejibei all over, isn't it? Do what you please. Now, young lady. Go ahead. No need to feel embarrassed in front of this old man. You say you don't have any talent? You even offer to give us a massage. But if you can manage to show us your one dance, then I say you are a true geisha. Do this one thing, and you'll feel better about the tip you're going to be getting. We definitely want to see you perform. But do as you please. We're not going to force you to entertain us."

"What kind words the man has spoken!" the maid said. "I don't know what sort of dance you have in mind, but even if it isn't polished, who's going to mind? Not at all. Now, don't you have to get ready?"

A Song by Lantern Light

"Yes, ma'am." Omie raised herself ever so slightly and turned her head so her lips almost touched the collar of her purple kimono. Her once full figure now seemed sadly gaunt.

She lowered her head and looked down at her chest as if embarrassed. She almost touched her chin to the skin showing at the collar of her kimono. She pulled a slender, deep-purple silk pouch from her bosom, quickly turned it over, and from it produced a silver fan that flashed in the candlelight. The fan seemed to rest heavily in her slender, pale fingers. As if bowing to it, she held it to her forehead like a jeweled hairpin, then gradually opened it. As it spread like the outflowing tide shimmering beneath the moon, her face disappeared behind it, leaving only her thin white fingers, bent back against the fan's outer ribs.

Like the tide flowing into the mouth of the Ibi River, the sound of the people celebrating in the adjoining room fell quiet. On the silver fan glowed scattered clouds of gold and the round orb of the moon, painted in dark blue. And through the light of that moon came Omie's clear voice as she began her dance.

> Then the diver made her plea
> To the Dragon of the Sea —
> "If the jewel I fetch for thee,
> Make my son thy Hope."

> Upon his eager affirmation,
> N'er a moment's hesitation,
> Snaked 'round her waist her son's salvation—
> A thousand-fathom rope.

> "If the jewel I forthwith take,
> Feel my tug upon this snake,
> Then pull until your sinews ache,
> And rob the Ocean Slope."

Omie found the rhythm.

> With their promise
> She unsheathed a sword . . .

She closed her fan and moved her sleeve with skill and practiced mastery. Her refinement and maturity were as fine as the kimono she wore. Her eyes were fixed in concentration.

The moonlight flooding through the window illuminated the undulating waves of the frosty river. Upon the tatami where she placed her knee, the light of the lantern flowed like flowers.

Suddenly, Nejibei called out with new strength in his voice, "Hold it. Right there."

18

Nejibei reached out and pulled the brazier closer to him. "I wonder if I could get someone to put a little more fuel on this fire. No, wait. No need to get up. We'll just move this kettle over."

Osen suddenly became tense, sensing something about the situation.

He turned his legs to the side while she quietly moved the coals around in the brazier. His luggage was in the adjoining room, but he had kept one item close by. There in the alcove was the bundle he had carried from the station in the *furoshiki* that was tied around his neck. He picked it up carefully in both hands and, as if it were heavy, placed it on his lap. Looking away from Osen, he held his hand over the brazier and warmed it on both sides.

"Omie, is it? Young lady, take your hand off the floor. Look at me."

Nejibei had stopped Omie as she was about to stand with her sword. She was holding the opened fan close to her face, close enough to reflect the red blossom of her lips. She was looking down, bringing the fan to her forehead, just as the other hand touched the floor. At the sound of Nejibei's voice, she lifted her head slightly and closed the fan. Yajirobei, who had been watching intently, closed his eyes. Without saying a word, he held a trembling hand over the edge of the brazier, as ashes fell silently from his cigarette.

Nejibei let one knee slip off his cushion.

"We'd like to see the full performance again. But first, come here a minute. The dance you were just doing—the form, the style. How well it was taught! And how well it was learned! As far as we

A Song by Lantern Light

know, there's only one person in this entire country who could have taught you to dance like that. We think we know who it is, and we'd like to know how that came about."

Nejibei cast a meaningful glance at Yajirobei, who was sitting beside him. "And you, you be quiet and listen. So then, how and from whom did you learn that dance?"

"Well," Omie answered tearfully. Already, she had returned to her innocence. "As I said before, I'm a clumsy person, and hopelessly tone-deaf. I also have a hard time memorizing pieces. I couldn't pluck the first note of the easiest ballad. But there was a woman in Yamada, where I used to be, who did her best to teach me how to play—in the mornings and afternoons, even in the evenings when she had time. Three times a day—explaining things in the simplest way so I would engrave the music in my heart. But it was sad, even to me. It took me ten days just to learn a line or two. I finally got to where I could follow the notes. But then on the third line my hand would slip. I had the music in my heart, but my fingers would go to play the third string and hit the first string instead. It sounded terrible.

"More times than I broke the strings on my instrument she scratched my throat with her plectrum or struck me on my chest with her smoking pipe. She wasn't trying to be mean. Compared to what I had been through in Toba, before that."

"So you're from Toba. That's in Shima, isn't it?" Yajirobei suddenly asked.

"No. I'm actually from here, in Ise. After my father died, my stepmother sold me. They called it 'service to the family,' but it turned out to be nothing like I thought it would be. They told me to go along with what the customers wanted. If I didn't do it on land, then I'd do it on water. There was a dock beneath a cliff, where the male servants would grab me and throw me into a small boat at night. Even if the moon was shining, they'd head for the places on the islands that were hidden in the shadows. It was so dangerous I shook with fear. We drifted about on the water like a leaf fallen from a tree, and I would sing songs on the silent ocean. On nights when we didn't get any customers, they said this would be the magic to make sailors want women, or the punishment to take away our bad luck. They'd make us get off the boat and jump into the water. We'd go to the rocks that were exposed in the low tide, and they'd make us cry into the cracks—'Love me! Love me!'—as if we were calling for men. The male servants on the boat would wait near the bow, and when our voices got so hoarse that we couldn't yell any more, they'd throw empty turbot shells at us. The ocean wind was damp, and even the summer nights were cold. I was there in the middle of winter, when every one of those eight hundred and eight islands was white with frost. The wind was freezing, and the edges of those rocks were like needles. And on top of that, I'd have to shout out, 'Love me! Love me!' My lips would go numb, and I'd start crying. My throat would split, and my tongue would freeze. My clothes were drenched with ocean water, and the cold would go straight through me. If I started to faint, there would be the turbot hell. When I came to, I'd be in the boat. It would be dark, and I wouldn't know which boat I was in. I'd be looking up at a mast towering above me like a monster's walking stick. Huge leathery hands would reach out and grab me.

"The stars in the sky were blue, and the ocean was black. I felt as if I had fallen into a dark lake of blood. Am I still alive? The plovers would cry. I would cry. It was all so shameful."

With her sword, her dancing fan, pressed to her tear-soaked sleeves, Omie hid her face. No one spoke as the candle shed its white drops.

Ah, the heights of Mount Hiyori, the scattered islands of Shima, the placid ocean, and cranes circling over lakes of mist. You who hear this story, what do you think about the glorious scenery of Ise now?

19

"I cried constantly, so the boatman—that crude fellow—told me that with the money it cost to buy me, he'd rather sleep with the sea slugs of Cape Irako, or amuse himself with the squid of Yashima. Any other boat would have thrown me into the sea!

"I'd be taken to the rocks again, along with the gusts of freezing wind, and I'd cry out, 'Love me. Love me.'

"All I wanted anymore was to cry into those rocks, even if my arms and legs froze and I turned into a clam. I wanted my voice to go through those cracks and spread over the water, even to the ends of the earth. Let the boat leave me there! Let the tide rise! I wanted desperately to turn into stone, because, sir, I . . ." Omie bit the rumpled sleeve of her undergarment and blushed slightly around her eyes.

"Because I had been thinking of someone for a long time, though only in my heart. This sounds presumptuous for a person like me to say, I know—since I have neither talent nor looks. But I knew I had made a pledge in my heart to someone, even if they killed me, or if I happened to die.

"One night, I was bought by a party boat; and because I didn't do what the men wanted, I was going to be taken back to my original boat. I sat in the stern, straddling a foot warmer and drinking cloudy *sake*. The young man taking me back told the others that if they would stand the cost of the fee, he'd make a diver woman out of me before their very eyes. It was a bright, moonlit night.

"He made me take off my kimono in the middle of the boat. Then he tied a rope around my waist and threw me headfirst into the ocean. I went down and down until I thought I must be at the bottom of the sea. Then they pulled me up like a well bucket, and dangled me from a pulley. Before the last drops of water fell from my hair, they'd plunge me into the water again.

"There happened to be a young man who said his uncle from Nagasaki was on the boat and that he had come aboard to get some spending money from him. He was young. It was the middle of winter, and all he had on was a shirt and a pair of trousers. He had come to collect fees and was staying for a few days in the area. He drove a carriage from Futami to Toba and he told those men that what they were doing to me was cruel. When he got back to Ise, he reported what he had seen to the people there; and that's how I came to know the woman I was telling you about earlier. You know the one. . . .

"In Furuichi, where I had been until recently, she paid my owners a considerable sum of money and brought me here. She implored me to learn the arts well so I could avenge myself against those fiends in Toba, and to make myself into a splendid geisha. With tears in her eyes, she beat me with her plectrum and tried to teach me how to play the samisen.

"But for some reason, I just couldn't get it. With two fingers—

my first and second—I practiced a short piece three times a day for a week straight. I drove everybody in my neighborhood crazy. They even said that my playing made them lose their appetite.

"Again, it was a beautiful moonlit night. My mistress' kindness made it even harder to bear. Physical pain or anguish end once they kill you. I considered going back to Toba and crying 'Love me! Love me!' into the cracks of those rocks again. I thought of being tied to a rope and thrown into the ocean again. That would be easier to bear than what I was going through. In my mind's eye I could see the islands and the oceans. In a daze, I pictured a messenger bird from hell coming through the moonlight to take me away. But then I heard the song of a street musician, right in front of our door.

"In the moonlit streets of the quarters, like the dew about to fall, came the shimmering sound of a samisen and the most beautiful voice I've ever heard.

A Hakata sash wrapped 'round
A dappled Chikuzen kimono.

"'Sorry about the noise,' he said, then started to walk away.

"'He's so good he makes me shiver. Quick. Go to him. Pray that he'll give you some of his talent. And take this, as an offering.'

"My teacher was so engrossed by his music that she almost let the sleeves of her coverlet touch the ashes in the hibachi. Rustling her kimono, she quickly took some money from a drawer in the brazier, wrapped it in some paper that she took from her smooth satin sash, and told me to take it out to him. I placed the money on a tray. By the time I opened the front door, he was already a few yards down the street. The moon was between us, joining us together with its light.

"I ran to him. 'Dear sir,' I said, and held out the tray. He turned around and took the money. As he did, I suddenly reached out and grabbed his hand. Tears came to my eyes. Even though he was a man, if I could take just one finger of his hand and put in on my body. Thinking that, I couldn't stop my tears.

"He was wearing a towel over his head. He took my hand and held it. Without saying a word, he stepped to the side, and asked me gently, 'Why do you cry?'

"That's when I forgot my embarrassment and told him about my troubles learning the samisen."

20

"He listened carefully and gazed at my face. Then he said, 'Tell your employer you're going to pray to the gods to learn how to perform. Before the sun rises in the morning, I want you to come here again. Come to the woods at the base of Mount Tsuzumi. Three days should be enough, but ask for seven. We'll start right away, from tomorrow morning. Understand? The path for a young woman is perilous. I'll come and wait for you at the front door. Don't think I'm a monster about to put a spell on you.'

"After he said this, he brought his samisen to his chest and walked away into the shadows, along a black fence.

"I didn't tell my teacher about him, but when I asked her if I could go out and do ritual washings from three in the morning until dawn, she happily agreed. I was ready to be killed if it came to that. She had always been good to me. Thinking I might never see her again, I lingered there beneath the eaves, looking back at the gate. Then someone suddenly grabbed my hand from behind. 'Come.' It was him. I was ready to go. Still, I felt like I was being snatched away by a Tengu.

"What happened after that was like a dream. A few days later I returned to the house at dawn feeling as if I were in a daze. In the darkness of the woods at the base of Mount Tsuzumi—the wind moaning in the pines and the waters of the Isuzu River rushing by—I took lessons from that man. He taught me a dance—how to move my hands. He held me from behind, and my body started dancing. That's all I know.

"Of course, I told him about how those men had thrown me into the ocean. Strangely enough, he told me that the two of us were enemies, and that there was more to our relationship than I realized. And he made me promise not to tell anyone about what we were doing there at the base of Mount Tsuzumi. So I couldn't say a word.

"On the fifth day, he told me I was ready. 'Do this dance for your guests. And they will never say you have nothing to give.' As a memento, or a sign, he gave me this dancing fan."

Omie took the fan from her sleeve and held it tightly to her chest. Her shoulders quivered, and a few strands of her hair fell into her eyes.

Nejibei sighed and nodded. "I understand. The way he taught you. The way you learned. I knew all of that without your having to tell us. So then, how did you fare in Yamada? They didn't think much of your new dance, I suppose."

"No, they didn't. When I performed it the first time, some of them started laughing. Others said it was terrible, frightening. They started this rumor that a Tengu had had his way with me for four or five days in a row."

"Yes, but if your teacher hadn't been a demon, you wouldn't have been able to learn how to dance like that. I understand that even here in Ise there are a handful of people who know something about nō. Did you show your dance to them?"

"I did. There was a gentleman who wanted to see me perform, just out of curiosity. He himself offered to sing the libretto. But when I started dancing, he said I didn't know what I was doing, and he made me stop."

"The strong rhythm of your footwork would have made a mess of a weak accompaniment. The singing would have fallen apart. In any case, that's how you came to be transferred—if that's what you call it—to Kuwana."

"Everyone said I was crazy. A fox! Badger! Bewitched by owls! Those howlers couldn't handle it. My mistress said she was sorry to let me go. But the others wouldn't have me around. My teacher told me she wasn't that close to the owner of the Shimaya in Kuwana, but they were related. So she sent me here temporarily."

The older man said, "I see. And you're still having your share of troubles here, I suppose? We can talk about that later. I must say, dear child, your dance surprised me, too. For someone like you—a young woman, and not some evil spirit—to be dancing with such grace was so astonishing I had to interrupt. I hope you'll forgive me. Now, back on your feet. Let's see the rest. I hate to trouble you again. It's been a while since I last saw that dance. You make me want to see the young master again."

A Song by Lantern Light

As he says this, see what emerges from the scarf now untied on his lap. It's a small hand drum so elegant it could have been painted by one of the Tosa masters. It has tuning cords of crimson, like the maple trees of the Tatsuta River, and two round heads like faces of the moon. Its sound was like the striking of a jade fulling block. So let the angels come and hear! Inlaid in its lacquered barrel was the name Kumoi, "a well of clouds." With aged hands, the man warmed Kumoi high above the brazier's fire and tightened the cords as his hand struck it like a shuttle skillfully weaving a length of brocade. At the sight of it, Osen held her breath and immediately bowed. She pressed both hands to the floor.

The power of art is indisputable. Who was this Nejibei? None other than the seventy-eight-year-old Henmi Hidenoshin. His reputation as a musician was above question. Having recently passed his responsibilities on to his grandson, he had taken the name Sessō in his retirement. As a master of the small drum, he was without equal in all the land.

And the younger man? He was an elder of the most famous school of *nō* actors in Japan. Onchi Genzaburō. None other than.

Having recently been invited to participate in a program sponsored by the Marquis, Lord of Tsu, and having just finished their performance in his temporary lodgings near the great shrines at Ise, these two gentlemen—Henmi Hidenoshin and Onchi Genzaburō—were leisurely making their return to Tokyo, a la *Shank's Mare*.

21

Back at the noodle shop, the street musician continued: "He made a number of conceited motions, and then the bald-headed man started to chant. He was actually better than I thought, not the kind of performance you'd expect from a blind masseur. If you dumped his voice into the howling gusts of wind outside, it might have carried as far as the whistles of the blind. I could see why so many of my colleagues deserved to be called 'those other guys' by this man.

"To me, though, he was little more than an inconvenience. And yet, art demands respect. I knew I shouldn't make light of him. Concentrating on the music, I started to tap out the rhythm on my knee."

The young man sat up, and the blind man who had been massaging his shoulders recoiled, pulling the street singer's kimono back until the collar touched the front of his neck.

"I tapped out the beat on my knee. It wasn't just any ordinary tapping. It was a transmission from one generation to another, passed on to me as a child sitting on the lap of the man who was my adoptive father, my teacher, and uncle. I cut the rests in his rhythm by tapping just off the beat. I threw the weight of his voice off. And with a thrust to the throat, I shattered his breathing. To a beginner who is blind and deaf to timing and rhythm, it means nothing. But to a man who was a professional of sorts, hearing one misplaced beat made his voice get stuck and his tune fall apart. It's the same with the timing of the samisen. So how do you like that? Our stylish gentleman started behaving like a boor. Once he lost the beat, it was like plowing sand, or like beads of water rolling off a duck's back.

"I have to give him credit for knowing as much as he did. But with one slap of my professional hand I subdued his voice, and the tightness of his performance immediately went slack. Now that I think back on it, the foolishness of youth made me do it. Mine was the folly of a beast that knows no better. His was the sorrow of a novice.

"Wretched Sōzan! As I watched him try to wring music out of that dying voice, sweat began dripping down his forehead, drenching him from chin to chest. His huge lips became parched like dried sea slugs. His tongue hardened, and he panted for breath. As he sang, his trembling hand started to grab at the tatami as he searched for his *sake* cup. Before he had finished even one page of music, my well-timed clapping echoed in his soul and pulled the bottom out of his performance.

"He coughed up a flame-like breath and collapsed forward. He dangled his tongue and licked the tatami like a dog.

"'Master, you're not feeling well?' I smiled. 'But I must hear you sing. I beg of you, Sōzan, even if you become both blind and deaf, I won't be able to go to my grave without hearing one song.'

"I clenched my fists and asked in a loud voice, 'Masseur, how far it is to the Fujiya from here?'

"'Why do you ask?'

"'Because I'm afraid my voice has a way of carrying. I came here secretly tonight, and wouldn't want my uncle, who's asleep at the Fujiya, to hear me. They say that a great warrior can sense the stirrings of frost. A wakeful old man like my uncle might be having trouble sleeping on a windy night like this. I wouldn't want him getting up in the middle of the night. Here's your fee. I'd better be getting back.'

"Sōzan's eyes began to move about wildly beneath his eyelids. 'Wait! You keep the beat like that. You say that the people in Onoe-machi might hear your voice all the way from here. The arrogance of your words. Your youth. I've never heard you sing, nor have I ever seen your face, but you have to be Kidahachi, the adopted son of the current master, Onchi Genzaburō. That's right, isn't it, Onchi?' He called me by name."

"By god, I'm drunk," the street musician dropped his cup. "It's not that I can't tell you my name. It's my uncle. He wouldn't like that. Both of you, never mention this to anyone." He cautioned the woman and the masseur, then continued his story.

"I straightened my jacket. 'Maybe you're right. Maybe you're wrong. Anyway, think of me as one of "those other guys" from To-kyo. You call yourself Sōzan, do you? Master of the main school? Well, Mister Sōzan, why don't you fix up a gift, maybe a little sea-weed or something, and crawl your way up the Tōkaidō. If you come around to the kitchen of the Onchi residence, maybe some poor top-twirling fledgling will take you where my uncle can't see you and teach you a few easy lines from *Takasago*.'

"I stood up to leave."

22

"The white eyes of Sōzan's pockmarked face glared at me as he struggled to his feet and said with indignation, 'Dear Young Master. My sorrow as a blind man is not being able to see your face. Let me touch it. Let me hold it. Let me feel it. Just once.'

"Let him touch my face? Good god!

"I tried to slip by. But it was a small six-mat room; and even though he was blind, he knew every inch of his house.

"He quickly blocked access to the stairway, thrusting out both arms. His shadow appeared on the ceiling—a huge black monk, dripping with oily sweat and pawing the air. Even now I can't forget the sight of his fathomless jealousy, that bizarrely menacing countenance.

"'You'll never touch me. Never!' I desperately tried to make my escape. I moved to the side. He stopped me. I ran the other way. The second floor of his rickety house creaked beneath our weight. The wind howled and pummeled. I felt like I was being enveloped in a veil of dark clouds. It was terrifying! Dreadful, yes!

"I ducked beneath his arms and made it to the staircase. As I was thundering down the steps, I heard Sōzan call out in a hoarse voice, 'Sode, stop that man!'

"There were three or four women on the first floor. As I was opening the front door, about to get away, one of them, a beautiful young woman, came over and grabbed me. In the punishing wind, the crimson skirts of her kimono wrapped around me. It was her, the young woman I had seen earlier with the ribbon in her hair, the one who was massaging the blind man's shoulders and had brought him tea. 'Sōzan's concubine,' I thought.

"I looked into her eyes. They were clear, expressive, alive. I knew I would never see her again. I started to leave.

"'Pretty girl. Look, you might get killed. You might die. But never let yourself become some man's toy.' I blurted this out, and pushed her away. I faced into the wind that scattered the voice calling after me, and in a cloud of dust I plunged ahead and hurried back to the inn.

"Afterward I learned she wasn't a concubine, at all. That pretty one, Osode, was Sōzan's daughter. Had I known that, had I understood that then, I wouldn't have put her father to shame like that, even if I were one of his enemies." The young musician suddenly bent over and started searching the floor for the wine cup he had dropped. The blind man's hands slipped over the tops of his shoulders.

"I instructed the people at the Fujiya. 'If a masseur shows up, tell him I'm not here.' Fortunately, my uncle was sleeping peacefully. I slipped into the futon laid out next to his. I pulled the covers over my

A Song by Lantern Light

head and had a good night's sleep. That was the last good night's sleep I had. Why? Because Sōzan died in his anger that very night. He resented me for the way I had disgraced him. Being the arrogant man he was, he broke in two like a dried reed. He scribbled out a death note, cursing my posterity for the next seven generations, and killed himself in the foothills of Mount Tsutsumigatake. He was dangling from a tree in the clearing there. They said his body was still swaying when the storm let up at dawn.

"Of course, I didn't know anything about what had happened. The wind died down. The weather was fine. And my uncle was in great spirits. We left Furuichi and went to Futami. Sometime that morning, we checked in at the Asahikan; and since we planned to stay the night there, we thought we might go on to Toba and take a look. We immediately hired a carriage and took the mountain road above Futami Bay. The two of us spent half a day there, with the hills as our gallery and the ocean at our feet. And when we finally returned to the Asahikan? Guess what.

"There was a huge crowd in front of the inn, and the hallways inside were packed. I'm not exaggerating. They had come from Ise to meet us. By the end of the day, everyone in Japan had heard of the blind man's death and about the letter that he had left behind. They weren't interested in that, though. Those people, dressed in their formal kimono and frocks, came to us and said, 'You great artists who could put an end to Sōzan with the power of your art, we must have you come to Yamada for a day and perform for us.'

"My uncle was more than just angry. He called me the most disgraceful person in all of Japan. Right there in front of the crowd, Onchi Genzaburō proclaimed that from that day on I was never to sing the nō libretto again. I was disowned on the spot. My uncle went on, 'People like Sōzan, this blind man who had killed himself because he realized the paucity of his performance, these are the true gods of art.' He promised the crowd that he would respectfully attend Sōzan's funeral and, as an offering, sing at his grave. Then he sent me away.

"I don't know what happened after that. I started wandering the land, and began this fragile life as a street musician."

23

"I found an old samisen, also abandoned by the floating world. Someone had left it in a pawnshop in the back streets near the Ōsu Kannon in Nagoya. That was my beginning. I arranged to make payments. I earned a few coins here and a few there, but rarely enough to get a room for the night. During the days that followed, I slept under the stars about half of the time, making my way west to Kyoto, Osaka, and eventually as far as Hakata.

"But somehow I couldn't forget about Ise, and, strangely enough, I hurried back.

"I learned that the young woman I had warned never to become some man's plaything was following my advice, even at risk to her life. Meeting that pretty girl was the only memorable event in my life. Nothing could ever come of it, though, and so I quickly left again. Then in Yokkaichi I got sick." He addressed the noodle shop owner's wife directly. "Ma'am, there was another kind person like you who helped me get back on my feet. Things were all right in western Japan. If I happened to overhear someone play a line from a nō play, it sounded like a peasant blowing on a bamboo whistle, signaling that the bathwater's ready. But as soon as I got as far east as Hakone, once I reached the pass there, I could hear the drums of Edo echoing. How could I control myself? I might break into song. So I never ventured farther east than Imagire in Shizuoka Prefecture. From here, I was planning to pass through Age to the Ōgaki Road. I thought I'd head north to Gifu, then travel the circuit through the North Country. I was over in the Tomita area for three days, and came here to Kuwana yesterday.

"But then, what happened tonight? I saw two unlikely old men. And that upset me so much I came barging into your shop. Then the whistles of the blind masseurs started to pierce me—more sharply than ever. And then I saw shadows. One was beautiful, the other horrifying. The blind men of Kuwana are out to kill me tonight. But who cares? Let them murder me! I found one who reminds me of the other, and I had you come into this shop. Ready to die, I asked you to massage my shoulders. And now I feel like my muscles are torn out, my flesh plucked, my body ripped apart."

A Song by Lantern Light

The musician fell forward again. This time, the blind man's hands, having slid forward off his shoulders, were visibly trembling. The masseur's frowning face touched the young man's back. The musician's pale chest—veins pulsating visibly beneath his skin—showed against the faded color of his kimono's open collar. Poor man! He looked like a Hakata willow being captured by a huge mud spider.

"Who's that!" the woman suddenly cried out in surprise. Over in a dark corner beneath the votive shelf, a wet spot appeared on the paper-covered doors and a hole formed. The shopkeeper's wife called out, having caught her husband spying on them. He stepped back with a clatter. Apparently, he wasn't alone. He had brought two young men with him, both armed with sticks.

"Sir."

A dignified Onchi Genzaburō looked on as his partner Sessō tuned his drum. "Thank you for condescending to play the accompaniment for this young woman. She *and* I are forever in your debt." He placed a fan on his knee and bowed.

"Incompetent as always." Sessō returned the greeting and slid off his cushion.

"Is that really necessary?"

"It would be disrespectful to your school to play while sitting on a cushion."

"I see. So you're going to pay your respects to my nephew by way of this young lady's performance. In that case, let me join you." They tossed their cushions to the right and left.

"My daughter. My daughter." Genzaburō called her twice. "So you're Omie. I consider you my nephew's wife. I'm Kidahachi's uncle, Onchi Genzaburō. We'd like to see your performance again."

The two distinguished musicians assumed their positions.

With dignity and grace, Omie fixed her eyes on some distant spot and drew back a few steps. Her shoulders and arms were supple and delicate, her black hair set off beautifully by her wisteria-colored kimono. Once again, the fan she held was a sword, and her voice was strong and resonant as she began to sing.

> Say you'll pull me
> From the deep.
> Then, well promised,
> This sword I'll keep.

The shadow of Henmi Hidenoshin's hand danced on the drum as he held it above his shoulder. The barrel of Kumoi glistened, and its cords suddenly burned like a scarlet flame. The master, flower of his well-practiced art, in full blossom and imbued with honor, struck the drum and called out.

"Listen!"

Staring in the direction of the Minatoya, Onchi Kidahachi, once the rising star of the *nō* world, a crane hidden away by dark clouds and sorely missed by his many admirers, rose from the stool where he had been sitting. He placed one foot on the dirt floor of the noodle shop. "Sessō is playing his drum!" He leaned forward and held his chest. He reached out for a towel, quickly covered his mouth, and coughed up a spot of blood. He threw the towel down and grabbed the blind masseur by the right hand. "Curse me, Blind Man. But you're coming with me to the Minatoya! Now you'll have the performance you've been waiting for." He pulled the masseur to his feet, and together they quickly stepped into the moonlight.

> Down into the waters deep
> Down to where the dead ones sleep,
> I looked about and there I saw
> The gleaming tower of jade.
> In it lay the precious jewel
> 'Mid flowers bright and beautiful,
> With guardian gods there keeping watch,
> Eight dragons at the gate.
> Wicked fish and crocodiles
> Swarming 'round with vicious smiles,
> How was I to stay alive,
> To taste the breath of day?
> 'Twas no surprise when came to me
> Thoughts of home and family,

A Song by Lantern Light

> Memories of my foolish son,
> Amid the crashing waves.

With Onchi Genzaburō now singing accompaniment, Omie reached a point in her dance where her heart overflowed, and the ribbon in her coiffure broke, sending her lustrous black hair spilling over her shoulders, flowing in the water and in the flickering of lantern light, as she made each movement with utter perfection, dancing upon the tatami floor that had turned into the ocean beneath her kimono's train.

> I know my son remains alive,
> So does his father yet survive.
> Still, parting thus
> Is sadness hard to bear.

Remembering the son he had vowed never to remember, Genzaburō's voice became choked with emotion. And when his song began to falter, from outside the Minatoya came the clear voice of another that resonated in the room and took up the melody just where it had begun to fade. Like a white rainbow, the singing suddenly flooded Omie's dancing form with its brilliance.

Now it was Kidahachi, her beloved, singing to her every movement.

> Tears now rushing to her eyes,
> With resolve she starts to rise . . .

"This is it. Don't falter now." Genzaburō suddenly rose to his feet and steadied Omie's back with his hand. Supported by his timeless strength, she placed the wave-patterned sleeve of her kimono on the old man's arm and quickly brought her fan up and touched it to her glistening black hair. She quickly spread it open; and the clouds painted on the silver fan joined with the image of her lover, reflecting a brilliant light that made the lanterns dimly pale as she continued.

Dance the dance! Sing the song! Joining the secret rhythms of Sessō's accompaniment, the waters of Kuwana Bay reverberated like a thunderous drum, and the Hibi River added a higher pitch of lapping waves. Towering in the moonlight, as if seated around a stage, the snow-covered peaks of Mount Tado, Gozaisho, Kama, and Kamuri together witnessed the performance.

The night deepened. The town of Kuwana grew cold and frozen. When the notes of a blind man's whistle sounded again in the night sky, Onchi Kidahachi stood alone. Singing in the darkness of the Minatoya's eaves, his silhouette was blue and his shadow dark, as the moon that brightened the roof tiles splashed his face with the silvery light of a fan. One fan touching another, two sides of the same, Kidahachi and Omie joined, as she brought her hands together in prayer, and he continued the song.

> "Extend to me your saving light,
> Through the course of this black night,
> Let your powers join with mine,
> Oh, Kannon, Merciful One."
> To her brow, she puts the blade,
> Now left, now right, all guardians fade,
> She steps ahead, death's price now paid,
> Into the Dragon's Palace!

The singing and the dancing trailed off and came to an end.

"Lend me your back, Sōzan." The exhausted Onchi Kidahachi seemed to reach back and rest upon the back of the large, shapeless shadow that had been crouching at his feet. At last, he had vanquished his enemy.

From the inn, a road led off in a white line, set off by hanging lanterns flickering here and there in the deepening night. A crowd of people had gathered, among them blind men walking with sticks.

A Quiet Obsession

"A Quiet Obsession," (Mayu kakushi no rei, 1924) is a round-about translation of this story's title, which would more literally be rendered as "The Eyebrow-hiding Spirit." This is a cultural reference that would be missed by all but the most sophisticated reader, who would understand that, in Japan, it once was customary for married women to shave their eyebrows. The immediate allusion, then, is to Otsuya's obsessive desire to be considered not only the most lovely of all (for Kyōka, the eyebrows were a particularly important sign of beauty), but married as well. This is a modern ghost story par excellence, made up of a number of narrative layers that occur within each other. Kyōka's mastery of narrative structure sets the reader up to experience the bare logic of obsession and ghostly appearance. The ending comes suddenly, as the past bursts into the present, and the dead are no longer contained by death's veil. Finally, note once again the many references to Ikku's Shank's Mare, *a book that Kyōka took with him whenever he traveled.*

1

Located on the Kiso Road, the village of Narai lies three thousand two hundred feet above sea level. It is one hundred and fifty-eight miles from Iidabashi, the starting point of the Chūō Line. That would be one way to begin this story. But perhaps the better method of evoking the spirit of travel would be to allude to Jippen-sha Ikku's famous *Shank's Mare*.

Ikku's heroes, Yajirōbei and Kidahachi, have managed to make it over the Torii Pass. The sun is nearing the mountaintops to the west; and from the inns that line both sides of the narrow road a number of women emerge. They plead with the travelers, "Won't you stay the night with us? Our bath water is already hot. This is the place to stay! Stay here!"

To this, Yajirō says, "Still a bit early to call it a day."

But Kidahachi disagrees, "No. Let's call it quits. How about it, ma'am?"

"Stay with us. Would you like rice or noodles for dinner?" she asks. "If you want noodles, we have the lowest prices in the village."

"The cheaper the better! How much are the noodles? If you don't mind my asking?"

"116 *sen*."

Always short of cash, they are persuaded to spend the night here.

They finish their bath, and the promised noodles arrive. They dig in without hesitation. "Not bad. But the broth's a bit weak."

"Maybe so. But the hands that brought them couldn't be prettier." Yajirō flirts with the serving girl. "Ma'am, how about another bowl?"

"I'm very sorry," she replies. "But we're out of noodles."

"What? No more noodles? You mean we only get two servings each? That stinks. I'm still hungry."

Kidahachi adds. "Cheap is cheap, but this is a little much. You expect us to get full on two servings?"

"They're making fools of us. We'll pay more. Just bring us some rice!"

What little money they have, they've wasted on noodles. How utterly depressing!

That night, the two run into a well-to-do acquaintance, Kanbei, a knob maker from Drawer Alley off Dresser Street back in their hometown of Edo. Together they visit a temple to pray, and hear the cries of a stag. . . .

Contemplating this scene in Ikku's novel, our hero received the impression that he ought to spend the night here in Narai. He told me

A Quiet Obsession

that the train was already starting to pull away from the station when he made up his mind to get off.

My friend, Sakai Sankichi, had actually purchased a ticket to Agematsu to see the famous suspended bridge and the "frog boulders" of the Kiso River. It was the middle of November.

"I had some strange connection with those two bowls of noodles . . . ," Sakai said.

The night before, he had stayed in Matsumoto. As you probably know, one has to change trains in Shiojiri to get to Matsumoto, so it's unusual to stop there if you're on the way to Agematsu from Tokyo. It would be easy enough to say he had some kind of errand to take care of in Matsumoto. That would explain everything. But it would weaken the story. Of course, there's no need to scrutinize the matter too closely. Although he had only a limited number of days for this trip, Sakai left Ueno Station for Takasaki, desiring to taste the pleasures of the road more fully. With the sight of Mount Myogi in his eyes, he proceeded to Yokokawa, then to Kuma no taira and Asama. He passed through Karuizawa and Oiwake, where he changed to the Shinonoi Line. With the sight of Mount Obasute in his window, he made plans to stay one night in Matsumoto. He'd been told by a well-known painter about "an inn with nice young women. I'm a regular there, so I'll introduce you." Sakai would have been better off not getting involved in the matter, but the man gave him a letter of introduction.

Last night, upon finding the inn, he saw that the girl at the front desk seemed to be one of the "nice young women" the painter had mentioned, even though the person who showed him to his room was only a maid. He handed the letter to the woman, but no young beauty seemed to appear. In fact, all that materialized on that frosty night in mid-November was a single cup of tea that had been brewed long ago, say nothing of a late-night snack or dinner. At least his room was tastefully done. The table was made of rosewood; the brazier large, though its fire was weak. Huddling around those cold, white ashes, he suggested something warm to eat and perhaps a little *sake*. To this, the maid replied, almost curtly, that the cook had closed the kitchen for the day, and that there was nothing she could bring him. It was cold enough, all right. The place was quiet, as if all fires had been extinguished, even though it wasn't even eleven.

"How about some *sake*, then?"

"I'm sorry."

"You mean you're out of wine?"

"All out."

"Then what about beer?"

"I'm very sorry."

Sakai sat up straight and addressed the maid. "Young woman, couldn't you run out and get a little something from a shop close by?"

"I'm afraid it's too late. All the bars and eating places are closed."

"Bars and eating places, indeed!"

During the rickshaw ride from the station, near the bridge where he had heard the cold sound of rushing water, he had seen what looked like teahouses on both sides of the road, their red lanterns flickering. That wasn't so far from here. Ah, if he had known it was going to be like this, he wouldn't have finished off the bottle of *sake* he had purchased in Karuizawa—lapping it up like Master Jirō's hungry dog, as the song goes.

He sighed. His stomach grumbled loudly. With sadness in his voice, he inquired, "So you don't have any *sake,* or beer, or anything to go along with it. Any food? What about the meal you served here tonight?"

"Everything's gone. And we've put out the cooking fire for the night."

What had he done to deserve such abuse? This was beyond getting the cold shoulder, it was totally absurd. And thanks to that unsolicited letter of introduction from the painter, he couldn't very well put on a fighting face and announce he was leaving to go to another inn. Rather than do that, he surrendered to his fate, telling himself that he must be being punished for something he had done in a former life. Could he at least order a bowl of *udon* or *soba?*

He asked with fear and trembling, and the maid replied, "If it's *udon,* I can ask."

"Good, then I'd like two bowls, if that's possible."

The maid, who had been straddling the threshold of the room, pulled her knees in as if to make a quick escape. She stood and briskly walked away.

Sakai waited a short while. Soon, she reappeared at the door carrying a bowl on a tray. Famished, he remarked with a tone of rebuke in his voice that he had ordered two bowls, not one.

"The cook put two servings in this one bowl."

Before he could say "Oh, I see. Then you may go now," she showed him her backside and quickly walked away. With the eyes of a neglected stepchild, he watched her shuffle down the hall. Then he hugged the bowl of noodles and lifted the lid to see that, yes, the cook had indeed thrown in two servings of *udon*. But there was only a splash of soup in the bottom of the bowl, leaving the top of the noodles high and dry.

He felt like crying but all he could do was laugh. No doubt he had chanced upon an inn for people abstaining from food as they made their pilgrimages to the Akiba Shrine or to the Izuna Gongen in Nagano.

He thought of the previous night's two servings of noodles and compared them to the *soba* purchased by Yajirō and Kidahachi of old. Perhaps this is making too much of a small thing, but it did seem like a strange coincidence—their two bowls and his—which is exactly why he suddenly decided to spend the night in Narai.

The last rays of sun were showing above the Kiso mountains when a quick shower started to fall. But Sakai had come prepared for rain.

Rather than take one of the *rikisha* waiting in front of the station, he put up his umbrella and made his way down a lonely cobble street, following a row of dark, overhanging eaves. He was ready for anything. Bring on those two bowls of *soba*. Last night's *udon* had been a surprise. But tonight, he'd even welcome *soba*. Hoping to savor the pathos of travel, he passed up two modernized inns with glass fronts, and, like a crow, peered into an old and weathered inn that had a rustic mountain palanquin and dried vegetable leaves hanging together from its eaves. Inside, there was a dirt-floored area and a split-wood fire burning in the hearth. Dressed in a black overcoat, he called into the open doorway and stepped into the entrance to see a man with a bandanna over his head, tending to the fire. The doorway was very wide, the hearth huge. Suspended from the soot-darkened ceiling was a square hanging lantern, a perfect complement to the palanquin outside. At the front desk, in the shadows of the staircase, sat an interesting-looking bald-headed man.

"Welcome!"

Two bowls of *soba*. Two bowls of *soba*. Expecting nothing more than noodles, Sakai watched the man quickly jump to his feet and bow. It was as if an insubstantial gluten ball in his bowl had turned out to be a solid piece of fish cake.

"We have a customer," the man called out. "Put him in the Crane Room, Number Three."

The maid, a young woman with a fair complexion, wore a simple cotton dress and a clean, carefully pressed apron. She led Sakai up to the third floor. Together, they climbed a staircase and passed by windows through which many pines peeked in from outside.

His accommodations turned out to be a comfortable ten-mat room. The pillars and ceiling beams were made of sturdy logs, and the display in the alcove was tastefully done. Contrary to the initial impression he had received from the building's entrance, the inn was, in fact, solidly constructed.

The bedding was thick and warm and a beautiful bear rug was spread on the floor. So this is what people were talking about when, in the age of *Shank's Mare,* they spoke of people selling monkey fetuses, snake livers, and animal skins along the mountain roads. Sitting on the bearskin, Sakai was fancying himself as a fun-loving daimyō when a maid came up the stairs. She brought a fire pan, and from it transferred a generous amount of hot charcoal into the copper-lined hibachi. The heat it generated was impressive. The tip of the blue flames molded themselves around the edges of the charcoal and flared red. Suddenly, the cold mountain winds that had been seeping through the windows seemed to vanish. One hesitates to think of what would happen if an earthquake struck with such a fire blazing away on the third floor.

Sakai took a bath.

As for dinner, when he inspected what had been brought to him on the small lacquered butterfly-legged table, it far surpassed the *soba* to which he had resigned himself. There was nothing so luxurious as a piece of teriyaki yellowtail, but they did serve a thick, smoky-tasting slice of freshly prepared eggs, along with a bowl of fish cake glazed with a thick broth of grated arrowroot. There was also a plate of what was considered a delicacy in the area—five fragrantly broiled thrushes that had been cooked whole—their heads arranged so that their mouths were open like small *sake* cups, plump thighs pointed away, breasts facing up.

"Wonderful. Truly delicious."

Sakai had the maid pour *sake* for him, and even found pleasure in the rather unrefined way she did it. He thanked her politely, feeling as if he were riding a bear and being feted by a mountain wizard. "That was a great meal! Thank you so much."

The compliment came from the bottom of his heart. And because there was no trace of mockery in his voice, she answered with equal sincerity. "Sir, I'm glad you're enjoying your food. Another cup of *sake*?"

"Thank you. That would be nice. And while we're at it, I have another request. Could I ask you to bring me an extra serving of those small birds? And this time, could we set up a pot of water here in my room so we could boil them? How many do you have left?"

"Three more baskets. Plus there's another bundle hanging on a pillar in the kitchen."

"What luck! I wonder if I could get a few extra, so I could cook them here. Do you think that would that be all right?"

"I'll go ask the cook."

"And while you're at it, if you could bring a carafe of warmed *sake*. This fire here is so nice and warm that I could just set it here and it would never get cold. Sorry it's such a long way to bring everything. Bring three at once. How about that? Do I sound like Iwami Jūtarō?"

She laughed.

This morning in Matsumoto, his soul had been as cold as ice, like the water that washed his face. It didn't occur to him then, but now that his heart had been thawed by this warmth, he understood why he had gotten the *udon* treatment the night before. The painter who had written him that letter of introduction had only recently established his reputation. As a young man wandering the back roads of Shinshū, he had probably holed up at that inn for five months or more. He had mentioned how thoughtful the people were, how they didn't press him for the money he owed them, and how they even gave him traveling money when he left. That had to be it. They had obviously treated Sakai coolly because of that letter. They must have thought he wouldn't pay his bill promptly either, and that he would also expect traveling money from them.

"Sir, forgive us for the poor meal we served you tonight."

A man appeared at the opening in the sliding doors and politely bowed. He was thirty-six or -seven, had short cropped hair, and was wearing a navy-blue padded jacket with narrow sleeves and a wide apron made of the same navy-blue cotton. He was thin and had a sallow yet dark complexion. He seemed gloomy but honest.

"To the contrary. That was a tremendous feast. You must be the manager?"

"No. I'm the cook, and an incompetent one at that. I'm afraid we had nothing better to offer you in this out-of-the-way place in the mountains. I'm sure we didn't meet your expectations."

"Not at all. Everything was delicious."

"The maid informed me you would like to have boiled thrush. As I was thinking of how I might prepare the birds for you, it occurred to me that maybe she didn't quite understand what you were asking for. The women here are country girls. Forgive my rudeness, but I thought I might make an inquiry just to be sure. That's why I've come to bother you like this."

Sakai was embarrassed. "Well, that was very thoughtful of you. It's a long way to come," he said, then regretted his words. "I'm joking, of course. But three floors—"

"I don't mind at all."

"Please come in. Are you busy?"

"Actually, no. Dinner is served. Other than you, there were only two other groups tonight."

"Then do come in. Right over here."

"Thank you."

"Sorry if I'm being too forward. But how about a drink? Here comes more wine now. Ma'am, if you could pour for this gentleman."

"Thank you, but I don't drink."

"Come on. Just one drink. Sorry. All this fuss just because I wanted to eat thrush from a boiling pot. What I had in mind was—"

"Sir," said the maid. "The man at the front desk also said the best way to eat thrush is to *broil* them.'"

A Quiet Obsession

"That's how we served them to you tonight. It's customary to eat them head first. They're delicious if you suck the brains out and crunch down on the head with one bite. I guess that's a pretty crude way of doing things."

"I certainly have no complaints about your cooking. Sorry if I've given you that impression. Actually, I was at a banquet once where one of the geisha who was present said something about thrushes in Kiso. We all had had plenty to drink, and everybody was singing folksongs. That's when someone started into a Kiso-bushi. There's always been a warm place in my heart for this part of the world. Even now I have a faint recollection of how it went. Something like—

> The rice you send to Kiso,
> To Kiso,
> To Kiso."

"Yes. That's it." The cook set his *sake* cup down carefully. Then he took his pipe from his tobacco pouch and, without hesitation, started knocking the ashes out against the hibachi's metal edge.

> "Surplus rice
> From Ina
> And from Takato.

That's how it goes. Rice happens to be this girl's name, too. She's called Oyone."

"What are you talking about?" The maid looked over at Isaku the cook. She made a face and laughed.

"Sir, this man's from Ina."

"I see. Then you're from the same place as the famous warrior Takeda Katsuyori, Shingen's son."

"That's right. But even Katsuyori wasn't as handsome as our cook."

"Of course he wasn't." Without as much as a smile, the sullen cook continued cleaning out his pipe.

"And that's why he was partial to the village of Ina. In Kiso, they sing it a little differently.

> The rice
> From Ina

And from Takato
Is surplus rice
From Kiso.

That's what they say anyway."

"Well, whichever it is, I was just telling you how I came to be interested in the geisha's story about the thrush, triggered by the 'To Kiso, to Kiso' song. We were all drunk. I couldn't tell if she was talking about Niegawa or Yabuhara or Fukushima or Agematsu on the other side of the pass. The geisha told us a story about how she had gone with a customer to set a bird net to catch thrushes. They walked up a mountain road early in the morning before dawn. They put up a net and set out decoys where their guide told them to. Just before sunrise, a flock of birds emerged in the glow of the morning mist and flew from Onoe on the other side of the valley to the ridge of the mountain where they were waiting. Beating their wings, the thrushes flew right into their net. They slowly drew it in, grabbed the birds, and immediately roasted them over an open fire. She told us how they ate them while they were still dripping hot, sucking them down and enjoying their wonderful flavor."

"Sounds delicious."

"It was terribly cold so they drank warm *sake* while devouring the birds. Contented, they rested, squatting close to the fire. Then one of the geisha stood up, and the two hunters who had come along as guides cried out in horror. The geisha's mouth was filled with blood from the half-cooked birds. When the woman who was telling us this story unconsciously put her handkerchief to her mouth, red blotches seemed to form. I watched her face. She was a slender, inviting young woman. Just hearing her story makes me hungry. But what an unearthly sight that must have been! Even imagining it in Tokyo, I could see the whitely breaking dawn on the high, steep mountain ranges and valleys of Kiso. Then the woman's beautiful head rising up through the mist, higher than the peaks around them, with flames licking at the hem of her kimono in the darkness."

"Sir, you shouldn't say things like that."

"I don't tell the story well, but it gets to you, doesn't it? Her mouth dripping with blood—"

"My goodness."

"So I asked the woman, 'How did you get out of there alive?' When she asked me why I'd ask such a question, I told her that someone who looked like that would surely draw fire from some panic-stricken hunter, taking aim from a flat of bamboo grass on the other side of the valley. The place and time, too. They used to say that trapping birds at dawn leads to spirit possession and other strange things. And that's just what happened. Didn't she immediately turn into a beautiful demon? 'And why not?' That's what she said as she pressed her handkerchief to her mouth. 'I am a demon, after all. It's better than being eaten by someone. . . .' Frightening, isn't it? Chills ran down my spine."

"No kidding." The cook, lost in thought, spoke in a subdued voice. "That's quite a story, sir. You know, it really is dangerous. In those circumstances, someone always gets hurt. The woman's lucky she survived. I don't know where she was hunting. We always catch more birds on the Mino side of the gorge—at the foot of Mount On, upstream from Niegawa. Where in Tokyo was she from?"

"Somewhere downtown."

"Yanagibashi?" The maid looked intently at Sakai.

"Or maybe Shinbashi?" the cook asked.

"Actually, right between. Closer to Nihonbashi. The only time I heard her tell that story was at that banquet."

"If you don't think she would mind, I'd like to ask her where it happened, just for my own information. Sometimes our understanding is no match for the mysteries of these deep mountains."

The maid nodded, and a dark shadow passed over her face.

As anyone might do, Sakai followed the lead. "Why? Did something out of the ordinary happen here, too?"

"Nothing in particular. But just as a river has its rapids, the mountains, too, have their deep places. You have to be careful. You know the thrushes we just served you? The hunters caught them at the summit for two days straight. It doesn't happen that often."

"And that's it." Sakai raised his cup, signaling the maid to pour another round. "Cook, sir. When I saw your wonderful presentation of thrushes tonight—so fragrant and juicy—I couldn't help but think of the geisha with the bloody mouth. I'm no monk, or vegetarian, or anything like that. I could ask for half-cooked thrushes, too. But take a look. Outside the window. The rain, the maple trees, the mist covering the mountains. And the peaks. You can see those snow-covered ones that tower up and pierce the clouds. For whatever reason, if I suddenly stood and my mouth turned bloody and my head rose into the air, a face like mine wouldn't be anything like that geisha's— impressive and beautiful, like the metamorphosis of some mountain god. Rather, some crow would think it was a persimmon fallen from its branch. It would peck at it through the window. I don't know. Somehow, I'm starting to feel uneasy."

"Oyone. Aren't they late with the lights tonight?" The cook spoke in a subdued voice.

The rain had cleared, and evening came to the Kiso mountains. Rising from below, they could heard the echoing rapids of the Narai River.

2

"Is something wrong?"

"Oh, it's you."

Night had fallen, and Isaku, the cook, was standing in the snow-covered garden.

"The herons come and try to eat the fish." The cook passed close by, just outside Sakai's window, as if he were walking across the water.

"I thought maybe someone had fallen in, or otters or something were running around out there. What a racket!"

Twent-four hours had passed, and now Sakai Sankichi was staying in one of the first-floor rooms.

He had decided to remain a little longer in Narai. It wasn't because of the snow that had been accumulating since morning, nor was it because he had anything in particular that he wanted to see. Last night, after their conversation, the cook had responded to his request for boiled thrush. What he had in mind was setting up a brazier next to his serving table, just as one would cook woodcock or chicken. Isaku brought up a plate piled high with cut-up pieces of thrush, a basket filled with chopped scallions, and some soy sauce and sugar.

A Quiet Obsession

Oyone made sure the fire was supplied with charcoal.

In Sakai's hometown along the northern coast, the local appetite for thrush was extraordinary when the season rolled around. All the eating establishments hung out signs advertising the small birds—to be stewed or grilled to one's liking. Even the noodle shops put out flyers for thrush *udon* and thrush *soba*. The thing about thrush, though, was its price. With thrush added to a dish, it suddenly became haute cuisine. Although the servings were small—three or four tiny slices of meat—Sakai wrapped them in scallions and tossed them into a boiling pot, which produced a column of steam that warmed his heart.

And to top it off, he drank warm *sake* while sitting cross-legged on the bearskin.

The geisha with the bloody mouth became a mountain bandit.

When it was time to retire for the night, he had the warm quilt with sleeves to slip into and the bear. He quite enjoyed putting his arms into the sleeves, pulling the bearskin over him, and tucking his feet in. Snow was predicted for the following day. And yet, with the wine in his blood and an animal skin on top of him, he gave no thought to the night storm seeping into his bones, or to the menacing rush of the Kiso River in his ears. He spent a warm night on the third floor sleeping soundly; and because of that solid night of slumber, he also enjoyed breakfast the next morning—blowing on and sipping hot tofu soup.

It was a far cry from what he had eaten the morning before—cold broth like skimmed-off gutter water, with a few small clams tossed in, half-boiled and foul-smelling.

The mountains and sky became clear as ice. While the sun sparkled brilliantly in the pines and other wintering trees, something white began to fall from the sky. In the deep mountains, where bears stood on their rear legs like human beings, the snow came down like needles.

Shortly after breakfast, Sakai started feeling pain in his stomach. He visited the toilet two or three times.

It was the *udon*. It couldn't possibly have been all those little birds he had eaten last night. It had to be those two helpings of poisonous, half-cooked noodles served all together in one bowl. He tried to control his bowels. But the very thought of *udon* made his stomach ache. Of course, even if needles were flying outside, and if even his stomach hurt a little, he could still ride a train with no problem. Still, unbeknownst to anyone, he decided to stay on at the inn, taking advantage of the comforts that allowed him to compensate for the place he had stayed the night before.

As for the room. Was it the second time he went to the toilet? On his way back to his room on the third floor, he stopped on the staircase and looked down to the second floor, where he noticed, under the stairs, a broom and a duster leaning against an open door, and a room with a *kotatsu* and an alcove, which he could clearly see. On the floor was a piece of luggage, and two bundles wrapped in faded yellow scarves and tied with flat straps. A middle-aged peddler was warming himself at the *kotatsu,* his back leaning against the alcove; and across from him was a maid of about the same age. She was kneeling, leaning slightly forward with her hands underneath the *kotatsu* blanket. She was looking up, conversing with the man.

It was like a scene from the floating world, taken from the most remote spot on earth and placed in the inn.

All he had in his room was the bearskin. Suddenly feeling as if he had been abandoned in the mountains, he began to long for home.

Two days before, he had visited the castle in Matsumoto. He had climbed the castle tower and, reaching the frost-covered fifth story, had come to a window and a close view of endless ranges of mountains rising to the clouds. The sight overwhelmed him. He found some ivy growing over the mossy stone wall of the broken-down moat and thoughtlessly wrapped a strand of it around the handle of his wicker suitcase. The small, frost-bitten crimson leaves were like the dripping blood of thrushes. Suddenly, he felt lonely.

"Oyone-san. Do you have a room on a lower level? I'd like one with a *kotatsu* in it so I can take a nap."

Because the rooms on the second floor were frequented by peddlers who came and went, he was taken to a ten-mat room in a different wing of the inn, slightly separated from the main building by a long plank walkway.

The room had a low window, through which he could see the garden and its pond. Amid the whiteness of snow, the crimson backs of the red carp and the purple fins of the black carp were strikingly beautiful. The garden was dressed with a few plums and pines. But the rest were all large oak and zelcova trees. There was even a huge magnolia, two arm spans in diameter. Needless to say, the deciduous trees had all lost their leaves, and were as naked as a mountain wizard.

It was probably about three in the afternoon. He had been staring out at the branches and twigs, now blossoming with snow, with his body bent in the shape of a *hiragana "ku"* as he lay on the floor at an angle to the *kotatsu*. He wouldn't mind showing those trees to one of the "good women" his friend had talked about.

Gazing out the low window, he noticed the cook standing beneath a camellia bush, staring at the pond with his arms folded. He wore the same navy-blue padded jacket, with the apron wrapped around his waist and tied so it covered his buttocks. A hunting cap protected his head from the snow, but it didn't seem as though the cook was peering at the fish in the water. He looked more like a giant moorhen zeroing in on a loach. The mountains and peaks, buried deep in the clouds, framed the sky.

Sakai felt the deep emotions that the mountains evoke in travelers. He called out, "Cook, are you planning to slice up one of those fish for dinner tonight?"

"Oh," Isaku raised his dark face. He laughed, removed his cap, and bowed. He put his cap on and backed into the shadows of the trees with a rustle, out of Sakai's view.

The front desk in the main building was far away, and the snow started to fall harder.

Just then, he heard the sound of rushing water. "Someone forgot to turn off the faucet again." This was the second time. This morning, before he moved down to the first floor from the third, he had gone to wash his face. The maid told him the lavatory was quite nice, if a bit out of the way; so he followed her there from his new room in the detached wing, and discovered that of the three faucets not one of them produced a drop of water when opened. He didn't think it had gotten that cold, but maybe they were frozen. He clapped his hands loudly, and the maid said, "Oh, let me go prime them." By and by, the water started running. Later, when he went to the toilet after changing rooms, he tried one of the faucets again since he didn't have a washbasin at his disposal. This time he got a few drips out of the tap, just enough to wash his hands.

A short while after that, he heard the sound of running water coming from the washing area. He left the warmth of his *kotatsu* and walked down the wooden walkway to take a look. He could see water flowing full blast from all three faucets. It seemed like such a waste, so he took the time to make sure all three were turned off before returning to his room. He noticed the cook at the edge of the pond as before, standing with arms folded. It's a bit tedious to say, but this was the second time the cook had been there by the pond. The first time was about ten in the morning. When the cook disappeared, the sound of rushing water started coming from the lavatory again.

Once again, all three faucets were running full blast. Someone was wasting water. There wouldn't be any left to wash his hands, so he had gone to turn them off.

Now it was around three o'clock in the afternoon, and again he heard the sound of running water. A small stream was running through the garden, and he could also hear the rapids of the Narai River. Coming to Kiso and being bothered by the sound of running water was like riding a boat and trying not to see waves. He liked the sound of water and had never tried to avoid it before. But, try as he might, he couldn't help but be bothered by the thought of someone leaving the faucets running like that.

So Sakai left his room once again. Just as he thought, all three faucets were running full blast.

"Sir, are you going to take a bath?" It was Oyone, who had brought a fire pan and was about to tend to the hibachi. She could see that he was carrying a towel.

"Is it already that time?"

"The water will be ready soon. Today, we're using the bath in the new wing."

As a matter of fact, he could smell the scent of heated water amid the falling snow. The swinging door next to the lavatory was apparently the entrance to the bathhouse. He could see it from his window. There was also a place where newly erected pillars were partitioned off with piles of straw mats, an area where scaffolding had been set up next to a shed that had lumber in it. The place looked more like a deserted horse stall covered with leaves. To the original inn—once the spacious estate of an established family that offered lodging to the vassals of lords on their way to and from Edo—an addition had been built in response to the new wealth generated when both mulberry leaves and silkworms were king. When the economy in this part of the world flared like a fire, the Niegawa, Sacrifice River, became Niegawa, Boiling River, and every attempt was made to establish a hot-spring resort anywhere warm water bubbled from the ground. The addition had been started, but except for the room where Sakai was staying and the bathhouse, the project had not been completed as originally planned. Or so he later learned.

"Why do you run the water like that?"

He watched the maid open all the faucets he had just closed, one by one. He couldn't help the tone of reproach in his voice, but soon he understood the reason. The pond drew water from the river behind the inn through a pipe that was buried under the trees. Once or twice a year, the river level would fall and the pond would begin to dry up. The fish would gather together in one spot and gasp for breath, weakened by the low levels. To save them, the people at the inn drew water from the well, poured it into the kitchen storage barrel, and piped it all the way to the lavatory. From there, the water would flow under the bridge and into the pond.

Lying with his body deep in the warm *kotatsu,* and with two or three recent volumes of *Travel in Kiso* scattered on the floor around his pillow, my friend Sakai said to Oyone, "I have a special favor to ask of you." When he saw her shyly cast her eyes downward, he suddenly remembered Kidahachi, Ikku's rambunctious hero, and laughed out loud. "*Ha, ha!* Don't worry. It's not that. Thanks to you, my stomach problems are over. I didn't eat anything for lunch, so I suspect I'll try to make up for it tonight. Isaku-san has just been out staring at the pond with his sour face. My guess is that he's checking out how fat the carp are. He's thinking fish for tonight, I'll bet. This isn't quite last night's thrush story, but now that I've moved down here by the pond, I've become a neighbor to those carp. I don't think I could stand seeing one of them plucked from the water and sliced on a cutting board. I'm sure he has to make plans as the cook, and it's not my place to say anything but. . . .

"I'm not in the mood for sashimi, but I wouldn't mind a nice fish soup. I was wondering if we could arrange to get the fish from somewhere else, maybe at the fish market or wherever. This is none of my business, I know, but if it's just one or two fish—I don't know how many customers you have for tonight—I don't mind paying for whatever you'll be using."

"Oh, we never use the pond fish for cooking. The owners of this inn actually release fish into the pond on holidays to celebrate the mercy of Buddha—carp and other kinds. The cook's the same way. He loves those fish and takes good care of them. That's why he stands there looking at the water whenever he has any free time."

"Then that's perfect. Thank you so much." Sakai felt so pleased that he thanked the woman.

At dusk, the electric light in the room came on like a star descending to the snowy peaks. Just as the light went on in one of the rooms across the way, the maid came to tell Sakai that the bath was ready. "Bring my dinner right away," he said and hurried to the bathhouse.

He opened the door that stood beyond the sink and faucets, and entered a dressing area. It was pitch black inside. No, no. Actually, there was a faintly glowing paper lantern. The tub was apparently on the other side of the second door, which was closed.

The bathhouse was still unfinished. Maybe that explained why there was no electric light yet. The lantern, he noticed, had a swirling comma pattern painted on it. He had seen the design many times before, as it was also the family crest of Ōboshi—or was it Ōishi?—Yuranosuke, the heroic leader of the forty-seven loyal samurai. In this part of the world, though, the gloomy *tomoe* pattern reminded him of Kiso no Yoshinaka and his love for Tomoe Gozen. It had a sense of refined elegance.

He undid his sash, but then he heard a sound—*chaburi*—as if someone were in the bathtub. Just then, the sound of the running faucets suddenly stopped.

Sakai hesitated.

Anytime would be fine. I told them to let me know when the others were finished and the bath was free. No one's in there. Still, he retied his sash, and when he leaned over the lantern and pressed his

A Quiet Obsession

cheek against the door to listen, the place near his sleeve went dark, and the candle brightened again. The shadow became a birthmark, a swirling comma that showed on his face and dismally soaked into his cheek. Just as he was thinking this, he heard the sound of water again, coming from the other side of the door. Suddenly, through a crack in the walls, he smelled plum blossoms, the scent of white makeup washed off a warm body.

"A woman."

Even if it were a man in there, with people in the water, how could they prevent shoulders and hands from tangling in the darkness? He might even touch someone's breasts by accident. Noisily, he put on his slippers and retreated.

"Finished with your bath?"

It was a long way to the kitchen. Thinking she would serve him some warmed *sake,* Oyone had brought a carafe of heated wine.

"I'll take it later."

"Are you that hungry?"

"I'm hungry, all right. But there was someone else in there."

"Really? We haven't used that bathhouse for some time now. Maybe I shouldn't tell you this, sir, but since it's been a while, we cleaned it thoroughly and heated the water especially for you. After you go in, we'll go in. No one else has—"

"Well, that's all fine and good. But I'd rather take my time. Seems like it was a woman."

"What?"

The maid suddenly made a strange face, as if she were about to cry. The carafe she was holding in her hand rattled against the side of its warming kettle. She moved backward, suddenly stood up, and stepped out into the hall. She was quiet for a moment, but then started down the board walkway to the main building, making a terrible racket as she ran.

Sakai stared in wonder. "What was that all about?"

When dinner appeared, it wasn't Oyone but an older woman who brought it.

"So, you're the one from the mezzanine," he said to her. She had seen the woman being so hospitable to the traveling salesman. "How's your man doing?"

"Who knows?"

"I'd certainly like to know." He lowered his voice and said jokingly, "Looks like you have ghosts here. But in the bathhouse? Surely."

"Well, sir, we did have quite a laugh about that. Oyone thought there wasn't anyone in there, and that's why she said what she did. And then you told her there was a woman in the bathhouse. The truth is, Oyone-chan's a coward. Since we hadn't used it for a while, the mistress thought she might—"

"Oh, I get it. I was wondering myself if—"

"No need to worry. Ghosts don't appear in the bathhouse anyway. They do come out in the guest rooms occasionally, though. Like this one here. What do you think about that?"

"Fine with me."

A little excitement would only make his wine taste better.

It was already dark and the snow was falling quietly. After the bedding was laid out, he'd have another round of *sake*. Then he'd enjoy a good night's sleep. He finished his dinner, and the maids came to take the serving table away.

He heard the sound of footsteps. The noise continued down the hall and seemed to gather around the lavatory. Once again, he heard the sound of running water. He recognized a man's voice among them. When the noise died away, Oyone's face appeared at a crack in the sliding doors.

"Coast is clear for your bath now."

"You're sure of that?"

She laughed as if slightly embarrassed. She stepped back into the hallway, and Sakai, carrying a bath towel, followed her.

Once over the rounded bridge, he saw the bald-headed fellow who had been at the front desk the night before, along with an older woman, perhaps the head maid or maybe the man's wife. There was also one other maid. The three of them were standing close together, looking his way. Then Oyone joined the group. He noted the whiteness of her socks as she hurried across the landing to the bridge and joined the others, as if jumping into their front pockets.

"Thank you for your trouble."

He thanked them since they were obviously waiting for him,

having investigated the bathhouse on his account. They bowed together, and crossed over the wooden walkway where the thatched roof hung over the dirt-floored area. The group of four became swallowed in darkness when, as they reached halfway down the walk, two electric bulbs dimmed and the bridge and lavatory disappeared.

He sighed. The vague outline of the paper lantern appeared next to the three streams of water flowing from the faucets. It glowed dimly, and bore a swirling comma, like a flame drawn in *sumi* ink, or a catfish leaping.

The electric lights would come on again soon, he guessed. Thinking to take the lantern with him into the bathhouse, he reached down to pick it up. But just then it suddenly disappeared, leaving him in the dark.

No, it didn't go away. There it was, inside the door, in the bathhouse, still burning as before. Drips of condensed steam fell from the ceiling and made the wooden floor wet beneath his feet. Now he could see that the lantern he had seen before was actually a reflection of the one in the bathing room. The lantern had never been in the foyer. For Sakai, it was like glancing down at a reflection of the moon in the water and trying to take it into his hand.

Feeling his way with his feet, he reached the dressing room. Then, just to make sure, he moved closer to the door to the bathing area and held his breath. Again, he heard a noise and suddenly felt a chill. It wasn't like steam from the bath condensing and falling on him, but more like melted drops of snow from the roof.

He heard the sound of someone moving in the bathwater. Once again, he smelled the ineffably alluring yet cold and lustrous fragrance of a woman's face powder, enveloped by the steam. He sensed the touch of warm skin on his shoulder, then fingertips caressing the nape of his neck.

He tightened the sash of the kimono he was about to take off.

"Oyone?"

"No."

After a pause, one breath of time, a reply came back from inside the bathroom. Sakai's heartbeat echoed in his ears.

Of course it couldn't have been Oyone.

The sound of the running faucets suddenly stopped.

Finding himself riveted to the spot, Sakai looked around and announced, "Excuse me, but I'm coming in."

"No. Don't do that."

He heard a voice—clear, distinct, and moistened with steam.

"Then do any damned thing you want!"

Sakai was already back in his room when he lost control of his temper.

Here the lights were bright. In this light, there were no more swirling commas. But, once again, the three faucets were gushing.

"Go ahead! Make a goddam fool out of me."

It was insulting, more than eerie or terrifying. Sakai lost his temper. He suddenly lay back on the floor, with his legs still in the *kotatsu,* and looked up at the ceiling.

A moment later, he bolt upright because he heard what sounded like a water fight coming from the pond.

"Now what?"

The splashing continued.

He heard someone rustling about the pond. He guessed it had to be the cook, because of his love for the fish. He had already learned that much about the man.

"What is it? What's going on?"

He opened the rain shutters and called out to a faint shadow standing amid the total whiteness of snow. The pond itself was white as the water level was so low.

3

"What was it? An egret? A heron?"

"Both, I'm afraid."

Isaku, the cook, came around to the window and stood with his arms folded, facing away from Sakai.

"They come from the woods over there by the trailhead."

As Isaku talked, the snow stopped falling; and the forest, black as lacquer, appeared at the clouds' edge.

"They don't usually bother us. But when the water is low like this, sir, the poor fish are almost half out of the water. They can't get away."

A Quiet Obsession

"Those birds are pretty smart."

"They are. And that puts us stupid human beings in a difficult spot. I feel sorry for the fish. But, then again, you can't stand here all night and watch the pond. Sir, it's cold. You'd better close your window. It's time for the customers to make special requests of the kitchen. Perhaps I could prepare something for you, too, although nothing I make is that good."

"If you have the time, why don't you come and have a drink with me? I'm a night person. And besides, if we drink here, we can keep an eye on your pond."

The cook paused before replying, "That's not a bad idea. I've already straightened up the kitchen, so I'll come soon. Those devils!"

Mumbling the rest, Isaku looked up at the sky and disappeared into the snow-covered trees.

Sakai didn't slide his window shut but left it open a crack. From where he sat in the warm *kotatsu,* the snowy pond and egrets coming to hunt the fish seemed like a scene from a fairy tale. If anything happened, he'd chase them off or scare them away, whatever seemed appropriate. In the first place, and in spite of himself, he even entertained the thought that the sound in the bathroom, which he had now heard twice, was the noise of a heron bathing, having come in with the snow through some crack in the walls .

As he sat, peeking out the window, he saw Isaku's faintly dark outline as he rustled through the snow and there next to his sleeve was a lantern with swirling commas, lighted and moving along with him. Sakai didn't remember the cook having a lantern with him when he was there by his window. And there was something else. The cook soon crossed the garden and went over to a porch or some kind of entrance, growing smaller in the distance. Then he seemed to turn around and come back, now growing larger, passing under the eaves of the thatched roof that ran along the walkway over the dirt-floored area, the lantern moving back with him, in this direction, until it was right here, coming in, lighting the darkness of the hallway. Was he imagining it? There it was coming over the bridge, with the lavatory on the one side and the bathhouse just ahead, and then. . . . My god! What struck Sakai with terror was the way he was seeing the approaching lantern, not by turning his head back toward the entrance of his room, but by stretching his body out the window, toward the garden.

Suddenly the light went out, and Sakai felt a chill start in his skull and move down his backbone. He turned around and saw, there in his room, the figure of a woman who was looking away. She seemed like a snowy egret, the nape of her neck purest white.

She was facing away from him, gazing into a mirror and sitting by the staggered shelves in the alcove, in the southeast corner of his ten-mat room. Her kimono was bluish-gray with a fine striped pattern, like a sasanqua blossom wilted by steam, wet, damply clinging to her figure. Her under-sash of white-and-light-crimson checks was loosely tied beneath her bosom, almost draping down. She sat with the skirts of her kimono flowing lightly onto the floor, concealing her hips. One knee was slightly raised off the floor, so the dyed silk fabric of her kimono spilled over it. Her hair was like a hanging drop of dew, done up in a rounded coiffure, tied with a dark-violet silk band that showed faintly blue. She held a hairbrush in one white hand alluringly covered by the pale edge of her light-yellow undergarment. Leaning slightly forward, she looked at her image in the mirror and fixed her makeup.

Sakai held his breath, unable to sit or stand.

Her kimono was like fallen maple leaves under snow—her snowy white skin enveloping those leaves. She deftly rearranged the collar of her kimono, which had been pulled down in the back to expose the nape of her neck. Then she reached over and grabbed the tissue that was lying on the floor near her knee. She rolled it, and wiped the palm of her hand. When she dropped the paper onto the tatami, it looked like white face powder spilling down.

She rustled her kimono, and he smelled the incense that had been infused in the silk, so much like the scent of human skin that he had encountered in the bathhouse. She turned halfway in his direction, and raised a smoking pipe to her lips. The mouthpiece was white, and the barrel of the pipe shiny and black.

Tōn, came the sound of ashes being knocked out of her pipe.

She suddenly turned fully toward Sakai. She looked at him with her melon-shaped face, her thick eyelids and straight nose. Her skin was frighteningly white. She covered both her eyebrows with the

A Quiet Obsession

paper, and looked directly at him with her big eyes. "Does this become me?"

She smiled and revealed blackened teeth.

Still smiling, she pulled the skirts of her kimono together and stood. Her face rose toward the lintels of the sliding door as she stretched upward.

Sakai's heart leaped. He felt as if he were floating and his shoulders were rising into the air. It was the sensation of being gently taken up into the sleeves of the woman's kimono. No, that wasn't it. It was more like being caught sideways in her beak, hanging in mid-air above the tatami floor.

The mountains turned pure black. When the whiteness of the garden beneath him blocked his vision, he left the room through the window, and his arms and legs sprouted into fins. He flapped like a fish while the woman floated sideways beneath the eaves, an angel of the transom.

Suddenly, the white forest and the white houses of the village were far below him as he rose into the air, as high as the towers of Matsumoto Castle. Then he heard the sound of water and felt himself falling head over heels into the pond. At that same moment, he returned to his senses and found himself at the *kotatsu*.

He heard the commotion of wings flapping at the pond.

How could he, the scarecrow, bring himself to run out and chase the birds away?

When he saw the bloody ivy on his suitcase, he let out a blue breath and suddenly felt limp and exhausted.

Someone was coming down the hallway. He held his breath and got to his feet. This time, it was the cook, carrying a wine carafe on a tray.

"Isaku. It's you."

"Sir."

4

"It happened a year ago, at exactly this same time of year."

The cook sat down, moved up to the table, hunched his shoulders, and began his story.

"This year, the first snow came this morning. We got more than last year. But I'll never forget it. The snow came the day before a woman—a stunningly attractive woman—arrived at our inn. It was about two in the afternoon. She was traveling alone. When I say she was stunning, I don't mean to say she was flashy or anything like that. She was charming and maybe a little melancholic. She was about twenty-six or -seven, and had her hair done up nicely in a rounded coiffure. She was good-looking—a slender woman, beautiful beyond compare, and too alluring to be called Madame. Me, I'm nothing but a country hick. But I've seen my share of customers. I could tell right away that she was a professional. Later, I learned that her name was Minokichi, and that she was from Yanagibashi. The name she wrote in the register was Otsuya.

"They showed her to this very room.

"She liked to bathe. Most people do, I know. But she went to the bathhouse twice, once right after she arrived, and then again at night. The inn had run into a few problems, and we had to put off the completion of the new wing. We did manage to put in a rock-and-mortar bathing area—the sort you'd see at a hot-springs resort—and our customers who were staying on the second and third floors of the old wing used to ask us if they could bathe there, even if it was a bit of a walk. To tell the truth, strange things happened there on occasion. We haven't used the new bathhouse for a while. Same goes for this room. We were thinking, sir, that if a gentleman like yourself used it, then perhaps the occurrences would stop of their own accord. We talked it over and—maybe I shouldn't be telling you this—we heated the water up today and used the bath for the first time in a long while.

"As for the woman, Otsuya-sama, after she took her first bath in the middle of the day, she started asking around, 'Could you tell me how I might get to the village shrine?' She actually visited the spot, located on a hill along the Niegawa Road. It's a Sannō shrine. Legend has it that they used to perform human sacrifices there. The woods are thick. It's a lonely place.

"Although there are other shrines in the village, she took a special interest in this particular one. The people at the front desk told her what they knew, and she headed up the mountain all by herself.

A Quiet Obsession

Seemed she was having some sort of trouble with her eyes. Apparently, the glare of the sunlight off the snow bothered her. She wasn't overly concerned with appearances out here in the country. So she purchased a simple pair of sunglasses, put them on, then set off, using an umbrella for a walking stick. It seems her trip to the shrine was her way of thanking the people of Narai.

"She came back safely. At dinnertime, she asked to have a small order of food brought to her room. Perhaps I shouldn't say this in front of you, sir, but because she had most graciously sent a tip to the kitchen, I went out to greet her. That was when she told me that she had taken an offering of persimmons and small dessert forks to the shrine. 'The woman at the shop at the bottom of the stone steps told me about a deep forest behind the shrine. She said there was a place called the Bellflower Flats and that there was a Bellflower Pond where a beautiful woman lives. Is that true?'

"It is true. Without having heard the entire story myself, I told her it definitely was true. Facts are better than theory, I said. For better or for worse, I had actually seen her once myself."

Sakai didn't say anything.

"They call it the Bellflower Flats. The autumn blossoms there are beautiful. It's not just bellflowers, though. The water in the lake is blue, like blue bellflowers. The bellflowers there are actually white.

"Four years before, right at noon, on the other side of the pass, a fire broke out in Yabuhara. As everyone knows, if a fire gets out of control in the middle of the day it can turn into a huge conflagration.

"I climbed the hill by the shrine to take a look. The fire had seven branches, all of them crackling loudly, as if you could grab the sound in your hands. The noise was like a waterfall in a mountain valley, or the sound of water rushing from a pump. The south wind was blowing hard, and the flame quickly spread to the forest. People started to worry that the fire might come up to where we were. Some started running. Others started to make a commotion. People like me were more like sightseers than anything else. A crowd of us congregated there in front of the shrine.

"It was still the latter part of August and we were experiencing a terrible heat wave. That's why I moved into the woods a little at a time as I watched the fire. It was a place you'd usually never go. But

I wasn't worried since it was only a half a block or so from where the crowd was. I didn't go that far from the shrine, maybe half a block. I knew I'd be safe there. I'm a quiet person and don't associate that much with the younger men in the village, so it wasn't like I would have invited anyone else to come along with me, anyway. I ventured into a stand of cryptomeria and cypress. The woods weren't as extensive as I thought, because I soon found myself standing in a grassy plain blooming with flowers. Amid the white bellflowers was a large lake with pure blue water. And there by the lake, not more than fifteen to twenty yards away, was a person—a beautiful woman, who was turned diagonally toward a long mirror on a stand. She was putting makeup on her face.

"I stood and watched. I noticed her hair, what she was wearing. There's no way to describe how overwhelmed and frightened I was. Even now, when I recall that moment, this wine turns into ice and pierces my chest. I get the chills. And yet, she was so beautiful. Perhaps it's presumptuous of me, but I—a man with no house of my own nor a Buddhist altar to put in one—wanted to make her reflection in the lake the object of my worship. Now a day doesn't go by when I don't see her face in the pond here. At that time, though, I didn't know what was happening. Like a bird with a broken wing suddenly falling from the sky, I ran through the woods, not knowing where I was headed. I ran for my life, down the tall flight of stone steps. The people who saw me said they had never seen anyone look so frightened. The crowd of spectators that had gathered in front of the shrine turned into an avalanche and ran down the mountain. A gust of wind, cold enough to put out the fire, came rushing from the woods behind us and chased us like a huge snake. They said that, in my attempt to get away, I looked like a rabbit—jumping and falling, jumping and falling.

"So I told all this—to Otsuya. And she asked me why I called this beautiful woman Madame instead of Goddess or Your Highness. Well, that's just the point. My eyes were clouded, but according to the people who had seen her before me, she had shaved off her eyebrows."

Sakai shivered with horror, and turned away from the *kotatsu*.

"I didn't know to whom she was married. I just assumed she was married because of those eyebrows. Sir, when I told all this to Otsuya, she listened very carefully. Then she asked me if it meant that there had been other people who had seen this married woman. And the answer was yes—at the mountain edge on a moonlit night, on the paths near the blooming foothills, in the shade of fireflies, the lanterns on a rainy day, along the river during snowstorms—there are a lot of people in the village who had caught a glimpse of her. When Otsuya heard me say this, she sat her cup down and looked sadly down at the floor.

"I don't know why she did that. But I do know, sir, that she had a reason for coming to these mountains."

5

"At that time, we had just witnessed the strangest love affair you could ever imagine, right here in this village. A case of adultery.

"There was a woman who lived at the fork in the road, just as you enter the village. We called her Madame Governor. I suppose we could have called her something less grating to the ear, like the village headman's grandmother, or something like that. But we called her Madame Governor because, as the nickname implies, she was an awful, authoritarian woman. She wore her pedigree on her sleeve, so that everyone knew—'My family used to serve as provincial governors for the old regime.' She bragged about it whenever she got half a chance, and she delivered the message with a vengeance. Well, since that was her attitude about things, even though she was still middle-aged when her husband passed away, she managed everything by herself.

"She did a grand job of raising her son, bringing him up to become My Son the Scholar. For a while he lived in Tokyo. But with the small pittance of his salary, he eventually bought a second home here—a small, broken-down house. From about three or four years ago, his mother and wife—that would be Madame Governor and the one we call Young Madame—have lived there together. They survived on next to nothing. Since the old lady was too cheap to buy soy sauce to cook greens, daikon, and eggplant, she planted every square foot of their yard into onions, leeks, garlic, and scallions, all members of the five spices that she could easily pickle with a little salt. You could smell their house from a mile away. That's why we called the mother Madame Governor of the Garlic Mansion.

"As for the scholar's wife, she was the daughter of a merchant from Fukushima. She had been to school, but, unlike women of this generation, she was quiet and gentle, perhaps a bit too withdrawn, if anything. Of course, if she hadn't been that way she never would have been able to live with Madame Governor. The daughter-in-law was about as ungarlic a person as you could find. She quietly endured every task set before her—the spade, the hoe, the rope basket. It was painful to see.

"Now, about halfway through November, a visitor from Tokyo suddenly showed up at the Garlic Mansion. He was the son's friend, a man who hadn't held down a regular job. He was supposedly a painter, so I guess it makes sense that he didn't have a real job. My Son the Scholar, on the other hand, had a respectable position as a principal at a middle school in Tokyo. Well, the reason the painter had come unannounced to his friend's house was simple: he had no money and needed to get away from Tokyo. To get to the point, he was in a tight spot because of an affair he had had with another woman. People had been merciless in their criticisms; and when his wife finally confronted him, he lost his temper. 'What are you saying!' He whacked her across the face. After doing that, he couldn't stay in his house any longer, not there in front of the Buddhist altar where he would be seen by his ancestors. He knew he was the one who should have been whacked, so he immediately ran out into the street. Considering how he had been confronted by his wife, he didn't have any friends or acquaintances to turn to. So he sneaked out of the city that night and escaped here to Kiso. He actually ran away. Turns out that his wife had once been his lover, and for them to get married had required great efforts on the part of My Son the Scholar. It was only because of him, in fact, that they had been able to become man and wife. So this place was a most convenient place of refuge for him.

"Now this unfortunate painter's lover was none other than Otsuya-sama, the one who came to our inn on her own. She came, despite the snow, and not because she was looking for the painter. Or at least that's how I see it. About two weeks separated their visits, and it was during this interval that the adulterous affair that I mentioned took place."

Here, the cook took a short rest.

A Quiet Obsession

"The Madame Governor had a strange habit. More than a habit, it was a sickness. According to what I learned from someone who knows about such matters, it's called litigation sickness. If her onions died, she took the matter to the village hall. If a child looked at her the wrong way, she was off to the police box, the police station, the courthouse. Whatever it was, she felt compelled to take all matters to the proper authority, and with reason on her side! Madame Governor was always convinced of her righteousness.

"Now at the approach to the village, on the road that leads to the fork where the Garlic Mansion is situated, there lived a hunter named Ishimatsu. He was in his forties and lived in a cave-like hollow with his many brats. Before Madame Governor and her family fell on hard times, he used to work for them as a manservant, and his wife worked for them as a maid. The Madame treated him as if he were her retainer, and Ishimatsu the Hunter, being a hard man, served his master with undying loyalty.

"The evening rains turned to snow. That first storm of the year hit harder than people expected. In the mountains, the wild boars and rabbits went crazy, and Ishimatsu knew that this was his big chance. He got up late at night, checked out his rifle, ate some rice with tea by the fireplace, and put on his monkey-skin hood. Just then, the sixty-nine-year-old Madame Governor came barefoot through the snow and stopped by the entrance, where a thin straw mat was dangling down. Her gray hair was hanging loose, and her underwear was the color of buckwheat noodles. How repulsive! Around her shoulders she wore the usual threadbare pink shawl. The hem of her kimono was pulled up in the back and tucked under her sash. 'There's a monster in my house!' she said. 'Come quick!' Her face was flushed. She gestured with her arms. She struggled for breath.

"'A gun comes in handy at a time like this.' Ishimatsu tossed a bullet into the chamber.

"The widow of his lord had come barefooted, so he too went without shoes. They cut across the road and made their way through the snow over the patches of leeks, scallions, and onions. They were out to find a monster. Quiet now! With Madame Governor leading the way, he entered through a shed in the back and sneaked into the dirt-floored kitchen. Following the direction of her pointing finger, he looked through a crack in the wooden door. And what did he see? There behind the six-panel folding screen were two pillows placed side by side. The two lovers weren't lying down, though. The young wife was dressed in a long crimson crepe undergarment, with the collar of the sleeved coverlet slipped off her shoulder. Her white hand was on the painter's knee, and she was leaning forward, facing the floor. The man was apparently running his hand over her back. The young bride who had always dressed in coarse cotton and a padded sleeveless kimono was now dressed in silk and sitting with another man! No doubt this surprised Ishimatsu more than if he had seen a real monster.

"'You wretch! Beast! Whore!' Madame Governor moved into the room with the quickness of a mud spider. 'Don't move an inch! Move and you're dead! Dead!' From the other side of the screen where he had taken position, Ishimatsu, looking like a toad that had grown hair, glared at them down the barrel of his rifle.

"Judging by the look on his face, he was ready to pull the trigger. No doubt, the painter was in a tight spot. 'The punishment of heaven is about to strike! Make one move, and I'll turn you into a public display—with four legs, four hands, and two faces!'

"While Madame Governor ran off on her own to round up four villagers from the neighborhood, Ishimatsu kept his gun trained on the couple so others would find them in the same compromising position. The old lady's plan was to take them to the police station first and then to the family temple at sunrise. Under these circumstances, the scholar's young wife and the lady-killer painter were like a many-colored sea slug, cold as snow and limp with exhaustion, her dappled silk girdle turned to straw.

"There wasn't much she could do to the man. But when the Madame produced a rope to tie the girl's hands behind her back, the policeman scolded her. And that made her all the more furious. She was beside herself with rage, saying that she was going to get the court, the village office, the police station, and the town council to bring charges of adultery against her daughter-in-law. They decided to take them first to the family temple in order to keep them under confinement, so to speak. The Madame wouldn't let her daughter-in-law put on any clothes, as she wanted 'living proof' of the evil she had done. So the policeman put his snow-covered overcoat around her shoulders. Even the little girls in the village trailed behind her as they started for the temple."

Sakai sighed many times as he listened.

"I suppose they let him go. Sometime during the night, the painter disappeared from the temple. And that was how it should be. The story I heard from them went like this. He was a close friend of the Madame Governor's son. They were like brothers, and so the mother had thought of him as her own son. Because her daughter-in-law had been lonely, alone at home for half a year at a time, the Madame Governor encouraged her to think of him as if he were her husband and to talk with him about all the things that were on her mind. The mother-in-law had made her put on makeup, arrange her hair, and change her kimono. When bedtime came, the smiling Madame Governor made her spread their beds out on the floor, side by side. Why should we be surprised, then, that her daughter-in-law would lay her head on the man's knees and shed a tear or two over the things that were bothering her? The painter, a man who knew enough about the ways of love to get in trouble with a geisha, couldn't help but caress the young woman's back.

"Imagine how angry this turn of events made Madame Governor. She sent a telegram off to her son, telling him to come immediately. No matter how people tried to calm her, she wouldn't listen. She insisted that her son bring his wife up on charges of adultery. She didn't care what others might think of their family. A governor belonged to the sword-wielding class! To a samurai, life is all about rewarding virtue and punishing vice. When she got that crazy, it was impossible for anyone to deal with her. 'If you don't bring this matter to court, I can't go on living. I'll put a rifle to my windpipe! A scythe to my belly! Do you know how deep the pools of the Narai River are? I'll drown myself in the Bellflower Lake.' What a bag of bones she was! Did she have any idea? Drowning in the Bellflower Lake? If she threw herself in, the waves would spit her back."

The cook started to laugh. Sakai could feel an edge in his laughter.

"My Son the Scholar was not the kind of man you often meet these days. He had studied ethics, morals, spiritual training. He had even taught those subjects. When it came to filial piety, he was nothing less than extreme. He already had a solid reputation. But to anyone on the outside who might look upon his wife with any amount of sympathy, he was too weak, if anything. Finding himself in a tight spot, without any other recourse, he decided he'd have his friend come back to Narai, if just once. Everything would rest on that. That was My Son the Scholar's request of his painter friend.

"Well, for the painter, this was more horrifying than a duel to the death. There are people in the village who would stone you and spit in your face for the cause of preserving morality. Sir, how could the painter possibly bring himself to make an appearance in Narai again?"

"No. I don't suppose anything he could say would make his friend show up."

"And yet the painter felt as if he owed it to his friend to come. And where do you think he was then? Having disgraced himself because of a sex scandal, he was hiding under his wife's sleeves, this woman he had whacked, covering his head so he couldn't see his parents' memorial tablets, his ass and legs shaking with fear. What a coward!

"'I'll bring him back, if it's the last thing I do!' Making this promise to his mother, My Son the Scholar returned to Tokyo. And it was while he was away that Otsuya—Minokichi from Yanagibashi—showed up here in Narai."

6

"How could I send her out by herself? It was already the middle of the night when Otsuya told us she wanted to go visit Madame Governor. The people in the village were already asleep. She said if we could just tell her how to get there, she'd be fine. But we thought that if it were unacceptable to have someone go with her, we might protect her secretly by watching from behind a fence or a back door. We discussed the matter at the front desk. And guess who was chosen to go with her? This fumbler—me.

"'Whenever you're ready,' I said. I came here to this room. I brought a lantern with me."

"Yes. The one with the swirling comma pattern on it." Sakai couldn't resist the comment.

"That's right." Isaku responded darkly, seeming to swallow his words. "You seem to know a lot about it."

"Twice. In the bathhouse. I saw it."

"What? We don't keep a lantern in the bathhouse. Not unless—"

Given Isaku's response, this was hardly the time for Sakai to say he had just seen the lantern again, just now, when the cook walked across the garden. "You were saying," he urged the cook to continue his story.

"Sorry. I feel a little—. That's right. When I got there, she had just finished her preparations. She had put on a little makeup after her second trip to the bathhouse. Her kimono was bluish-gray, but against her face it seemed more like violet. Her complexion was white beyond compare . . . there in front of the mirror."

Needless to say, Sakai turned around and looked over toward the corner of his room.

"The mouthpiece of her smoking pipe was gold, and the rest was plated with an alloy of copper and gold. She had dyed her teeth, it seems. She took out some paper, held it up to her forehead, and looked at me with her oval face. That's when she asked, 'Does this become me?'"

Sakai's words, "I see, I see, I see," seemed to turn into a chunk of ice that lodged in his throat. He became speechless.

"The edge of the room seemed to grow white with bellflower blossoms. 'It more than becomes you,' I told her.

"She took the paper from her forehead, and I could see the pale freshly shaven skin where her eyebrows had been. 'How do I compare to the Bellflower Lake woman?'

"'Like a sister. No, I'd say you're twice as beautiful.'

"I'll be cursed for saying that, but I couldn't help it. Now listen to this."

"'So, Otsuya, how are we going to handle this?'

"It was a day of snow mixed with rain. The painter's wife came dressed in a ragged livery coat and carrying a dilapidated paper umbrella. She looked chic in her tawdriness. She didn't intend to accuse Otsuya of stealing her husband. What good would that do, given her plans to find a way out of the impasse? Otsuya's eyes were bothering her, and she had retreated to an attic room in her owner's home, where she practiced her instruments and made a little money teaching ballads to the young girls and children. Imagine her surprise when the painter's wife paid her a visit.

"'Otsuya, this is what I've been thinking. If I were as attractive as you, the fastest way to get to this old woman who's been calling my husband an adulterer would be to say to her, 'Look. He has this wife. Why would he be interested in some woman from Kiso?'

"'That's exactly right,' Otsuya responded. 'And on top of that, I might say, 'This is all a kept woman really is' —and show myself to her. He has someone better than me—a wife, a person of real substance. And in addition to his wife, he's also involved with me. So why should he get greedy and go for some country girl? Let's say that to the old hag. For the sake of her son's bride.'"

"After it was over, we found something in the will that Otsuya left behind, some notes she had scribbled down. I'm afraid this is all very. . . well, personal. It hadn't been her idea to get pulled into this. So why should she fear some beast in the Kiso Mountains? I suppose she wanted to see for herself how the women here in the country handled such matters. She probably had that in mind when she went to pay homage to the Sannō shrine. That was when she heard about the mysteriously beautiful woman of the Bellflower Lake, how the people in the area sometimes saw her. She assumed that, naturally enough, Madame Governor had also seen her. She seemed to be thinking that if her looks didn't stand up to the comparison, if beauty alone couldn't win the day, she had brought a straight-edged razor with her. . . . If all else failed, she'd make the world a better place by getting rid of the old hag. That was also in her diary.

"We walked through the snow, as far as the fork in the road at the edge of the village, then made our way along the moonlit dike of one of the tributaries of the Narai River. The moon was like ice, shining brightly down, the mountain air frozen and enveloped in mist. Flowing among the boulders, the waters of the narrow valley stream were partially captured by the icy weather—*sara sara, sara sara.* It was that same sound. Just like the water running from the faucets."

"By the way, do you mind turning that water off? It gives me the chills."

"Same here. But . . ."

"You don't want to go alone?"

"Do you?"

"Forget it. So what happened next?"

"There was an earthen bridge between two cliffs. On the far side was a dead pagoda tree. When we saw it in the moonlight, waving ominously on the water, the candle in the lantern I was carrying started to drown and dim in its own melted wax.

"'When the lantern goes dark like that, those two swirls become one, black like the soul of a person walking.'

"In response to Otsuya's words, I quickly took a look. I realized my error. Had I been distracted by her beauty? The candle was almost gone, and I had forgotten to bring a spare. I was there to guide her, but there was nothing on our moonlit path that needed to be feared. Besides, this lantern with our crest on it carries a lot of weight around here. Still, I did it for her. We had come only about half a block anyway, so it was only a short run back to the inn. I started back. And that was my mistake."

For a while, the cook seemed speechless.

"I had passed an earthen wall and was approaching the door to the kitchen, when—*don*—I heard a sound like a meteor falling from the sky. And then—*don*—an echo. It was the sound of a gun."

Sakai, too, became speechless.

"Surprised, I ran back to the dike. I looked for Otsuya's thin silvery figure by the river where we had been. 'My god!' I threw the lantern and everything else down. I ran to find her. I discovered her a short distance from where we had parted. She was leaning back on the snowy dike. Her hips had fallen onto the rocks of the riverbed. 'I'm cold,' she said, as if dreaming. 'I'm so cold.' With those words, three threads of blood spilled from her lips.

"It was all so tragic. I tried to cover her legs. The disheveled skirts of her kimono were already frozen to the rocks; and in my hands, the many colors felt like frosted autumn grass. When others came and tried to help her up, her crepe undergarment crackled like ice. It was like ripping a painting from an old sliding door. To me, it was the sound of a body being torn apart. The pool of blood on her chest flowed warmly despite the cold.

"Ishimatsu shot her. His family had been suffering from poverty. He thought that snowy night, if any night, was his chance to make a kill. So he left a rice cake at the shrine and prayed to the gods of the mountain. For his own use, he took along a few rice balls on a stick, coated with miso and grilled over a fire—the kind they say attracts evil spirits. He started across the bridge over the river. Otsuya saw him coming and tried to hide. The water was low. She stepped onto the rocks of the riverbank. Thinking she was the ghoulish woman of the Bellflower Lake walking across the water, Ishimatsu fell down on his stomach. He took aim. He'd put an end to evil! He'd do it for the people of the village!

"Ishimatsu never recovered. Even now, he's still mad.

"As for me, sir, look! There I am! Coming from the bathhouse, over the bridge. Sir, that's me, coming this way. See! A madman, like me! I'm coming here! And there, at my side. That's her, Otsuya!"

Sakai clenched his teeth. "Isaku-san. Don't be afraid. She doesn't blame you for what happened."

But then the electric bulb in Sakai's room became a swirling comma. It floated darkly in the air, and suddenly a paper lantern appeared above their *kotatsu*.

"Does this become me?" the beautiful one asked. And suddenly, the room filled with water, and snow carpeted the tatami like bellflowers blooming whitely at the water's edge.

The Heartvine

"The Heartvine" (Rukōshinsō, 1939) was Kyōka's last story, completed shortly before his death. It takes place at a Buddhist temple on Mount Utatsu in Kanazawa, across the Asano River from the neighborhood where he spent his childhood and youth. In this strongly autobiographical attempt to sum up his life as an artist, he nostalgically recounts the most unstable period of his life, when as a young man he considered suicide but was saved by the intervention of a young woman who did, in fact, kill herself on that same night. Struggling mightily to finish this final statement, Kyōka was able to leave behind a quiet yet powerful testament of beauty, eros, and death.

1

See them
'neath a blade of grass,
Waiting for
The storm to pass.

Hiding from
Our prying eyes,
Whitened silk
and crimson dyes.

Two red leaves
on purest snow,

Izumi Kyōka

Wings erect
In love's sweet glow.

By lightning flash,
We see, we stare.
We fear and scorn
This tangled pair!

Oh, dragonflies
Stitched red on white,
Which one of you
Will die tonight?

"Tsujimachi-san, your lantern."

"My lantern?"

It was two in the afternoon. Standing a shoulder's height above the old man, a young woman of thirty extended a pale, white hand and asked, "Should I take it? You'll bump it on the steps."

She is the old man's cousin. Oyone is her name, and she is slender and graceful from head to toe. Her husband is a lacquerware artisan who works in one of the well-established shops in the area. Her mother, Okyō, passed away just year before last.

Oyone's hair is done in the proper fashion for a married woman—tastefully quiet, gentle yet inviting, tapering to a well-defined hairline at the nape of her neck. For a winter's day in the north, the weather is unseasonably mild, too warm for a coat. Indeed, it's a shame she has to wear a kimono at all, so pure and white is the hand that holds the offerings for her mother's grave: one small white candle; two sticks of incense bound together with a strip of colored paper; and a bouquet of small chrysanthemums of pure white and yellow, mixed with light-purple cockscombs, and a sad-looking flower that people in this part of the world call the Priest's Blossom. They are considered a must for this time of year.

Her hand reaches out. She asks, "Should I take that?"

The two were climbing a steep, slightly overgrown flight of broken-down steps leading to the two-story gate of the Senshōji, Oyone's family temple. To the people of this castle town, the place is more widely known as the Lantern Temple.

Last year . . . no, every year, the people in the North Region

The Heartvine

celebrate the Bon Festival by offering lanterns at the graves of the dead, small candles that express the feelings of their hearts. As has always been the custom here, the lighting of fires to welcome the spirits of the dead begins on July thirteenth of the lunar calendar. Communicating with the deceased—whether family members or friends—the candles begin to appear everywhere, not just at the temple graveyards where you might expect them, but in the fields and mountains, on boundary markers, anywhere you might find a tomb, or an ancient burial mound, or the unmarked graves of those neglected souls who seem to have barely missed being forgotten forever. Delicate blossoms of damp moss bloom within the flicker of small paper lanterns, as the sad and faintly white pathways of spirits appear, partially hidden in the grass and trees, dim and dark, prominent in the shadowy night, obscure in the moonlight. Perched high atop a steep almost cliff-like hill, dangling from the branches of a great nettle tree in the graveyard behind this temple, the light of a huge hanging lantern can be seen from the tangled crossings of city streets below, or from the surrounding lakes and marshes, or from the banks of the large rivers. Even from the distant sea to the west, if one were to pause and look toward the temple, one could see its pattern against the sky; and thus the name.

A visitor to this Lantern Temple, Tsujimachi Itoshichi carried his own lantern. Dangling there at the end of his coat sleeve, it seemed strangely out of place in the middle of the day. A gust of wind blew through the pines, and two or three crimson maple leaves sailed by, as if bursting into flame. They landed upon a spot of sunlight that fell warmly on the grass growing by the steps. Failing to seize the moment, Tsujimachi seemed as if he didn't know whether to stretch out an arm and yawn or draw it back and sneeze.

As if yawning and sneezing at the same time, he spoke in a loud voice, "You want to take this lantern? Up we go!"

He climbed a step.

"And up!"

Oyone smiled. "Judging by all that noise you're making—"

"I'm not tired. Even if I were, what difference would this lantern make? If it starts getting heavy, or if it gets in my way, I'll just leave it here in the grass."

"Well, this *is* a temple. Hardly anybody comes here. No one would think to take it. You're refusing my help because you'd rather carry it yourself. Is that it?"

"That's right. By myself."

"Don't act so innocent. You know you couldn't leave it here. How would you deliver it to the person you've come to see? That wouldn't do."

"Thanks for the lecture. So, tell me, then. Who am I giving this to?"

"I wonder." She smiled again. "See how hard you're breathing? Maybe we should take a little rest. This is a nice spot."

They had come to a landing halfway up the flight of stone steps, to a level spot about the size and shape of a front box at the theater. Oyone moved over toward the base of a brilliantly colored maple tree and looked down at the ground as she extended a hand from the sleeve of her kimono. She turned her hips away, pliant as a willow. The pale crimson of her undergarment spilled out from beneath her kimono's cool snowflake pattern that showed against the darkness of her lacquered sandals. She stepped closer and reached to take the lantern in her hand.

Oyone was an attractive woman. But she was here only as a guide for Tsujimachi, who, because she was married, did not allow himself to hold her beauty in his heart. She received the lantern from him and turned it around so its handle pointed toward her. Against the darkness of the black lacquered wood, her hand, reaching out, seemed whiter and gentler than before.

Tsujimachi was circumspect with good reason. The stone steps were like a lookout tower built by a band of mountain thieves; and as they lived among the rooftops and the crisscrossing streets, among the willows at the crossroads, half-concealed and half-revealed by wooded areas here and there, the people of the town could see Oyone and Tsujimachi should they turn their eyes that direction. To the townspeople, it would seem as if an overcoat-colored cicada had alighted upon a dyed silk sleeve draped over a railing in midair.

The cicada laughed to itself, and flew deftly into the shadows of the maples.

Well, maybe not so deftly—not this cicada.

The Heartvine

"Thank you for helping me with the lantern. My one hand gropes, and the other holds a stick. And I can't get used to this cane. It's like a damned oar I found on the beach. See how it gets caught in my sleeve? It's like I have a cane in each hand."

"You shouldn't talk like that."

"I guess I really am helpless. Maybe we should take a little rest, as you suggest. There couldn't be a nicer spot—this cool-looking moss, this warm sunshine. As for the lantern, let's just set it aside here. Trees above, stones below. Quite a luxurious setting, I'd say! But the truth is, I feel like a monk begging at a festival. I should be laying out a straw mat and beating on a bell."

"Wait. You'll get your kimono dirty if you're in such a hurry."

"Who cares? This is nothing but a rag anyway. A monk's black robe."

"Well, whether you're a nameless priest or the great poet Kisen, there's no stage here for you to sit on."

"I wouldn't ruin that nice handkerchief on my account."

"It's not nearly as nice as these maple leaves. It's almost a shame to brush them away."

"What color would you call that? Thanks to you, the moonlight is falling on this rock, just as planned. And look at that view! This has always been a good spot, but today! The ocean over there, and the castle."

Yellow ginkos, autumn reds, green pines. As Tsujimachi's eye moved over the wooded landscape, he saw scarlet maples mixed into the expanse. The green of not-yet-fallen willow leaves formed a thin, patterned veil from which the tower of the castle rose even higher than the snow-covered mountains in the distance. Down and to the side, the ocean formed a line of dark blue where it met similar colors of the sky, encircling paddies and fields, the castle and streets of the city. The ocean, even on this quietly pleasant day, was topped with whitecaps that spread and flowed like white chrysanthemums. As if it had donned a many-colored kimono, this Snow Country town showed whitely through a thin covering of mist. Off to one side, where the sleeve would be, he could see the oval of a lake, shimmering like a half-moon at midday.

"Oyone." The old man turned to her. "This scenery's not the

only point of interest here. Did you notice how the man at the lantern shop was acting? What was that all about? When you asked him, 'How much is a lantern?' he said, 'Go ahead, take one. Pay me later.' And what about me? I'm the visitor from afar, but he didn't even offer to wrap my things in a newspaper, let alone in something decent. I have to say, dear, that man had eyes for you."

"What are you talking about?" The tone of her voice changed to one of reproof. "How was he supposed to know you were from out of town? It's not like you were wearing straw sandals or something. How could he tell by just looking? And by the way. We pay for things twice a year here. Even if we didn't, whenever we go to the temple we have to pass by his place on the way back. That man's known me ever since my mother used to lead me by the hand to and from the temple. So keep your empty praises to yourself. You shouldn't be saying things like that on the way to the temple, anyway. Trying to get away with it, under pretense of flattery."

"Okyō! Just a minute. I mean, Oyone," he corrected himself. "Okyō was your mother's name."

"Thanks for reminding me." She laughed.

"Sorry. I suppose I should have called her by her posthumous name—Lady of the Something Something. That's why we're here, after all, to pay my respects to your dead mother."

"No need to apologize for that. I know you've come to visit my mother's grave, and I'm grateful. But you're also here to see someone else . . ."

"Someone else? I'm afraid I don't know what you're talking about."

"My mother always said that about you. That you're a dead end when it comes to getting to the point."

"Well, I do live on a cul-de-sac."

"Sorry, I shouldn't say things like that. There's no reason why you have to hide it from me. Maybe you really don't remember. Maybe you've forgotten. I feel sorry for her if that's true. That would be heartless."

"Now wait a minute. This is a total surprise. I honestly don't know what you're talking about. I might look bad saying that, but I really don't have a clue."

The Heartvine

"You mean you forgot? And you think that's all right? You're lying, aren't you? Don't you think that's a little much? Now I really will have to tell you. I guess I'll be the inappropriate one here. Look what you've tricked me into. That woman. You know, that woman. The one you were about to commit double suicide with . . ."

Tsujimachi didn't respond right away. Taken completely by surprise, he placed his hands over his chest and pretended to smooth down the bulge in his black coat. He could only stare at Oyone.

"Tsujimachi-san, I forgive you. I really did surprise you, didn't I? I thought you were pretending. But now you know who I'm talking about, don't you? That spring night, the cherry blossoms in full bloom. You there by the castle gate, at the edge of the dark moat, walking back and forth."

The way Oyone magically flitted her fingers as she moved her hand made Tsujimachi see in his mind's eye the shadowy figure of a little man emerging from the woods surrounding the distant castle. He was walking slowly, arms folded, eyes focused on the ground. Without a coat on his back, he cut a pitiful figure. Having gone without food for several days, he was determined to end his life then and there. That young man was none other than Tsujimachi himself, as he had been on that night so many years ago.

And there was someone else—a sad but beautiful young woman who appeared as if she had alighted from the blossoming clouds. Hidden in the dark shadows, she came slowly to the edge of the same moat and moved down the long slope that connected the castle with the streets of the city. Slightly hunched forward, she seemed to float her skirts above the ground as she continued, eyes upon the earth, the sleeves of her kimono held softly over her bosom. He caught a glimpse of the nape of her neck as she walked away quietly and calmly into the black night, the skirts of her kimono almost not moving at all. Spring flowers ablaze, beneath a canopy of cherry blossoms in full bloom, she moved gracefully down the slope, as if the earth had become a raft beneath her feet.

—Oyone. Hide your fingers, and pull up those sleeves. The whiteness of your neck and the graceful line of your shoulders mustn't resemble that unfortunate woman's.—

Before his very eyes, Tsujimachi saw a woman walking down the slope. She was only twenty years old on the night she threw herself into the Thousand Wing Abyss. . . . By gallantly leaping into the water, she died a noble death. Unlike her, he—the young man standing at the edge of the black water—was nothing but a coward. He went on living, shamelessly. And now he was an old man, the very one who had stopped to rest halfway up the stone steps at the Senshō Temple.

2

"I feel like I'm in a spell."

Tsujimachi felt the coldness of his palm as he pressed it to his cheek. The ashes of the cigarette in his fingers fell past his ear and onto the pebbles at his feet.

"It was like waking from a dream. I remember wandering along the edge of the moat until dawn. But I can't remember what happened next. Did I go home? Did I sleep under the stars that night or in my bed? I was completely out. When I awoke, I heard someone—it was Okyō—calling, 'Nii-san! Nii-san!' "

"Shall I answer?" Oyone asked.

"Could you?"

"Certainly." She laughed.

"Needless to say, she had a lively, young voice. And why not? We were both twenty. I heard later that the young woman who died that night was a year older than I. It had been raining, and the mist softened the brilliance of the cherry blossoms, as if veiling them in a thin layer of cotton. I heard your mother's strong voice calling to me from the street, and sat up in bed. I answered back, hardly able to open my eyes. I made my way to the door, and stuck my head outside. It was a beautiful morning, the very height of spring, bright enough to scorch my pallid face. Okyō was standing there, her hair freshly done up in a butterfly coiffure. The sharp brightness of her light-yellow collar and the luster of her black sash were enough to clear the mist away. 'There's been a suicide at the moat,' she said.

" 'That's a lie. I'm still alive,' I said carelessly, making it easy to guess where I'd been.

The Heartvine

"My grandmother was standing directly behind me, working in our dirt-floored kitchen. She was over seventy years old at the time, cooking a pot of watery gruel made from our last few grains of rice. Two years earlier, our house had burned down. The year after that, my father died. So our home wasn't much more than a shack. Where to live? What to eat? Life was so hard that, the night before, while walking around the castle, I even envied the crying frogs and the chirping crickets. Luckily, my grandmother was hard of hearing. Otherwise she would have heard me say, 'I'm still alive.'

"'What are you doing in bed? Get up!'

"Okyō knew I was in trouble. She was impatient and irritated, probably because she cared so much about me. She wrinkled her eyebrows—you know how she used to do that—and said, 'Right here in the neighborhood. I just passed by on my way here. The gilder's shop on the corner, where they make gold leaf. It wasn't a family member. It was the girl who had come to live with them. She worked at the handkerchief factory. Get up. Take a look. All those people standing there.'

"The morning was bright and clear; but the street was bleached and still, as if everything had been painted white. There it was, on our side, about a block down. Although they said the girl had died at the moat, it seemed as if that street stretched all the way to the ocean, and that the crowd of people standing there were huddled together, as if bracing themselves against the crashing tide. The entire street looked as if it had been drenched by the waves.

"The cherry blossoms scattered and fluttered before my eyes.

"Rich peoples' houses never burn down. Across the street from our shack was the residence of a wealthy man whose second wife was famous in our neighborhood for her bad temper. There's no trace of her anymore. But that morning she came rushing out and stood before her threshold. Like the rest of us, she stared in the direction of the gilder's shop, her hair done up like a swallow's tail, sticking up in back. Her stepdaughter was a kind, beautiful person of quality who disappeared like the melting snow before her twentieth birthday, like white plum blossoms scattered upon the water. The women of the neighborhood said our neighbor tormented her stepdaughter to death. From where I was, the dark woman's profile—her eyebrows and nose—seemed to be touching Oyone's bangs. 'Such a poor girl!' she said to Okyō. 'The young bride of your relative.'

"We didn't know the woman well, of course. But since she lived just across the street, we saw her when she passed by, and knew her well enough to say hello. Just picture us forcing a laugh, and saying to her, 'Whenever we see you, you always look so nice.'

" 'They say it was an unnatural death. But, you know, everyone gets what they deserve.'

"Our neighbor gave us a searching glance and then Okyō—this is your mother, right? You should never try to imitate her. She suddenly nodded her handsome chin so it almost touched her chest, and just as quickly said, 'Isn't that just the truth?' She was carrying a baby on her back."

Tsujimachi looked at Oyone's face and thick eyelashes.

"Your mother was dressed in a short-sleeved jacket, on her way to visit this very temple. Because the steps are so steep, she had strapped her baby to her back with a light-yellow tie-dyed sash, rather than carry it in front. 'Baa!' I hid my face with my hands and tried to make it laugh. And then your mother came right in through the front door, rattling her clogs. I blushed bright-red, right there in front of the rich man's wife.

"And who was that baby on her back? Why hide it? It was you, Oyone. And now you're a beautiful woman, standing here next to me. It's been a while since I last saw you. You were two then. Maybe three."

"Three. By the old way of counting."

"I see."

"My mother once told me she was pregnant the year your house burned down. She came running to see if she could do anything. That's why I have a birthmark."

Oyone's eyelashes trembled. Tsujimachi suddenly shrugged his shoulders, as if startled.

"Sorry. I shouldn't have said that. I didn't think you'd mind. It used to be red. Now that I'm older, it's become less obvious. It's pale bluish-green now."

Tsujimachi looked downward, as if training his eyes on the ground, and said, "No one can see it. You've nothing to worry about. Where is it, by the way?"

The Heartvine

"That's not a question you should ask."

"Well—"

"Over on this side, on my breast."

"I'm sure it's an attractive mark—like the shadow of a shaved eyebrow, or a spring leaf showing through melting snow. Well, when my father died, I came back to Kanazawa. But then I insisted on returning to Tokyo. That's why I wasn't around when the fire broke out. So, yes, it was my fault your mother had to rush to the scene. And you—this person I'm looking at now—you were a baby in your mother's womb. It's been about thirty years.

"Everything's a blur. I can still see that sad, beautiful person in the dim light. Far away. Closer up. Now disappearing. Now appearing right in front of me. I was there with her that night, also searching for a place to die. I wanted to be alone, and I thought she was getting in my way. She probably thought the same about me. It got late, after three in the morning. The hill that slopes down from the castle is a long one, so I eventually lost track of her. The one image that sticks in my mind is of her back as she was walking away, just before I lost sight of her. If she did kill herself in the moat, that must mean she went down to the city once, then climbed back up the hill.

"The next morning, I still didn't know if the young woman who had been living at the gilder's shop was the one I had seen earlier that night or not. I still don't know. At the moat, I didn't get a good look at her—not from the front nor from the back nor from the side. But that next morning, when Okyō told me what had happened, I immediately sensed it was her. I must have felt that way because we both shared the same death wish.

"So, to avoid the eyes of the woman across the street, Okyō came right in. And when I said 'Baa!' you had the strangest look on your face."

Oyone laughed. She brought one sleeve of her kimono to her chest.

"Your mother suddenly tapped my grandmother on the back. When she took the lid off the pot and looked in, a thin waft of steam rose up."

Oyone touched her side locks.

"To me, those weakly burning flames beneath that boiling pot

seemed to be warming the body of that young woman who had just
killed herself. In the flickering ashes, I could see her fallen figure—
her tangled kimono, sodden hair, and pure white face. I was convinced she looked like the woman's stepdaughter, the young woman
who, reproached for her love by the rich lady standing in her doorway across the street, had thrown herself into the very same moat five
years ago. I must have been out of my mind.

"From the depths of the broken-down well next to where I was
sitting, I heard the lonely sound of dripping water. In those echoes, I
could also hear the sounds of people running down the street, crying,
'There's been a suicide!' 'A beautiful woman.' 'Another young
woman in the moat.'

"The uproar continued like a great wave that fell upon the
neighborhood, the town, and everywhere around us. But for the
next three years, I said absolutely nothing.

"Okyō didn't talk about the girl either, nor did she allow me to.
'It would be like wind blowing through the same cherry tree,' she
said. 'I didn't want it to come back and tempt you.'

"I was sickened by the thought that I had come so close to being
the young woman's partner in death. Having survived, I always took
a detour whenever I passed through her neighborhood. I took an
alley along the mountainside to avoid passing in front of the gilder's
shop.

"I didn't have the money to buy a newspaper and read about
what had happened. Neither was I able to peruse the ones they put
up on the public bulletin boards. I was hardly in the mood to be
seen among the crowds that gathered there. I had come this close to
crossing the Mountain of Death and the River of Three Hells. Having walked the moat's edge with the dead girl, I lost all courage. I
tried my best to avoid everybody, to stay away from people and all
their rumors. What had made the blossom scatter? The rain? A
storm? Rocks thrown by others? Had her branch been broken off by
some evil man? Even now, I don't have a firm grasp of the details.
And it's already been thirty years.

"Oyone, I know they celebrate the Lantern Festival early here.
But it was after that, in August of that year, when the dragonflies—
the ones I'm so fond of—were flying through the air. That was when

I found a way to get back to Tokyo." Tsujimachi took a breath. He shifted his place on the stone, and lightly tapped his knee. "Oh, now I get it."

3

There was something strange about the lantern as it suddenly moved near the sleeve of Tsujimachi's overcoat. No, nothing strange. It was only the shadow of a passing cloud, showing palely on the white face of the lantern.

"Now I get it. You think I got this lantern for the dead girl."

"That's right." Oyone quietly nodded at the bouquet of mums and cockscombs in her hands.

"You probably heard it was a failed double suicide or something like that, didn't you? Your nosey mother told you all about it, didn't she? That's why you know about it, right? What a strange, weird connection I have with that girl! She sadly went her way, just as the cherry blossoms were reaching their peak. You're right. They put the poor girl's grave here at the Lantern Temple. She was too young."

Tsujimachi put a hand to his forehead and looked down at the lantern.

"What was I thinking? Just before I left for Tokyo, I made a point of coming here when no one was around. That sounds sexier than it really was. There I was, sneaking through the dark like a mouse, coming up the hill from over there in the corner, up those stone steps, carrying a small paper lantern, the cheapest one I could find. My chest was pounding. I could barely breathe.

"I forget what I was wearing, probably a *yukata* or something. I came to make an offering to that young woman—a bouquet of harlot's blossoms? bellflowers? bush clovers? eulalias? Dripping with dew, my image of that woman was more beautiful and sad than a pale-colored lantern.

"I got this far up the steps, right to here.

"And then what do you think happened? Oyone, you were joking when you said I was heartless. But even more heartless than a man's indifference is the thoughtlessness of thirty years. I brought this lantern here today, but, like they say, sometimes we don't see the forest for the trees. I had completely forgotten about her. I have no excuse. Worse than that, I have no dignity.

"Should I tell you everything? These red leaves were green then. I climbed through the shadows of the trees. When I looked toward the graveyard, the top of the hill was covered with mist, so I couldn't see a thing. It was as if the gravestones had suddenly vanished like a mirage. But through the nettle trees, I saw the light of the temple's tall lantern, coming to me through the branches, passing between the leaves, greeting the spirits of the dead, welcoming the dew, while above my head trailed the long ghost of a wisteria tassel, swaying before my eyes. I couldn't make out all the details, but it seemed that she was there, her sleeves waving in the air around the towering lantern.

"'You're hopeless.'

"There, right before me. Something white. Someone had come directly down from the temple gate, dressed in a dark-blue *yukata,* tied with a two-colored, reversible sash.

"'You're here to meet the dead girl, aren't you?'

"Of all the things to say! And who do you think said that? It was your mother, of course. Doesn't that sound like something she would say?

"What a sudden blow! There I was, a snot-nosed kid, eyes wide open with astonishment. Until then I had never visited my ancestors' graves once, not even during the Lantern Festival."

Tsujimachi placed a hand on top of the lantern.

"I just stood there with the lantern in my hand, like a badger lost on its way to buy *sake.* Okyō-san was quick to speak. Even if I had wanted to tell her I was on my way to put the lantern on a family grave, I couldn't have, having suffered that blow from her."

—As for Hatsuji-san's grave?

"Hatsuji. I had heard someone mention her name. The gentle, meek young girl who had taken her own life."

—Do you know where the grave is?

"How could I? Okyō told me I might fall and hurt myself. The rocky path was extremely steep and slippery with dew. Why not leave the lantern at the temple and come back when it was light? But how could I show up there during the day? I told her I'd leave the lantern here on this rock. I'd give up. But your mother made the point that if some nocturnal creature came and tread upon it, Hatsuji's beautiful ghost would tremble.

"'So let's go back to the temple.' She lifted the skirts of her kimono with one hand and led the way.

"I had made a point of coming to the graveyard at night so nobody would see me. I asked your mother what she was doing there.

"'I was enjoying the coolness of the temple grounds, away from the cares of the world,' she said. 'There in the tinted blue shadows of hydrangea bushes, with a watermelon cooling in the stream by the rear veranda and the priest enjoying the chilled vinegar noodles with spicy mustard that he had hidden away from his young acolytes, we were shedding cold tears, cooling ourselves in the darkness as we watched a number of spirits, half-hidden among the trees, being guided back to this world by over three hundred flickering lanterns. Among them was Hatsuji's ghost.'

"Okyō rambled on pleasantly. And afterward we rushed back to the temple grounds, where a priest was seated on a platform near the main hall. He was waiting for visitors who came to the temple at night after work. Beside him was an offering tray piled with red and white cords, mementos for those who had made donations to the temple. So guess what happened next? I kept my distance, but your mother grabbed the lantern right out of my hand and took it to the priest. 'Give this to that young woman who killed herself this spring,' she explained. 'It's from her partner, the one who survived their double suicide.'

"I ran to the gate. And your mother followed after me.

"'Look. I brought you this red cord,' she said. 'Maybe I should have gotten the white one—since your bride's already a ghost.'

"Blushing, I stumbled to this spot on the steps. Maybe I exaggerate a little. But lightning flashed over the dark ocean, and it started to pour, in the middle of the night."

Tsujimachi sat quietly for a moment, as if thinking back on that evening squall. When he spoke again, the tone of his voice had changed. "So, Oyone. You heard all this from your mother, I suppose."

"I did. But not until after I got married."

"Oh, really? So even your mother had enough sense to wait for an appropriate time. It's not a story you'd tell a young woman, I suppose." He paused. "Now, about this lantern. I can see now why you thought I brought it for the woman's grave, instead of those square ones they usually use around here. The truth is, my intentions were never so noble. I didn't buy this for the poor girl. I confess. I was in a daze. If I don't need a lantern on a moonlit night, how stupid would I look carrying one around in the middle of the day?

"Thanks for staying with me back there, even though I was acting like a lost tourist. I was in a daze, standing in front of that lantern shop in the alley down the hill. Looking at this, staring at that. The shop reminded me of another one—in a different place and time. There was a hollow next to the river, by a temple near my neighborhood grade school. The shop was there, a dingy place that sold lanterns not far from the temple gate. It was run by a bearded man who dressed in a navy-blue kimono splattered with white paint. He wore a low apron covered with blobs of green and crimson. His clothes were so plastered with color that he'd look like a dancing dragon were he to crawl on the ground. He painted peonies with a quick, heavily loaded brush, using a shading technique that allowed him to make crimson taper off to pink. He painted carp swimming up waterfalls. He did murals of iris and walkways for the local bathhouse. On my way home from school, I loved to linger beneath the eaves of his shop and watch as he leaned forward and painted flyer after flyer. He kept his brushes in a big bowl filled with water—the colors mixing together like yam soup. I remember the rain and sleet showers of late fall. School vacation during the summer. Cherry blossoms in spring. Snow in winter. The brilliance and sharpness of those peonies. Generous in his use of gold and silver powder, he sprinkled it on leaves and moss, so it sparkled like shafts of light that pierce through elegant corridors. In those days, every time I returned home from school, I could see his beautiful peonies blossoming near the bridge over the Asano River.

"At the lantern shop where we stopped today, they don't paint flyers or make things like that. But there were those white paper umbrellas lined up in the sunshine. They took me back to my childhood. I stood there in the shop so long I thought I should buy something. So I got this lantern.

"When the shopowner asked me what my family crest was, I answered, 'Peony.'

"It would have taken too long for him to draw something on the lantern. And I wasn't planning to use it for anything anyway. I guess I could just as well have gotten an umbrella. I would have opened it and followed up the hill behind Oyone, the Chrysanthemum Girl."

"That's right. Like an advertisement for a comedy team."

"There you go. But, seriously, do you remember those umbrellas lined up in the sunlight coming through those willow trees? They looked as if they had been covered with silver foil. And then there were those two butterflies on the flowers you were holding. They flew into the shop and danced above the umbrellas, above the snow peonies, like two pieces of silver foil floating in the air. I didn't put it all together, not even then—the silver foil, the grave nearby, the poor young woman taken from the water, the gold-leaf shop down the street from where I used to live. It's not that I don't have feelings. As we make our way through the trials of life, we can cut up the time from morning to evening as finely as we like. But the past still gets lost in the distance. It happened so long ago that even those sunlit chrysanthemums turned into a flowery mist before my very eyes and vanished in a hazy dream.

"I feel bad about what happened. After we visit your mother's grave, we'll go there. I just hope it isn't too close by. I'd feel awkward paying my respects in front of your mother, even if I am an old man now. Your mother would make fun of me. She'd laugh at me from beneath her gravestone."

"That's a scary thought. I wouldn't worry about my mother. I'm here, so she won't make fun of you. I think you really should pay your respects—to Itozuka-san."

"Itozuka Hatsuji? Was that her surname?"

"No. You don't know about Itozuka, the Thread Memorial? Some people also call it Itomakizuka, the Spool Memorial. There's a temple over there, across the valley, halfway up the next mountain. It's dedicated to Kishibojin."

"That would be the Pomegranate Temple, the Shinjōji."

"Excuse me. If you don't mind, I think I'll sit down, too. Over here, for just a minute. Oh, no. Why should that matter? These fallen leaves are like a brocade. If anything, they're too pretty to sit on. I still remember how I used to take off my sandals and sit at the temple among the fallen pomegranate blossoms. We'd call it Kishibojin's cloud. My mother would take me there. I wondered whose clouds the white, blue, and purple ones were. I always thought of Kishibojin's cloud as crimson."

The graveyard was nearby, but Oyone's eyes seemed to be focused on something far in the distance. Was she thinking of her mother as she spoke so dreamily of the temple? Hearing her words, Tsujimachi immediately remembered the three or four years he had spent in Zushi with his young bride, trying to survive the illness that nearly took her life. He could never forget how she had been saved by the mercy of Kannon. He remembered the Ganden Temple and the mountains behind the inner hall where, in the sunlight of spring at its height, he saw a white rabbit jumping among the fragrant violets and bowed his head to pray fervently for his ailing wife. With the clouds directly before him, he had intoned the words that could only proceed from a pained heart.

Oyone's profile was elegant and refined. She continued to explain. "The grave of the founder of Kaga *yūzen* is there at the Pomegranate Temple. For a while, no one visited the place. The moss, the ground beneath, everything dried up. But these days, people come from afar; and because the temple has come to be widely known, they've put up a new stone memorial for him. It's become a famous spot. That's why this temple decided to do something, too. They want to put up a memorial for Hatsuji-san."

"No kidding. So the priest here has his worldly ambitions, too. Using the dead to attract the living. Since she drowned herself, why not put up a billboard with pale watercolor washes?"

"You shouldn't say things like that. It wasn't the priest's idea. It was the temple's patrons, some people in the tourist bureau. The temple just loaned them the space."

"Not the spot where she was buried, I hope."

"No, a different place. They couldn't decide whether to call it the Thread Memorial or the Spool Memorial."

"I supposed they wanted *thread* to match the *dye* of Kaga *yūzen*, right?"

"No, it's not like they just made up some story. The woman

The Heartvine

worked in a handkerchief factory. She did embroidery. That's why she ended up killing herself—because she used red thread."

"You're telling me that's why she had to die? Because she worked at a sewing plant and embroidered with red thread?"

"You really don't know much about her, do you?"

"Some people commit double suicide for trivial reasons. No, I really don't know anything. Whenever you have your photograph taken with a large group, you lose track of the others one by one, whether to death or to life."

Tsujimachi turned to Oyone and spoke.

"'Every crab digs a different hole.' Is that a strange way to put it? 'Not every badger in the same den is alike.' 'A quart gourd holds exactly one quart.' Be that as it may, people naturally speculated about the usual reasons, like hard times. Everyone thought it was because of poverty."

And it actually was.

"So you didn't know. That's a shame, I feel bad for her, just thinking about it. She had to work for piecemeal wages to stay alive. But she used to be a high-ranking servant to a provincial lord."

"As good as a princess, was she? Then I guess I missed my chance, didn't I? Had we died together that night, I would have been reborn a fashionable man with a young lover. And as for her thread, I think it should be red."

"You don't know what you're saying. That thread caused her death. Hatsuji served a wealthy family, and her mother was a mistress. Even so, she enjoyed her share of privileges, at least until the new government abolished the samurai class. Her lord's mansion soon fell into disrepair, and her parents passed away. Some distant relatives to the lady she worked for took her into their home. They were the people at the gold-leaf shop you were just talking about. Since it was a difficult time for everyone, they had to struggle to make ends meet. She went to work in a factory. She had learned how to do sewing at home as a diversion, and so she was a skilled seamstress and embroiderer. In no time, she was the best of the women in her factory and made only the finest goods. Some of the handkerchiefs were done in subtler colors, of course. She did a beautiful job of embroidering flowers and butterflies on white silk. Her best works were the pride of Japan. They sold them as luxury export items to foreign countries rather than domestically."

"I see."

4

> "See them
> 'neath a blade of grass,
> Waiting for
> The storm to pass.
>
> Hiding from
> Our prying eyes,
> Whitened silk
> and crimson dyes.

"They sang that ditty at the factory. And it killed the girl, Hatsuji. Slender green leaves of grass sewn around the edges and, off to one side, two red dragonflies against a background of snow-white silk."

Oyone gracefully adjusted the collar of her kimono with two fingers.

"There might have been no problem had the dragonflies been separated from each other, or if someone else had done the design and she only did the sewing. But the real reasons she got in trouble were because she was such a beautiful woman and because her work was so fine. The others were jealous. They found fault with every little thing. And she did it all, including the design. It was a wonder where she got her ideas. Her red embroidered dragonflies were highly prized, especially in the West. People couldn't get enough of them; and the orders kept pouring in. That caused an even bigger stir, because her work came to be seen as an international embarrassment. They sang their songs as if the wings of the dragonflies were arms and legs, and their red was the inner lining of a woman's kimono, exposing naked flesh.

> Two red leaves
> on purest snow . . .

(Here two or three lines have been omitted because Oyone was too embarrassed to sing them.)

The Heartvine

"But isn't that ridiculous, Tsujimachi-san? Whoever heard of butterflies and dragonflies wearing clothes?

> By lightning flash,
> We see, we stare.
> We fear and scorn
> This tangled pair!

"It would have been better had there been only one dragonfly. But she sewed two together—tail touching tail, eight wings spread, each one stitched with silver thread. They weren't asleep. They were flying! And that's why—

"'Don't you have any shame?' they asked. 'What a disgrace you are!' they said. Everyone had a complaint to make, as if Hatsuji were trying to get rich by showing pictures of lovemaking to red-headed, blue-eyed foreigners. Accused by their nasty songs, the reserved, gentle, and refined Hatsuji blushed to her ear lobes. A touch on her kimono left a gash of poisonous fangs on her skin. Like a white camellia blossoming in the snow, she fell apart and scattered.

"Apparently, she wrote about it in her suicide note—about how terribly, terribly embarrassed she was."

"I can sympathize with that. It must have been a terrible experience. You know what they used to say about proper samurai women? If you couldn't make them talk with whips and water and fire torture, all you had to do was threaten to strip off all their clothes, and they would immediately comply. Unlike noblewomen . . ."

Because he was a weak-hearted person, Tsujimachi envied the tomboyish lady of Seville who made her living in a tobacco factory. He also thought of Oyone's mother. Had Okyō been at that factory, instead of cutting those workers' faces into shreds, she'd have flung noodles at them.

"Unlike noblewomen, the commoners' daughters would . . ." Tsujimachi carelessly said.

"Would what? Commoners' daughters would what?"

"Nothing."

"I'm a commoner's daughter."

Tsujimachi suddenly remembered the birthmark, the green leaf on Oyone's breast. He hunched his shoulders. "My apologies. I must say, this story of a woman in service to a bankrupt samurai's household is more moving than an old romance. So fleeting and sad. And so pure." "She was like Princess Chūjō, the Fujiwara daughter who wove mandalas. Her pale fingers would vanish as they moved over the smooth, white silk. The point of her needle would flash like a sparkle of dew, and the red thread dangling before her slender chest would dye the silk with its color. A few stitches more with the silver thread and several dragonflies would magically appear. 'I was sitting right there! I saw it with my own eyes!' An old flat-nosed factory woman, her mouth as smelly as pickled eggplant, would say things like that. When I think about those dirty-mouthed women singing their nasty ditties, it makes me wish I could have been there to stare them down. But it wasn't just them. For about a year after Hatsuji's suicide, people in town used to sing that disgusting song everywhere you went—at the bathhouse, in the streets. Even the weakest ones among them were saying that Hatsuji had embarrassed them with her embroidery.

> See them
> 'neath a blade of grass

"With silver wings like arms and legs, her two dragonflies were in the act of . . . well, you know."

"What's so bad about two dragonflies together? Those people were ignorant, that's all. These locals don't know anything. But then again, I didn't pay much attention to dragonflies either, not until something happened to me just recently.

"From the letters I've been sending, you probably know that the distance from my neighborhood in Tokyo to Tsukiji, across town, is about as far as from here to, let's say, the ocean over there in the distance. Just before I came here, I thought I'd visit my dentist since I had a tooth that was bothering me. Actually, my dentist is in Akasaka, so I went to Tsukiji to do an errand on the way. I left Kōjimachi by way of Yotsuya and Shinjuku, to Miyakezaka, Hibiya, then to the Ginza, right past the Kabuki Theater to my destination in Akashi-chō. Everywhere I went, the city was full of them—as high as the rooftops, above and below, left and right, vertical and horizontal, like a blizzard of cherry blossoms floating in a shining pale crimson rain, wings translucent, bodies red, a flood of dragonflies spilling over everywhere, not running into each other or dancing wildly in a maelstrom, but flying diagonally toward the sky, diagonally toward the ground, diagonally right, and diagonally left, all of them flying in unison to the north, perhaps to Asakusa, or Senju, and beyond? It was almost almost beyond my ability to imagine. A bioluminescence at Akashi-chō, right in the middle of the day! A reflection of the Sumida River in midair!

"Once I was finished in Akashi-chō, I hurried off to Akasaka. And there they were again, flying everywhere—masses of dragonflies. I got to my dentist's office and sat down in the seat. They were flying outside the window, seeming to thin out a bit. Even so, I'm not talking about just a thousand or two thousand. They came up to the dentist's second-floor window, about to the eaves of the house across the street, flying at about the level of the telephone wires—not much higher than that, nor much lower. Each of them filled the same layer of the sky. Passing by in countless numbers, their stratum was neither very thick nor very dense, more like a thin translucence, the fluttering wings of each insect.

"To my eyes, the low sky of Tokyo was a light crimson covered with coarsely woven silk and wrapped in a silver mist. The taller buildings and wooded hills looked like rocky islands sticking out above the white waves that were wrapped in the colors of the setting sun.

"'A lot of dragonflies out today,' I finally had to say.

"'It's been that way since early this morning,' my dentist replied. That was about four in the afternoon.

"On my way home, I mentioned it to the taxi driver, just as we got to Akasaka Mitsuke. He said, 'It's not as bad as it was. You should have seen them this morning at about six. When I came through here with a passenger, the dragonflies were everywhere—up and down, left and right, making this rushing sound as they passed by. The blue sky above Aoyama, up to the clouds on Mount Fuji straight ahead, like the Chinese milk vetch that covers the foothills, dragonflies were everywhere. They got under the car and lifted it off the road. For a while there, I didn't know what to do. Never seen anything like it!' The driver seemed truly frightened by what had happened.

"I myself had never witnessed such incredible numbers. The dragonflies came pouring into the city at about the same time each

year. Since childhood, I've always loved dragonflies. But I never realized that until recently, not until about eight or nine years ago—because I hadn't been paying that much attention, I suppose. It's always
the same month—the middle part of October, between the tenth and
the twentieth. For the past three years, they've come on the seven-
teenth. I know that because I've been recording it in my journal. I've
noticed that the pattern of the seasons and the weather doesn't change
much from year to year. The autumn rains come, the storms roll in.
Then right after a typhoon passes through, the sky is incredibly clear
and blue the next morning. As if they've waited for the moment, the
dragonflies come floating in waves upon the wind, rustling their wings,
like a lifting fog of light crimson as they pass by. How about here?"

"The same." Oyone's face blushed faintly, not because she had
been listening that intently to Tsujimachi's story but because of the
crimson maple leaves around her. "It's already late, and we haven't
seen one all day. When I came here to the temple last month to visit
my mother's grave, I saw them just as I passed through the front gate,
like a sudden downpour on a sunny day. Their wings were like silver
rain falling from the sky."

"Flying one by one, I suppose."

"One by one?"

"Not two by two?"

"I'm not sure. I didn't notice."

"No, I'm sure you wouldn't notice something like that. But
that's just what I wanted to say. You know the dragonflies I was just
telling you about? Well, they were all in pairs, every one of them,
flying through the air together, just like the ones Hatsuji embroidered. I wonder what kind of song the locals here would have come
up with had they seen that—a ditty like the one that killed Hatsuji?"

"What would they do? Declare them indecent? Pronounce
them injurious to society? A public embarrassment? Could the waves
of the sea wash them away? Could they be scorched with fire? Even
an earthquake wouldn't be able to get rid of them. A strong gale
could do them in, I suppose, as they filled the skies and covered the
earth. They're actually short-lived, in fact. Hatsuji took their ephemerality upon herself."

"That's why, Tsujimachi-san. That's why. Times have changed.

In order to placate her soul, and to console her, they've decided to erect the Thread Memorial in her honor, to praise her skill as a seamstress."

Tsujimachi said nothing.

"The monument's just about finished. They published the design in the newspaper. It has a big spool of white stone sitting on top of a base. They carved lines of thread into it and dyed them red."

"So the Yūzen memorial could have a partner? I guess that's not such a bad thing after all. Where's the spot? Where did they put it?"

"Would you like to go see? It's more than half-finished. Right next to the front gate."

Thinking of the red cord that Okyō had playfully given him that night, the small gift that the temple always gave in return for the square Bon Festival lanterns that everyone brought, Tsujimachi stood, lantern in hand, like a puppet being manipulated by some other power.

5

"A dragonfly . . . ghost?"

"There's no such thing," Tsujimachi spoke calmly and quietly. So who was it, just now, who shouted out, "Ah!"?

Tsujimachi had just embraced the moss-covered gravestone with one hand. No, wait. Better not say embraced. Rather, he had placed a hand upon what we might call the young woman's stone corpse, even though it was colder than frost. Of course, there was something on it—Oyone's pale-purple coat, its sleeves draped gracefully over the grave. Covering the stone and its ghostlike shadows with its woven background of slender willows and its delicately dyed pattern of asters and pale chrysanthemum-like flowers, her coat spilled over the white mountain soil. It bloomed among the dried grasses and below the sky-covering trees as they leaked a pale light that made it seem like a splendid, sorrowful lantern, woven with golden thread, its eyes cast upon the ground.

The two had come here by way of a boulder-strewn path that was steep, almost vertical it seemed, as if they were climbing up from the bottom of a broken V-shaped bowl, or the bed of a dry waterfall. On the grass-covered banks, graves were lined up one after the other, some of them leaning, others fallen.

Where they had climbed to the top, at the graveyard high above the temple, a huge Chinese nettle with its tangled roots sewn into the cliff towered higher than the mountains. There, among generations of ancestors, Oyone's mother slept fitfully, as if her eyelids would open at any moment. Her grave was dark and covered with shadows. From her bed beneath the ground, surely she was laughing at Tsujimachi for carrying a lantern in the middle of the day. White, smoky curls of incense twisted upward, and the naked flame of a candle flickered in the quiet breeze.

The cliff beyond the great nettle tree fell quickly away, forming a steep basin that extended to the foothills on the far side, forming the cemetery behind the temple. Hatsuji's grave was right across from Okyō's, slightly downhill and to the left, on one of the grass-covered banks.

Look! Oyone had folded Tsujimachi's overcoat and was holding it over one arm while standing behind him. He was crouched before the grave, with his hand reaching behind the stone and underneath the coat that covered it so alluringly. That hand was dyed a pale-purple because of the coat. And the other held a rusty pair of pruning shears.

The shears weren't an afterthought, there to prune back any branches that might be growing over the grave. They were there because Hatsuji's beautifully sad grave, now dressed in Oyone's coat, was dark and filled with spirits, along with the graveyard around it, like the night of the Lantern Festival grown late, when all the candles have burned out.

The shears had been dropped there. They had been thrown down on the ground when the old caretaker of the temple grounds, along with three day laborers, made their escape, scared out of their wits.

It happened this way.

When Tsujimachi and Oyone first came up the stone steps to the front gate, they entered the temple grounds, a wide open space without a belfry. Near the always open wooden gate to the graveyard, in a clearing in the pine trees, they saw the nearly completed monument. There was nothing fancy about the base. It was a huge, plain-looking slab of rock about three yards high. Sitting on top was the spool of thread, specially carved for the memorial; and into this cylinder a hole had been bored, indicating plans to do something more. The stick that would eventually be used to turn the spool was missing. Even Oyone didn't know what all was planned. As for the four handles sticking out from the bottom, fortunately they did not give the impression of a three-legged pot; for if they had, any person of gentle feelings would find the boiling and roasting too much to bear. Rather, the protrusions looked more like smooth, jewel-bearing branches of white coral.

"We'll take a closer look on our way back."

They were there to visit Oyone's mother's grave. Leading Tsuji-machi as far as the gate, Oyone seemed to take her time. "The path is broken up, so please be careful."

Just then, four men came rushing toward the wooden gate in a brown blur of bodies, huffing and puffing. They formed an avalanche of arms and legs that pumped and hurried down the hill. As the men passed by, their hurried voices and the drumming of their feet sounded as if they were about to crash down on them.

Oyone stepped nimbly to the side of the path to avoid a collision. The man in the lead, wrinkled in face and foot, turned his nose directly at Oyone and gave her a strange smile, "We just seen a ghost."

A ghost.

"No snakes? No adders?" Oyone furrowed her brows when she heard the man speak of ghosts. She was worried only about snakes.

"I'm not talkin' snakes."

Indeed, these burly, bare-shinned, determined-looking day laborers—dressed in jackets covered with shop logos, wadded cotton shirts, and short pants—hardly seemed the type who'd be afraid of a snake or two. They quickly passed by the Thread Memorial and huddled together under a pine tree. The old groundskeeper stood among them, his white eyebrows twitching nervously.

"Dragonfly."

"A dragonfly ghost," added one of the younger ones, who was wearing a straw hat.

"If it's a dragonfly, who cares about ghosts?" Oyone smiled. The collar of her kimono had come open slightly—light yellow against the snow white of her chest. Without bothering to adjust it, she started uphill through the gate, without looking back.

The boulders were jagged. The path steep. Oyone took the lead, her white socks like two butterflies that led Tsujimachi up the slope.

"Who was that man?"

"Kyusuke, the groundskeeper. He takes care of the graveyard. That was probably an after-tea prank. He still thinks I'm a child. He has no sense of propriety, even with you here with me. What a complete fool."

"Well, it's a pleasure to be teased with someone young like you. If he wanted to scare us, though, why talk about ghosts at a temple? Let alone dragonfly ghosts."

"As long as there are no snakes and adders. I'm not afraid of lizard ghosts or whatever."

"So they have them here?"

"Sometimes."

"Yes, I imagine so."

"But not this time of year."

"Good. Then I'm not afraid either. Still, I wonder. Maybe they saw one of those black dragonflies. What do you call them? The ones with black lacquer wings and slender blue bodies. I think they're called Kawara *tombo* or something like that. Maybe that's what they saw."

"People call the black ones spiritflies. But a ghost? The old fool."

And that was when it happened.

"Oh!" Oyone shouted out. "Oh, how awful! Look!"

No sooner had she spoken these words, than Oyone slipped off her coat. Somehow she managed to untie the string and slip her hands out of the sleeves while holding the bouquet of flowers. Like a single gust of wisteria-colored wind rustling over meadow flowers, her coat quickly covered the grave.

The stone had been pushed backward onto the grass. Coils of filthy rope were tied around it.

"Hatsuji-san!"

It was the girl's grave.

"Look. They didn't even bother to put a straw mat or anything around her. She's completely naked."

Oyone's face was flushed with anger and embarrassment. Although it might be inappropriate to put it this way, the sight of the grave entered Tsujimachi's eyes in the same way. Someone had manhandled the stone and moved it off its base. Here and there, its patina of green moss had been ripped off, leaving patches of bare skin to swell and recede in the shade of the lowering sun. It was as if they had cruelly tied her up, tightly binding the young girl's gaunt, pale body.

It wasn't hard to guess what had happened. For some reason, the workers had decided to haul the old stone to the new location where they were constructing the Thread Memorial.

And how else were they supposed to react to such a heartless act? Thankfully, Oyone's coat now covered the gravestone. Although she was a gentle young wife, the way she had reacted to the situation so aggressively, even dramatically, didn't take Tsujimachi by surprise. It was only to be expected. After all, she was Okyō's daughter. Had her mother been there, she would have done the same. Her mother, though, would have calmly taken off her coat, untied her sash, and continued disrobing until she was standing with nothing on but her undergarments. Rather than her coat, she would have put her kimono on the grave.

And what if it had been a blazing hot summer day, you ask? Such a cynical reader always poses problems for an author; but it would be cowardly not to respond. If it had been a hot day, Okyō would have stood there naked. If not, she would have made Tsujimachi disrobe.

They had already paid their respects to Oyone's mother and were on their way back when they saw the other grave.

Tsujimachi's immediate response was to cut the ropes and toss them away. Even for a brief moment, he couldn't bear the thought of others seeing the grave. And if it had to be done, then he would pitch in. As they worked together to free the stone of its bonds, neither he nor Oyone could bear to look at it.

He felt bad about undoing the ropes without first giving the workers some notice. But even that wouldn't be such a problem as he could easily make them see his point with a present of *sake* and rice cakes. If he signaled to the wrinkled-faced man to come, his wrinkles would disappear. Anyway, the legitimate daughter of the chief donor, who had won the right to make vinegar-flavored noodles in the temple kitchen, was right here with him.

No need to go borrow a dagger or a chestnut- or persimmon-peeling knife. The pruning shears had flown through the air like a bat's bones. Taking them into his hand, Tsujimachi positioned himself above the grave. Still feeling bad about not asking for permission, he couldn't bear to look at the fetters; and without removing Oyone's silk coat and while imagining the incense basket that burned beneath the scented sleeves, he reached in with both hands and . . . my god! The stone was slightly warm and fragrant. The grave's skin soft to his touch.

That was when Tsujimachi cried out, "Ah!"

"A dragonfly ghost, Tsujimachi-san."

"There's no such thing."

The snipping shears echoed near Oyone's breast, near her small birthmark, green like the mossy grave. Tsujimachi bowed once. He faced the stone, and said "If what I'm doing here is wrong, then let me cut my hand."

The bracing snip of shears at work cut the moaning wind in the pines. From the crickets came not one chirp.

"Oh, it's you. The lacquer man's wife."

The wrinkled face of the groundskeeper appeared at the wooden gate down the hill from the graveyard. He opened his mouth and called to them. Walking toward them in thin straw sandals, he avoided the rock-strewn path and skillfully climbed sideways up the grass-covered embankment until he came up to where they were.

Bringing up the rear, the gang of day laborers appeared at the wooden gate, lined up shoulder to shoulder.

"Greetings, kind sir. You seem to be enjoying yourself. Everything's just fine, is it?"

"Actually, my friend, everything's not so fine. I've just undone all the work you did. I'll buy you a drink later. As you can see, I've cut your ropes."

"Yes, well. Then you've done us a favor."

"That's not what I thought you'd say."

"No, no. You've done a good thing."

The Heartvine

"What do you mean, a good thing?" Oyone said. "You desecrated this young woman's grave."

"Well, Madame. We did use this twine. Dammit all."

The groundskeeper crouched down and slowly came forward on his tiptoes, as if smashing caterpillars with his feet. He pulled out pieces of the rope that had been cut from the grave and, tossing them over his shoulder, looked up at the trees and sky.

Strangely, as if answering orders, the men lined up at the gate crouched down and started searching the sky in the same manner.

"Looks like the dragonfly ghosts cleared up pretty well."

"What in the world are you talking about?"

"Ghosts. That's what I'm talking about. They came out when we moved that stone off this base."

"I assume this is about that Thread Memorial or whatever it's called. Maybe you dug up some bones, or something."

"No. We wouldn't do that. The stuffed shirts who wanted the memorial—you know, those fancy bearded men with top hats, leather shoes, and suits—they wanted us to dig her up. But the chief priest wouldn't have it. The woman's been buried here for thirty years. Besides, this has been an unmarked grave for a while now. Her family hasn't been around, and no one was here to speak up for her. So they talked it over and the priest decided that nobody was digging up anything."

"As he should have, I should think."

"But then they put up that roof over the stone spool. And they wanted this in there with it."

Standing in her simple kimono with its sash tied in the "bulging drum" style, Oyone looked truly elegant.

"She's a Buddha now, the poor girl. She has this coat of asters now, and this mist is her purple cloud to Paradise." The old man stroked the stone. His hand, too, seemed old enough to be covered with moss.

"That tickles."

"That what?" Without thinking, Kyusuke stroked the coat again. "We were going to trim this stone to size. The pavilion's ready—the beams are cut, and everything's put together. We thought we'd carry the grave to somewhere inside the temple grounds and get the measurements just right since, as you can see, the footing is so poor on this slope. The question was how to move it. To make sure we got it right, I asked the boys to carry it on a log. But just try to get those fellows to move. They sat there like a coiled-up snake. Put feathers on one end and shoot it down the hill like an arrow! Then we'll all be served a fine meal to celebrate the new construction. That's right. But this is the entrance to the graveyard, and they're the guardians of hell. I never imagined one of the lady's people would be here." The old man wiped his mouth with his shiny, muddy fist.

"See, we had to tie a rope around the stone to carry it. For that, we should have put some straw or something around it. I told them boys, but those knuckleheads said to me, 'Why wrap a gravestone? It'll just take time. No one's looking. Who cares?'

"The priest and everyone else were attending some big memorial service. So no problem. No one would know. We started wrapping it with rope. Then we tipped it over so we could roll it. It was just like you found it. Picture this. I was down with my knees and face against the stone. The others were leaning over from the other side, trying to put the log through the ropes. And that's when it happened—right in front of my nose, and right in front of the others. Two red dragonflies came out.

"We hadn't seen anything up to that point. But then, those four men, eight eyes as round as chestnuts, watched as the dragonflies came out from beneath the ropes, right out of the stone! We tried to scare them away—'Go on! Get out!' But you think they'd move? Those boys are too young to know much about how the girl died. But when they got this job, they were told a few things about the Thread Memorial.

"Look! The dragonflies started coming toward us. One big fellow with a towel hanging around his neck, standing in front, had been working the log through the ropes. 'Is it the woman's ghost?' he said. And then another worker, the one with the beard, shouted, 'It *is* her ghost!' That's when the dragonflies darted, and two small flames flared up. Cold flames on sweat, a black gust of wind poured down from the mountain. We were blinded by the smoke and ran for our lives.

"So that's what I have to say about that."

"And that's why you're not mad at us for what we did?"

"Why should we be mad? You done us a favor. If you see the priest when he gets back, though, I'd appreciate your not saying anything."

At that moment, the other men lumbered back up the hill.

"Hey, Old Man, everything okay? All clear?"

"See for yourself. This woman's coat is more powerful than a priest's robe with fifty years of incense burned into it. They're gone now, the ghosts."

"I'm afraid of those things. If a dragonfly curses you, you can burn up with fever. That's the thing. If we put the ropes on again, they'll come back." The bearded man in padded cotton clothes made his complaint.

"If that's what you're thinking, why didn't you bring something to wrap the stone in? This Thread Memorial woman's a lady, you boys. You got us in trouble because you tied her up naked. Think of her as a peony bush in a teahouse garden, like you're protecting it from the snow."

"All right. I'll go get something." The man in the straw hat started walking away.

"Wait." Oyone reached out and stopped him. "Just tie the rope over my coat."

The bearded man reminded Tsujimachi of the lantern shop owner he met so many years ago.

"It'll ruin your coat."

"Doesn't matter."

"You say that, but when we tighten the ropes—"

"And you'll be right here watching us."

The beard and the straw hat exchanged looks and mumbled something to each other.

"Go ahead. I really don't mind."

The log looked like it was made of steel. The man holding it, with power rippling through his arms, said, "The stone's soft enough. It'll be like holding a woman in my arms." He tossed the log down and quickly tied the towel around his forehead. Putting both arms around the grave, he pinned the sleeves of Oyone's coat against his chest, embraced the stone, and stood. Thrusting his hips forward, he started down the slope. Apparently, that was the best way to hold the stone. He moved down the rocky path with his feet spread wide apart. His body swaggering from side to side, like a giant crab hugging the Sea Dragon's wife to its chest while climbing a rushing waterfall. Without stopping, he proceeded down the hill.

"Careful, Gonda. Don't hurt yourself." The bearded man followed after with small quick steps.

"I could've done that. I was just holding back. That's right. For whom, you ask?" The straw hat looked back at Oyone, grinned, then followed after the others.

"May the girl find peace in Paradise. Should I toss these into the river? Guess I should burn them."

Kyusuke began gathering up the pieces of rope. By the time he had them in a bundle, holding them on his hip, the three other men had already passed through the wooden gate and were no longer in sight.

"Kyu, sir. Just have them put my coat on the porch by the entrance."

Oyone found her coat at the temple, hanging on the black lacquered frame of a trapezoid-shaped window. She sat at a table by the window, engulfed by a spacious room that had been built to receive visitors to the temple. The winter sun had set—faster than a falling well bucket, even faster than a ripe persimmon knocked down by a rock. The tatami floor of the big room was dark with evening shadows.

Admiring the wonderfully clean sight of Oyone's neck, Tsujimachi sat with a cup of tea, gazing past the still unlighted hibachi that separated him from his lantern, which was now sitting on the table.

(Forgive my indulgence. But if I don't return to the lantern, I can't finish writing this story.)

Oyone dipped her brush into the inkstone that sat next to a small wooden stand on which were stacked numerous wooden tablets that had been brought to the temple by the faithful. She looked closely at the lantern, then dipped her brush into red ink, as if to draw an eyebrow.

"It just occurred to me that we should offer this lantern to Hatsuji's memorial on our way out," Tsujimachi said. "Make two red dragonflies, Oyone. And make damn sure their tails touch. You're a lacquer man's wife now, but you went to finishing school, didn't you? If it's too hard to paint, just make stick figures. Two red lines next to each other, and a shuttlecock feather for wings. Two thin carrots with some pine needles will do. Even a red pepper held between two fingers."

In the darkened room, the white of Oyone's stockings showed against the floor boards, which became as black as lacquer as they took on the darkness of sunset. Tsujimachi urged her on. It was time for the guests of the temple to leave and say their praises to the Big Dipper Bodhisattva.

She poured a generous amount of water into the inkwell, sucked the tip of the brush, which blackened her flower-bud lips, and carefully painted eight wings in light black. The Seto water dipper decorated with a tan-colored carp seemed to be made to order.

"You did it. That's good. Oyone, you look like a painting of Murasaki Shikibu, working there at that table."

"What a thing to say! I'll tell my mother. I'll have her scold you for that."

"My apologies."

His teacup was decorated with a red design. Apologizing for his words, Tsujimachi rose to get Oyone's coat for her, as if waiting on one of the Fujiwara ladies. In the light of the window—

"There's a lot of moss on the inside. That's too bad. Should I fold it up and carry it for you?"

He was still holding the jacket when Oyone reached for it. "I'll wear it."

"You can't. It's covered with moss from the stone . . ."

"It's a keepsake from the poor lady. A floral pattern on my coat now, *shinobuzuri.*"

Tsujimachi was moved by Oyone's compassion. He offered to help help her put on the jacket. "Here. Turn this way."

"Tsujimachi-san. Are you sure it's all right?"

"You're here as your mother's proxy. How could there be anything wrong in helping an old friend's daughter with her coat?"

"I suppose it's all right."

When she turned toward him, her hair brushed against his chest. To his surprise, he felt a chill run through his body.

"I miss my . . . mother."

Tsujimachi had had some professional dealings with the theater and the making of movies. A moment ago, he had been thinking that he could take a scene like this and exploit it for profit. It was an evil thought that secretly sprouted in his heart. But this time there was no allure, no desire. Tears came to his eyes.

"Thank you for being so patient." An elderly woman came out of the priests' quarters, holding a fire pan in one hand and a small, flickering candle in the other. "I'll leave this at the Thread Memorial. You'll want to keep on eye on it, though. You know what they say about crows playing with fire."

Oyone had already reached the platform.

"It's already late. No need to worry about that. The birds are already sleeping in the woods near the castle moat, at the Thousand Wing Abyss."

Tsujimachi looked out over the darkened castle town lying below. Flickering through the willow trees, the lights of the city flowed upon the surface of the river. Stepping down the long flight of steps, he and Oyone descended into the valley of darkness. The lights of the slums on this side of the river had yet to appear.

A tofu peddler making his way home in the dark stopped suddenly, as if to avoid a collision.

"Look. Dragonflies!"

Oyone immediately fell to her knees and pressed her hands together in prayer.

The paper lantern that Tsujimachi had hung on the handle of Hatsuji's monument, where the gravestone now rested, passed through the temple gate and slowly rose into the night sky. On a single gust of wind that blew down from the mountain, two dragonflies quietly stirred, and the images of two women appeared.

Essays

A Song by Lantern Light

In late November 1909, Kyōka returned to Tokyo from a trip to the provinces where, along with Gotō Chūgai, Sasakawa Rinpū, and others, he had ventured forth to stem the rising tide of the naturalist movement. The lecture tour had taken him to Kuwana, a small town in Mie Prefecture, which happened also to be one of the famous stops along the Tōkaidō, documented in Jippensha Ikku's famous travel novel of life on the road, *Shank's Mare* (*Tōkaidō dōchū hiza-kurige*, 1802–1809). Kyōka was so inspired by Kuwana in the moonlight that he began drafting a new story as soon as he returned to Tokyo. The sight of the moon and the waters of the Ibi River combined with an incident he had heard about in which a famous young *nō* actor had been ostracized from his family and troupe because of his arrogance. This fortuitous coming together of setting and theme resulted in the manuscript, completed in only one month, for *A Song by Lantern Light* (*Uta andon*, 1910). Along with *The Holy Man of Mount Kōya*, this novella is considered by most critics to be one of Kyōka's two or three most notable works. It is a complicated though fluidly written story.

Kyōka's appreciation of Kuwana is unmistakable. By way of the moonlit rickshaw ride of Onchi Genzaburō (as Yajirobei) and Hemni Hidenoshin (as Nejibei), we first see the town in bits and pieces. Perceived statically at first, lying cold and still in the January night, Kuwana suddenly begins to flow as a stream of images.

Charles Shirō Inouye

As the two rickshaw men raced off to the edge of the square, the pale lanterns of their carriages wavered in the moonlight. Rattling over the rocky street, they sped down a narrow alley lined by wooden fences, then turned at an intersection of earthen walls. They seemed to be taking a shortcut, passing through many lonely neighborhoods. By and by, they came to a row of two-story buildings, the road between them as narrow as a thread and shadowed from the moon by over-hanging eaves. Tucked into the darkness on each side were a few lanterns, glowing white; and above their heads, stars were sprayed upon the naked tendrils of willow trees, and walls were illuminated by the blue moonlight that appeared here and there in the night. At the end of a long road, a fire tower rose to pierce the mist of the distant mountains, casting the sharp silhouette of a fire bell that seemed as if it were alive, while the clapping of night guard's sticks—Beware! Beware!—sounded in the deepening night. Even though business is usually slow in January, the moonlight was still shining on the latticed windows. And yet, the girls of Kuwana seemed to be keeping early hours, for the pleasure quarter seemed quiet and desolate.

Beneath the spokes of the rickshaws, the street turned into a narrow river of quicksilver. Hanging from the eaves of black-pillared houses, rows of plain and patterned lanterns looked like river otters crossing a bridge on festival night. Suddenly, the rickshaw in the lead, the one in which the older gentleman rode, came to a stop.

Their movement is temporarily arrested by a street musician's song that fills the sky like moonlight, an image that Kyōka uses forty-six times in this story. The singer is standing among many plain and patterned lanterns and comes to be surrounded by the two *jinrikisha*. In this dramatic fashion, the reader is introduced to the story's title—song *(uta)* and lantern *(andon)*—although we must make the connection for ourselves. Constantly, our powers of association are tested by this image-laden story that establishes two narrative sites and two sets of characters. Until the two stories come together at the very end of the novella, we must be adept at jumping back and forth between them, making the connections as they gradually become clear to us. At the noodle shop, Onchi Kidahachi will relate his tale of artistic excess. At the Minatoya, the two elder gentlemen will meet Omie and learn of her artistic deficit. Separate yet proximate, these two sites provide a way to structurally express the story's main theme of reconciliation. The high regard in which this story is held has much to do with this boldly experimental structure. With an eye to the progression from estrangement to reconciliation, Kyōka develops the story along these dual tracks, maintaining a distance between the two main characters—the street singer and Sōzan's daughter—until both their stories unite in the final, climactic scene. This experiment in narration, this abrupt shifting back and forth, has been justly deemed cinematic by the critics.[1] As readers, we participate in the dramatic reunion only when we have fully understood the great distance that has come between Kidahachi and Genzaburō, his mentor. Certainly, this cinematic back-and-forth does make the point powerfully. As the distance contracts, we come to appreciate the characters' moment of identification as a time of forgiveness. By way of this dual structure, Kyōka moves us inexorably toward the truth that to know oneself truly is to be truly forgiven.

For most of the story, the singer is a nameless wanderer and the gentlemen are disguised as comic figures, Yajirobei and Nejibei, who try to textualize their existence through numerous references to Ikku's lively nineteenth-century travelogue. Both Ikku and Kyōka were modern in authorial preoccupation: both were similarly interested in questions of self and identity; and both exploited the eventful nature of travel to stimulate the discovery. Throughout the modern period, travel was an important form of learning, an extended encounter with difference that provided a means through which issues of identity and belonging could be articulated. Here we see how the space of Japan functions as a context that grants identity to those who occupy it properly, and how Ikku's written text about the modern discovery of Japan becomes a point of frequent reference for Kyōka.

The crucial difference between their two stories is the disparity between old Edo and new Tokyo, between the way *Shank's Mare* is satisfied to continue as a seemingly endless string of amusements whereas *A Song by Lantern Light* moves toward a serious, and even tragic, ending. Certainly, much fiction written after the Meiji Restoration of 1868 was dark; but it is also true that the shadows of this novella are heightened by the inclusion of Ikku's humor, in the same way that the solemnity of a *nō* play is set off by its *kyōgen,* or comic interlude. The lightness of *Shank's Mare* counters, for instance, the backdrop of militarism as introduced by the fleeting detail of the rowdy party in the room next door at the Minatoya. In the room across the way, the youth of Japan are being celebrated as they make plans to go off to war, a point thrown into relief by Yajirobei and Nejibei's equally ardent commitment to Hizakurige-inspired pleasure and entertainment. This mixed message of geisha and soldiers, and the suggestion of Japan's military dealings on the Asian continent, adds a touch of Meiji reality; although the darkest point of all, certainly, is that forgiveness for Kidahachi comes late.[2]

Reconciliation is a serious matter. So is love. Unlike Ikku's picaresque *Hizakurige,* Kyōka's *Uta andon* is a serious love story. Omie is a filial and loving daughter who serves her father valiantly. She is lovely and decent. She proves her integrity by not becoming the "man's toy" that Kidahachi warned her never to become— *"hito no omocha ni naru na."* But notice how it is only through the transformation of her character by way of the *nō* play *The Diver (Ama)* that her filial piety and decency become elevated to that point where decency and sensuality merge, where she possesses both the love of a mother and the love of a bride. Clearly, Kyōka drew upon this particular play for its combined values of maternal sacrifice and aqueous horror. In *Ama,* the protagonist is a mother who pays the ultimate sacrifice for her son's sake by diving to the bottom of the sea and giving herself to the Sea God. Performing this mother's role by way of the dance she has learned from Kidahachi, Omie becomes a beautiful young lover *and* a brave mother. Only in this dual role does she become a typical Kyōka heroine.

Elevating the status of women was something many Meiji-period writers considered. For one thing, the possibility of love required some attention to the emotional interaction between the sexes rather than simply to sex.[3] While what constituted an elevation was not precisely the same for Natsume Sōseki or Mori Ōgai or Higuchi Ichiyō, what we can say with confidence is that without the possibility of romance—as understood in this new, more egalitarian way—an interest in the suffering of women probably would not have led to their eventual emergence as sympathetic, empowered figures.

Kyōka could not separate suffering from love. In the case of Omie, her identity is created through her many trials on the one hand, and through her dance of "courtship" and her faithfulness to Kidahachi on the other. Coming to the discourse of love *(ren'ai)* with fresh eyes, the author sensed its essential nature with great insight. In *A Song by Lantern Light,* he shows us how the tender feelings shared between lovers are a form of worship, grounded in and supported by paradigms of beauty and salvation (as expressed in the *nō* play *Ama*). But he also reveals how romance, like beauty and salvation, is supported by violence. His emphasis on displaying rather than curing weakness lies here; for the dramatic reward of salvation occurs only when the obviously weak are helped by the obviously strong. Although pain and suffering might seem to be incompatible with tenderness, in truth a broad affirmation of violence underpins the culture of romance for the very simple reason that love is a form of salvation.

For all its leveling effects, romantic love requires a savior, and a savior must be someone who has endured more than the saved. This explains why Kyōka's lovely heroines, Omie among them, must suffer so much. They are, again, an expression of violence to the strong on behalf of the weak. In Kyōka's world, women are almost always the saviors. They are stronger than the men who need them. Consequently, they must suffer more, and they must suffer beautifully. Here, Omie's trials as a geisha prepare her for the more important role she will play as mother/lover. As a geisha, she is beaten, thrown into the ocean, doused with cold water. But it is only by finally assuming the role of sacrificial mother in the play that she eventually provides a way for Kidahachi to repent of his part in Sōzan's suicide and to be reconciled with his uncle.

Of course, Kidahachi suffers, too. He gives her the gift of dance as a way to pay for his salvation. In this way, their mutual giving establishes the kind of attentiveness that we associate with romance. But the insight Kyōka presents to us is that love's ethereal and tender qualities follow, not as a natural expression of human affection, but as an impossibility, as a dislocation of the established order that requires, as Itō Sei has argued, a kind of fiction *(kyogi)* to keep the illusion of mutual caring alive.[4] In this illusion lies love's threat. And herein also lies its narrative and dramatic possibilities.

Charles Shirō Inouye

Rooted in ancient paradigms of sacrifice, romantic love most often sublimates the violence it presupposes. In the Christian tradition, which provided much inspiration for Meiji-period writers on the subject of love, the passion of Christ and his adoration establish a foundation. Consider the example of European painters, from Giotto to El Greco, who took upon themselves the task of transforming crucifixion into a beautiful, worshipful moment. In some cases, as Dostoevsky and others have expressed, the representation of that suffering was made too real to engender the requisite complex of emotions, which would have to include both revulsion *and* gratitude. In short, the torture of the savior must be made attractive, even alluring, if the narrative of love is to succeed. A beautifying scene must engender feelings of tenderness while never separating itself from the realities of suffering and death. Death's pain must instill a complicated emotional and intellectual engagement rather than simply fill one with disgust; and so the artistic difficulty follows from the complex nature of the spiritual truth to be communicated: that the greatest is the least, that violence received should not be turned into violence returned, that we should totally love and forgive one another as we have been loved and forgiven.

In Kyōka's case, blood and horror are effectively tempered, but not by Christian doctrine. Rather, it is the author's sense of fear—as horror *and* reverence—and his unwavering belief in the meaningfulness of death that mollify. Reverence mutes horror. It allows a high degree of aestheticization. For Kyōka, beauty expresses the implausible nature of romantic love, this fiction that must be true. In this story and elsewhere, he portrays love as just that—miraculous, alien to the crass sensibilities of the real world.

To be sure, he was working within his own established traditions of love and death, some of them already ennobling and sacrificial. Yet, generally speaking, throughout the extended age of the samurai that was coming to an end in Kyōka's day, the prevailing vector of ultimate sacrifice was directed upward, as in a retainer's complete loyalty to his lord (in battle or in *junshi,* i.e., accompanying one's lord in death), rather than downward or horizontally, as is the case for the typical Kyōka heroine. A loyal retainer dies for one's lord (and for the honor and preservation of his own family); but a lord is not often expected to sacrifice his life for his retainers.[5] As noted by Fujita Yūkoku, Aizawa Seishisai, and other late-Edo-period ideologues, sacrifice that is directed downward was the radical, potentially destabilizing point of Christianity.[6] Kyōka shows us how it is also the ideological foundation for the much vulgarized practice of romantic love as it came to flow from this radical realignment of established hierarchies. This potential for realignment was threatening to Aizawa, who both vehemently resisted the spiritual dynamism of Western culture and also considered reproducing its vast reach and influence for what eventually became the cult of the Meiji emperor.

Unlike the idealized discourse of *bushidō*, or way of the samurai, less hierarchical forms of sacrifice, especially as they flowed from sexual rather than martial passions, were treated as a problem. The playwright Chikamatsu Monzaemon and other seventeenth-century writers often took up the theme of double suicide, where lovers had no recourse but to kill themselves. To be sure, this grisly resolution was often given a saving, Buddhist twist, as there was a chance for lovers to be reborn on the same lotus leaf in the next life. In comparison, Kyōka's contribution to this developing desire for salvation through love was to push the possibility of devotion much further. He combined the already well-established male need for female comfort—as expressed in late-Edo period *ninjōbon* such as Tamenaga Shunsui's *Plum Calendar* (*Shunshoku umegoyomi*, 1832–1833)—with the gallantry of Shiranui and other heroines of popular illustrated texts of roughly the same period, such as *The Tale of Shiranui* (*Shiranui monogatari*, 1849–1885). In doing so, he produced a Japanese heroine who is nothing less than heroic and self-sacrificing in her nurturing *and* eroticized love for (weaker and not-so-physically aggressive) males. This reversal occurred, then, as love (in the form of sacrifice and service) was directed not upward to a lord but downward to a helpless lover, and as women were assigned the (more Christian-seeming) role of victimized saviors. Perhaps it was the difficulty inherent in such a radical breach of tradition that required the very noticeable distance that opens up between lover and loved in Kyōka's stories and plays.

At once the loving gaze is mutual and distant, making possible a sublimation of the erotic savior who, in the end, becomes nothing

Charles Shirō Inouye

less than a maternal lover, a nurturing temptress. Thus, Omie is a be-loved in mind more than in flesh, possibly because an incest taboo is implicitly added to this departure from the more obviously carnal tradition of *iro,* or sexual desire. To state the obvious, Kyōka's hero-ines are a complex of seemingly incompatible values. They are conflicted and typically modern as they come into being by way of the essentially impossible requirements of romantic love: they must be at once strong and weak, maternal and seductive. These ill-fitting values are brought together and made compatible by the lyrical forces of art, which, like the enabling edge of spiritual truth, allow the imagination to affirm the impossible as possible.

This imaginative embrace that can even bring the dead back to life is often pointed out as being essential to Kyōka's work. What has not been sufficiently addressed in the critical response, however, is the ideological mechanism by which this process occurs. I have slowly and reluctantly become convinced that the romantic paradigm we see in operation here owes more than we have previously thought to Kyōka's exposure to Protestantism. No doubt, this assertion will sound heretical to generations of Japanese readers who have carefully preserved Kyōka's reputation as a truly native (Japanese) writer. Con-sider Tanizaki Jun'ichirō, writing in 1939, who portrayed the author as Japan's most "purely Japanese" writer.[7] Indeed, Kyōka himself proudly posed as one of a few Japanese novelists who owed nothing to Tolstoy. Despite his reputation as a thoroughly Japanese man, however, the possibility remains that the paradigm of the beautiful, suffering savior, one who endures even violence out of love for the weak, is a nativized permutation of Christian soteriology.

We know that Kyōka was exposed to Christianity as a youth during his three-and-a-half-year tenure at the Eiwa Gakkō, a mis-sionary school in Kanazawa. More to the point, while a student there from 1884 to 1887, he was clearly taken by the foreign beauty of his American teacher Francina Porter, who later became the model for Milliard in "The Maki Cycle" (Ichi no maki to Chikai no maki, 1896–1897), who appeared as Lyrica in "Chronicle of a Beautiful Princess" (Meienki, 1900), and as Benten in "A Throw of the Dice" (Machi sugoroku, 1917). His erotic understanding of Christianity probably has its beginnings in the way he described this Tennessee woman as both lover and mother. The essential tie between these two identities is, certainly, her whiteness, which establishes an aesthetically pleasing contrast with red—as blood, as crimson undergarment, as passion, as Japan? Although Kyōka rarely discussed Christianity and came to downplay his dealings with the West in general, it is not impossible that he, like many writers of the generation that followed, felt drawn to certain aspects of Christian aesthetics, especially because of its dual and conflicted emphasis on body and spirit.

In Kyōka's case, the influence seems to have occurred at the deep (and therefore well-disguised) level of blood atonement. While Kunikida Doppō, Arishima Takeo, and many other writers flirted publicly with Christianity, Kyōka did not affiliate himself with Uchimura Kanzō and other leaders of the Christian movement; nor did he openly express the rather more intellectual interest of someone like Akutagawa Ryūnosuke. His involvement was certainly not an assimilation of Christianity as such. Stated bluntly, he seems to have responded principally to the notion of beautiful bloodshed, in much the same way that the ancient Japanese poets took wholeheartedly to the Buddhist notion of ephemerality. Perhaps as a response to Christian patterns, and modulated by his own Buddhist understanding of death, Kyōka came to devise a very personal narrative of hope against hope, where the dead are revisited and made to live again. To be sure, the implausibility of the paradigm is precisely what makes his narratives so powerfully insistent and miraculous, for they express the heart's desire to trespass where reason dares not go.

Driving the creation of such a myth was the personal loss that Kyōka suffered because his mother died when he was nine years old. Of more concern to him than the sinfulness of human nature was his primary desire to be reunited with her. This explains why closure comes in *A Song by Lantern Light* as Kidahachi's reunion with a young mother figure, and is accomplished as a realignment of the supreme, uncontestable principles that made reunion (and salvation) possible. Placed in this nexus of Kidahachi's sin-against-art and loss-of-home, we can appreciate the power of this story because of the way in which the two-track narrative expresses the difference so subtly. In the final analysis, Kidahachi's greater offense was not causing Sōzan's suicide. His real "sin," if we wish to call it that, was that he did not understand the power and proper uses of art. In Kyōka's world, there can be no greater offense. According to this author's plan of salvation, beauty is always more important than spiritualism or ethics. This is simply because beauty alone, as a manifestation of Kannon's divine powers, is the true antidote to fear.

Kidahachi understands his folly after his expulsion from the society of true artists, such as Onchi Genzaburō—his uncle, adoptive father, and master singer—and Henmi Hidenoshin—an equally accomplished *nō* musician who travels with Onchi to Kuwana. Kidahachi has been left to fend for himself as a wandering street minstrel. Having drifted about as a vagabond, he eventually attains the wisdom to perceive Sōzan's arrogance for the provincialism that it is.

> Later, after I came to my senses, I realized that farmers in Shinshū make fun of Tokyo theater because we don't have real boars running across the stage. If Miyashige radishes are the finest in Japan, then the local pickles, too, must be unparalleled in all the empire. And broiled clams the equal of Kuwana's are nowhere to be found in the cities of Tokyo, Osaka, or Kyoto. I should have realized it was nothing but provincialism.

In other words, Kidahachi's faulty and immature standards of performance caused him to condemn Sōzan (even though Zeami recognized different standards of excellence for *nō* as performed in the city and in the provinces). In this allegory of salvation, Kidahachi does not, therefore, comprehend his proper role as one who has talent. *Nō* (which literally means talent, accomplishment, ability) should be performed in service to truth and compassion.

Art and beauty do not always kill. But they do instill powers of judgment, whether informed or not, whether enlightened or not. Herein lies their destructive potential. What Kidahachi needed to learn was that, ultimately, the value of great art lies in its ability to inspire rather than dismiss, to forgive rather than condemn, to obscure rather than clarify differences according to the demands of compassion.

We know that Kyōka himself had great respect for *nō* and its aesthetic principles, even at a time when support for traditional drama was waning. With the revoking of the samurai's hereditary privileges in 1869, patronage fell off sharply. The newly disenfranchised members of the old regime struggled to adjust to a new economic order. Some succeeded. Many did not. In either case, there was little interest in maintaining the theater at previous levels of support; and as the son of a family with direct ties to the *nō* theater, Kyōka had firsthand knowledge of the decline. His mother's family were *nō* musicians, brought to Kanazawa from Tokyo by the Maeda family who, having themselves retreated to their provincial home, pitied their former associates' extreme poverty.

In *A Song by Lantern Light*, Kyōka expresses his reverence for *nō* in many ways—in the careful manner with which the two elderly men transport their instruments; in the miraculous nature of Omie's mastery of the dance; in Henmi's refusal to play while seated on a cushion; and, of course, by the extensive use of the play *Ama*. Most important, the author's respect for *nō* manifests itself in how this play, *The Diver*, allows all the main characters of *A Song by Lantern Light* to identify themselves and to identify with each other. Kidahachi finds long-lost companions: "Sessō is playing his drum!" They find Kidahachi: "As far as we know, there's only one person in this entire country who could have taught you to dance like that. We think we know who it is, and we'd like to know how that came about." And because of her performance, Mie is also identified: "So you're Omie. I consider you my nephew's wife." In the climactic scene, Kidahachi rushes out into the moonlit street. He pulls the blind masseur along with him. Standing outside the Minatoya, he finishes the song that Onchi Genzaburō cannot complete because the old man has become overwhelmed by Omie's startling performance. Omie herself is nearly overwhelmed. With Genzaburō's help, she struggles to finish the dance—her hair spilling over her shoulders in erotic splendor—and the music and dance of *Ama* unite master and disciple, lover and beloved. In other words, by way of art, Kidahachi has found all his loved ones. By way of art, he has also found forgiveness. By way of art, he has even found himself.

As already noted, forgiveness and reconciliation come late for Kidahachi. Weakened by poverty, the former star of the *nō* theater has contracted tuberculosis, the quintessentially modern disease that will soon kill him. He will never be healed physically, though spiritually he has "vanquished his enemy" by performing before the blind masseur whom he considers to be the dead man's ghost. The "large shapeless shadow" of the man joins the ranks of Japanese *onryō*, or vengeful spirits who remain behind after death, driven by a need to claim justice. The arrogant Sōzan died bitterly. He could not rid himself of his attachment to this floating world. He was humiliated by Kidahachi who, by correcting his wayward rhythm with a slap on his knee, displayed a superior mastery of *nō*. Sōzan wanted to touch the young man's face and, as Kidahachi perceived it, to hear a superior voice; but he died without satisfying either desire. Now, having delivered this final miraculous song by lantern light before Sōzan's proxy, Kidahachi is ready to go home. His final resting place lies not through an opened door to his forgiving uncle or in the arms of his "wife," Omie. It is, rather, the white (and therefore deadly) night of flickering firelight, where blind men walk with sticks and young men go bravely off to war.

The rather unresolved nature of this resolution comes as a surprise, perhaps. But could there be another way to end this story? Certainly, the way to self-knowledge is, in fact, tragic. In the cultural realm of love, estrangement, and reconciliation, knowledge always comes late. We are expelled from the womb and are forever needy. We live both beyond and before paradise, trapped in between like a song sung by lantern light. Our only comfort is a mythical, aesthetic one—of echoes, of endings that both mean and do not guarantee a needed kind of closure. Story after story, play after play—even the sort of manic repetition that sustained Kyōka until his death in 1939—did not bring salvation, save for brief, literary, repeatable moments. And so we resign ourselves to calling the irresolute sadness of endings beautiful—a moonlit night, the roundness of glowing lanterns, the empty feeling that follows a masterful performance.

> From the inn, a road led off in a white line, set off by hanging lanterns flickering here and there in the deepening night. A crowd of people had gathered, among them blind men walking with sticks.

So ends Kyōka's famous novella. Like a *nō* play, *A Song by Lantern*

Light builds to a crescendo and ends abruptly in enlightenment. As the actors quietly shuffle offstage, "blind men walking with sticks," we must wonder if the emptiness we feel as we ponder the silent, emptying stage is the nothing that is nothing, or the nothing that is everything. Perhaps no work since Zeami's plays has so effectively raised this question.

"A Quiet Obsession"

By Kyōka's day, the slow and laborious travel that was captured so memorably in Hiroshige's famous woodblock series *Fifty-three Posts along the Tōkaidō*, or by Ikku's comic rendering of common life along this same road in *Shank's Mare*, was made much faster and certainly no less pleasurable by the implementation of rail service. Today, Narai is still a train stop. But during the Tokugawa period, Narai-juku was an important resting place for the foot-bound as they made their way along the Nakasendō, a more mountainous, alternate route taken when the rivers along the littoral Tōkaidō were too swollen to ford safely. Winding through narrow, deeply cut mountain valleys, the Nakasendō posed its own difficulties. Situated near one of the most arduous passes along the way, Narai prospered because of its location. Travelers would customarily stop to rest before attempting the climb, and so the numerous inns that lined both sides of the narrow mountain road enjoyed steady patronage.

As briefly mentioned in "A Quiet Obsession" (Mayu kakushi no rei, 1924), Narai experienced a second economic boost during the Meiji period as sericulture developed and the towns of the Kiso region profited from supplying both mulberry leaves for silkworms and the labor, usually young girls, required to unravel and spin the fibers of silk cocoons. Today, the silk industry is all but dead in Narai. This village is a protected historic district. It exists as a tourist destination for city dwellers seeking the coolness and solitude of the mountains. The inn where Kyōka probably stayed, the Tokkuriya, still stands. However, it is no longer a place to stay the night but has become an eating establishment. From the small, one-platform Narai train station, the building itself is no more than a few minutes' walk. It has

Charles Shirō Inouye

deep overhanging eaves, a spacious entry, and a hearth—all mentioned in the story. True to the description, the inn is a solid, well-built structure. But it has two, not three stories; and the rear garden, around which most of the story's action takes place, is sadly run down. There are no fish in the pond. There is no rounded bridge, or walkway, or separate wing with its own bathhouse. What remains the same is the backdrop of dark, mist-covered mountains and the rushing river, which still give a feeling of quiet isolation. Situated between the Kiso River (which Kyōka sometimes calls the Narai River) and the mountains from which numerous springs flow, the village of Narai could not be a more watery, evocative place for this twentieth-century ghost story.

As is the case with practically every piece Kyōka wrote, water imagery performs the important function of establishing a border, and therefore the possibility of trespassing this border and entering into another world. It is in this crossing-over that the uncanny meeting of the living and the dead occurs. Like the rainy, snowy city of Kanazawa where Kyōka grew up and developed an appreciation for water's constantly transforming morphology, Narai is demarcated as an ideally transformational site by the rushing river and the moisture-filled forests that surround it. In the same spirit, the story's running faucets lend their own domesticated force of mystery, as do the fishpond and bathhouse. Finally, and no less important, Bellflower Lake adds an element of folklore that grounds this modern time of electric bulbs within a context of dimly glowing lanterns and inexplicable occurrences. Once again, this seemingly quiet mountain village, surrounded and penetrated by water, is the perfect scene for conflict, metamorphosis, and the subtle erotic tension that only Kyōka could achieve.

Although Kyōka is particularly insistent in the way he employs water's evocative powers, his use of water imagery to connote danger and transformation is not unusual. Writers within the Japanese literary tradition have frequently employed such imagery to signal violence, death, and metamorphosis. Relevant examples can be found in the oldest Japanese texts and traced to the present. These tropes are especially pronounced in *gōkan,* lengthy works of popular illustrated fiction to which Kyōka was exposed as a young boy by way of his

mother's library. We know that as an adult he made a point of ac-
quiring his own collection of these same texts; and we can safely say
that they contributed significantly to the iconography of this and
other stories. For example, in *The Tale of Shiranui* we find not only
images of dangerous water but also of threatening birds. Like the
high culture of the *nō* theater, which we have already discussed, these
works of popular fiction similarly ground Kyōka's work in a well-
established aesthetic tradition.

Perhaps, for some, they are too grounded. When we examine the
critical appraisal of Kyōka's writing by his contemporaries, we see that
his ties to the past were viewed by many to be problematic. During
his own very consciously progressive era, he was often considered ret-
rogressive, too obviously influenced by *Shanks' Mare, Shiranui,* and
other works of *gesaku,* or "playful letters," as popular Edo-period
fiction is called. For reasons already mentioned, Kyōka's was an age of
serious letters, a time when the pursuit of truth—accomplished
through the creation of psychological depth and realistic description
—was considered the purview of novelists whose status was evolving
from scribblers to respected intellectuals. Their calling was to explore
and express the trauma of their day, which they did with a sense of ur-
gency and professionalism.

Kyōka was serious too. His debt to Edo-period *gesaku* notwithstanding, it would be a mistake to say that the tenor of his writings was
frivolous. Indeed, he would not have survived personally had he not
written with such compulsive intensity about personal yet universal
matters: bereavement, desire for one's mother, fear of disease, and so
on. What we can say is that the manner in which he addressed threatening powers was, at least narratively speaking, unusual and noncon-
forming. While others distanced themselves from *gesaku, nō,* and
folklore, Kyōka openly borrowed from all three, creating an eccentric, highly convoluted narrative method that precluded his participa-
tion in the more mainstream attempt to accomplish an objective
description of an exterior world and a psychologically depicted realm
of an interior one.

With regard to the latter, the way in which psychologically oriented writing developed in Japan is still a relatively unstudied topic.
There have been numerous attempts to employ psychological theories

Charles Shirō Inouye

in the practice of literary criticism, and many readings that insightfully locate the psychological aspects of various works. Yet the more fundamental question of what psychology actually is and how it did or did not become a part of Japanese literary culture remains largely unexplored. This is a vast topic that cannot be treated in satisfactory detail here. Inasmuch as a critical reading of "A Quiet Obsession" begs for an explanation of how its narrative features produce meaning in a nonpsychological way, however, let me briefly begin to consider the questions that this enigmatic work raises against this larger cultural context of truth and realism. Complete with mirrors, numerous points of view, and a complex handling of various layers of time, "A Quiet Obsession" is a *Las Meniñas* of modern Japanese letters. Carefully scrutinized, its secrets yield many truths.

To move quickly to the central issue, Kyōka's narrative approach was noncompliant with the emerging methods of psychological discourse because his handling of space and time was unsystematic. His narratives neither maintain a consistently stable and omniscient point of view nor do they present time as a steady flow of logically connected events that are contained in the past. Both types of noncompliance can actually be found to some degree in the work of most Japanese writers of this period, including those of the naturalist persuasion who were among the most vociferous advocates of the True and the Real. Just as the development of perspective in the visual arts was relatively slow in coming, similarly gradual was the creation of narrative methods affirming the possibility of a universal, fixed system of perception that could improve upon and supplant earlier, less unified methods of perceiving and describing reality.

This newer method was deemed realistic. As a systematic and truth-seeking mode of ordering, realism tries to identify objects by clarifying their relationship to all others. In the visual arts, it places things according to their distance and direction from one or more common points of reference—such as a set point of view, a vanishing point, a source of light. These set, fixed points allow perception to be systematic because it allows the world to become similarly oriented. These supposedly universal sources of orientation make possible a regime in which objects are not only recognizable but also reproducible, since the mathematical relationship of various coordinates of a particular object to each other, and to other points that surround the object, are knowable and consistent. While these features of realism are most obvious in paintings of landscapes, portraits, and still-life compositions, the principles of perspective apply also to linguistic forms and, by extension, to the social structures that flow from all forms of expression. The fixed point of view of the realistic painter finds its analogue in the omniscient perspective of the authoritative author. More than merely a scribbler, the modern novelist tells true stories from a privileged point of view, and from a similarly fixed point in time (usually the present as explained by the past). An author's claims to truthfulness rest largely on such a consistent, objective point of view, as if that view were an integral, ordering part of the reproducible world that flows from it. Its very stability generates robustness as a true and principled source of truth; and its generality produces realism's utility as a nondistorting understanding of reality that allows us to describe the world as similarly recognizable and understandable to *everyone*. This possibility of widespread agreement allows a universal system of persuasion to extend everywhere; and it is this possibility that Kyōka consistently rejected.

Again, such a perspectival system includes both the objectively true exterior (realism) and the subjectively true interior (psychology) because everything, including the invisible realm, must be accounted for. The connection between the visible and the invisible is an enduring issue that cannot be fully treated here. For our own purposes, though, it is probably enough to understand that, in the effort to expand the borders of truth to universal dimensions, the essentially visible and the essentially invisible become tied to each other by various ideologies that either obscure the relativity of this procedure of ordering (and become history), or sharpen that relativity (and become fiction). In the modern period, history becomes the acceptable and plausible truth, while fiction, with its ability to delve impossibly into the emotions and thoughts of people, becomes the acceptable and plausible lie (or the imagined that is nevertheless true).

In other words, realistic truth makes fiction necessary. This is borne out by the dominance of the novel in the modern age, and by the reasons why Kyōka's stories are less novelistic and more like tales (of limited narrative omniscience) than most. Fiction derives compellingly from a central contradiction of modernity to which, because of his mythical concerns, Kyōka gave only limited credence. That contradiction is this: that only by surrendering oneself to a rational and atomizing system does one gain individual identity and the ability to think and act for (and by) oneself. Paradoxically, in order to be an individuated member of such a society, we must assume a point of view that everyone shares; thus, the fundamental irony implied in the notion of subjectivity, where the subject is supposedly both a follower (a loyal subject) and an acting agent (someone with subjectivity or the will to act independently),[8] and where the status of subjectivity is, on the one hand, praised as being emotionally true and, on the other, degraded as a lack of (objective) truth. The modern novel attempts to make sense of this paradox—this surrendering as empowerment—by raising the possibility of a true subjectivity, that is, fiction, within a larger context of objective truth.

Modern narrative does this by way of psychological insight. Psychology appears at that cultural moment when a transition from a discourse of sight to one of insight is required, where presupposed is the kind of thorough explanation that only an omniscient and stable narrative device can provide. Such a viewpoint is both impossible and necessary. It is, therefore, both false and true. We might understand it as a new, secular reformation of spiritual insight, broad and even universal in its reach. As truthful vision, psychological realism is grandly inclusive, able to see and understand the thoughts of strangers. At the same time, however, it is also strictly exclusive.

This second paradox of modernity can be demonstrated at the level of social structures, where the development of fascism in Japan, for instance, shows how the scopic regime of the Real and the True encouraged colonial expansion while being murderously restrictive about who counted as important and who did not. In other words, despite the panoramic and insightful characteristics of modern perspective, one consequence of this system seems to be a radical reduction in the range of subjects that are actually validated. In Imperial Japan, certain human beings were not considered human, as racism, sexism, and other forms of discrimination limited the franchised members of the expanded empire.

Realism is descriptive. It claims to see what is there: nothing more, and nothing less. At the level of literary texts, we can see how the more localized discourse of monstrosity and metamorphosis that had been central to *nō*, *gesaku*, and the oral tradition was outlawed because it did not conform to this new epistemological model. As an older mode of visuality, monstrosity was either dismissed as irrational and eventually excluded from most works of modern Japanese fiction, or it was later reintroduced to become an integral part of a larger, overreaching ideological system, as in wartime caricatures of the monstrous enemy during the 1930s and 1940s.[9] In either case, by the turn of the twentieth century, most writers came to focus on the project of making the language of fiction less figurative and more transparent, more a secondary tool of representation than a primary consideration in its own right. Just as *figures* of speech were to be replaced by a language that would approximate speech itself, so too were the figural subjects of language banished. In sum, the birth of objective description (as a universally valid discourse of the exterior) and psychology (as a universally valid discourse of the interior) made the accounting of the Real and the True the primary goal, so that the graphically rich and less systematically coherent world of strange forms and occurrences that interested Kyōka became anachronistic. In this late-modern context, the discourse of monstrosity came be dismissed as fantasy.

Of course, Kyōka would be the first to object to this categorization. His work was not realistic, yet neither were his tales fantastic in the usual sense. It could not fully respond to the call to modernize in a realistic way, largely because of his need for mythical structure, divine intervention, and beauty. Believing in the powers of art and artifice, he rejected the focus of realism especially as the naturalist movement steadily became obsessed with the perverse, ugly, and hopeless aspects of human nature. Perhaps the famous theorist Tsubouchi Shōyō could not have anticipated such a slide toward all things unpleasant when he embraced psychology in his influential treatise "The Essence of the Novel" (Shōsetsu shinzui, 1885–1886). He encouraged the project of novel writing to go beyond the idealism of Takizawa Bakin's dog heroes to something more penetrating, realistic, and principled. "A novelist is like a psychologist. His characters must be psychologically convincing. Should he contrive to create by

Charles Shirō Inouye

his own invention characters at odds with human nature, or worse, with the principles of psychology, those characters would be figments of his imagination rather than human beings. . . ."[10] For people like Tsubouchi, psychologically informed writing was a modern improvement upon less well-explained truths of Edo *gesaku;* and yet, psychology's continued reliance upon (and uneasy relationship with) monstrosity and other forms of visual display could not be more obvious. Could there have been *Freud's Interpretation of Dreams* without dreams? Or, for that matter, could there have been Descartes' cogito without a lump of beeswax upon which to meditate? It is probably safe to say that there would have been no conceptualization of either consciousness or unconsciousness without phantasms, since they were the original, raw material of the kind of interpretation of the invisible that eventually established normative behavior and began to create robust conceptions of consciousness.

Psychological realism destroys figurality. Even in a monster-rich country like Japan, the secondary status of the figure comes to be almost a given by the end of the Meiji period. As psychologically oriented novels developed within the larger modern trend toward phonocentric expression (of abstract and invisible principles) and away from pictocentric expressions (of concrete and visible figures), concepts of consciousness, interiority, and self provided enough intellectual yield to produce explanations rather than metaphors, and novels more than traditional *waka*. It is within this trend toward creating a transparent, nondistorting, phonetically oriented language for the representation of life as it actually is *(ari no mama),* that Kyōka's figurally rich style appeared as an anachronism. Because of this timing, his work was seen as a belated efflorescence of Edo-period visuality, accomplished now in an environment of considerably fewer illustrations because of changes in printing technology and because of the antifigural bias that steadily eroded Japan's visual tradition. Here I would hasten to add that it is also possible to interpret his highly figural style as being ahead of, rather than behind, the times, anticipating the present age of film, as already considered in my discussion of *A Song by Lantern Light.*

When we consider the largely unillustrated literature of Meiji, Taishō, and Shōwa Japan, it might be helpful to understand the

Essays

graphic orientation of illustrated Edo literature as a protopsychological stage, where attempts to express the "unconscious" that had begun as visions of monstrosity were not yet completely rendered into the kinds of more analytical discourse we find in the works of Meiji writers. To give just one example of this transition from monstrosity to psychological narration, in *The Eight Lives of Siddhartha, a Japanese Library* (*Shaka hassō, Yamato bunko*, 1845–1871), another work of *gesaku* found in Kyōka's library, we encounter the figure of Kishibojin (the Indian diety Hariti), a woman who killed one human baby each day in order to feed her many children. As the narrative explains and the illustrations show, Siddhartha follows a river of bloodied water to her home, where the horrific butchering takes place. He gives her a pomegranate as a substitute for red meat, and Kishibo finds it delicious. Satisfied with the fruit (which is still too meat-like for strict Buddhists to eat), she forsakes her murderous ways and goes on to become enshrined as a protecting goddess of children.

Kyōka's "Pomegranate" (Kisshōka, 1909) took up the story directly; and, eventually, the ambivalent nature of this "complex" of woman as mother, murderer, and protector of children became a part of Kyōka's general portrayal of the female character, which is often both maternal and threatening (in its erotic attraction). In "A Quiet Obsession," Otsuya's forbidding qualities probably owe something to this image, just as the curious reference to her head flying up in the air can be traced back to various Edo-period texts in which *kubinaga* (long-necks) appear. The simple point of this long digression is that Kyōka belonged within this lingering visual tradition even as it tried to negotiate a place for itself within the increasingly rational and phonocentric world of Meiji Japan and beyond. Because the imagery we encounter in his stories is only partially explained, a value-added psychological interpretation of a story such as "A Quiet Obsession" seems as easy as shooting fish in a barrel. Yet the very ease of such a process should make us sensitive to the author's reasons for *not* telling us what these characters are thinking and feeling.

Take Isaku, the cook. Without gaining a mediated, authoritative access to his inner mind, we nevertheless understand that he is haunted. He is dark and taciturn, polite to the extreme yet capable of humor. We know that he is obsessed—with water, with the pond in the garden and the fish in it, with the woman of the Bellflower Lake whom he accidentally saw one midsummer day, with the captivating woman Otsuya, "a professional" who came to the inn on a snowy day and was mistakenly shot to death on the frozen banks of the Narai River. Isaku blames himself for that death and is tortured by her beauty. He feels guilt, and also fear. The depth of that fear is confirmed by Sakai, who imagines himself being eaten by a bird and who comes to view Otsuya as a bird: "Suddenly the light went out, and Sakai felt a chill start in his skull and move down his backbone. He turned around and saw, there in his room, the figure of a woman who was looking away. She seemed like a snowy egret, the nape of her neck purest white."

When we add this layer of metaphor—men like fish, and women like fish-eating birds—we begin to understand how Kyōka's method of establishing character is imagistic and superficial rather than discursive and penetrating. As readers we are simply not given access to Isaku's interior consciousness. His interiority is not articulated by an omniscient author because we are presented with something that is both more direct and less mediated. We are given only the substance of a psychological interpretation that might easily be imposed upon the work; and it is this protopsychological quality that explains why Kyōka's work was dismissed as nothing but *kusazōshi*. As Tayama Katai put it, "You could hardly call Kyōka's work realistic. Gradually it became clear that the source of his romanticism was the old kusazōshi texts of the Edo period."[11]

From our present perspective, we can see how Katai's criticism marked an important measure of modern letters even though the comment is too general to help us understand precisely how a text like "A Quiet Obsession" actually works. In order to sharpen the point of this critique, then, let us examine the various layers of narration employed in this story. With a little clarification, we can see just how Kyōka produced an aesthetic compromise between an outdated, pictocentric mode of monstrosity and a more up-to-date, phonocentric mode of psychological narration.

We have only to count the layers of narration in "A Quiet Obsession" to see that the author's method was precisely *not* to establish

Essays

the single stable narrative position that is essential to psychological realism. The outermost narrative frame is the domain of the writer who supposedly heard this story from Sakai Sankichi.[12]

> Contemplating this scene in Ikku's novel, our hero received the impression that he ought to spend the night here in Narai. *He told me* that the train was already starting to pull away from the station when he made up his mind to get off.
>
> *My friend, Sakai Sankichi*, had actually purchased a ticket to go to Agematsu to see the famous suspended bridge and the "frog boulders" of the Kiso River. It was the middle of November.
>
> "I had some strange connection with those two bowls of noodles. . . . ," *Sakai said.* [Italics mine]

By naming Sakai Sankichi, by quoting him, by identifying himself as the author, and by describing Sakai's relationship to himself as "my friend," the writer establishes a distance between himself and this character. This story is not about the writer; it is about Sakai. For the sake of analysis, let us call this first level of narration N1.

Sakai is the person who gets off the train in Narai. He settles into an inn. Later that day, he encounters a woman in the bathhouse and in his room. At times, we are told what he witnesses—at the level of N1. But at other times he narrates his experiences directly, thus establishing a second narrative layer. Here is the bathhouse scene.

> Sakai hesitated.
>
> Anytime would be fine. I told them to let me know when the others were finished and the bath was free. No one's in there. Still, he retied his sash, and when he leaned over the lantern and pressed his cheek against the door to listen, the place near his sleeve went dark, and the candle brightened again. The shadow became a birthmark, a swirling comma that showed on his face and dismally soaked into his cheek. Just as he was thinking this, he heard the sound of water again, coming from the other side of the door. Suddenly, through a crack in the walls, he smelled plum blossoms, the scent of white makeup washed off a warm body.
>
> "A woman."

The first sentence in this passage refers to Sakai in the third person and therefore belongs to the outer narrative frame, N1. But from "Anytime would be fine . . ," Sakai suddenly emerges as the first-person narrator and tells the reader directly of his own experience. Because there are no pronouns in the original Japanese text, my willful inclusion of "I" in the translated version makes these subtle shifts of perspective clearer (and ultimately more confusing) than they probably are to the Japanese reader.[13] At any rate, this shift establishes a second narrative layer, N2, and a second narrative point of view that is different from and does not simply supplant the first. This coexistence is an important, often-employed feature of Kyōka's writing. Rather than replacing one point of view with another, he deploys both in order to create a deliberately unstable, multivalent situation. Notice how (throughout the story) he continues to supply references to Sakai Sankichi in the third person, thus giving the impression that N1 encircles N2.

At times, it seems as though these two layers meld, or that N2 is overtaken by N1. Consider the moment when Sakai meets the eyebrow-hiding ghost in his room for the first time.

> Sakai held his breath, unable to sit or stand.
>
> Her kimono was like fallen maple leaves under snow—her snowy white skin enveloping those leaves. She deftly rearranged the collar of her kimono, which had been pulled down in the back to expose the nape of her neck. Then she reached over and grabbed the tissue that was lying on the floor near her knee. She rolled it, and wiped the palm of her hand. When she dropped the paper onto the tatami, it looked like white face powder spilling down.
>
> She rustled her kimono, and he smelled the incense that had been infused in the silk, so much like the scent of human skin that he had encountered in the bathhouse. She turned halfway in his direction, and raised a smoking pipe to her lips. The mouthpiece was white, and the barrel of the pipe shiny and black.
>
> *Tōn,* came the sounding of ashes being knocked out of her pipe.
>
> She suddenly turned fully toward Sakai. She looked at him with her melon-shaped face, her thick eyelids and straight nose. Her skin was frighteningly white. She covered both her eyebrows with the

paper, and looked directly at him with her big eyes. "Does this become me?"

She smiled and revealed blackened teeth.

Still smiling, she pulled the skirts of her kimono together and stood. Her face rose toward the lintels of the sliding door, as she stretched upward.

Sakai's reaction is described externally in N1: he is "neither able to sit nor stand." But his inner mind is not explained to us from this (more objective) narrative level. We are not told how he *feels*. Rather, we are presented with what he *sees* at the level of N2. As readers, we too see this strangely beautiful woman and are left to interpret the image as we will. The slippage from N1 to N2 is subtle, not so unlike a description we might find in a more mediating, psychological mode of fiction. Indeed, with a little more pointing, this sighting of the ghost who hides her eyebrows could be easily framed within N1. But this is clearly not the author's intention.

As a related consequence of Kyōka's predilection for (presentational) narrative and (visual) directness, Sakai comes to function as a facilitator, rather than an editor, of Isaku's stories. He invites the cook to drink with him. And directly from Isaku we learn the story behind this beautiful specter. It is a story within a story within a story—how Otsuya came to Narai, how she heard the legend about the female phantom, a married woman who inhabits the Bellflower Pond and is feared by the people living in the area, how she is mistaken for this legendary beauty and is shot by Ishimatsu the hunter. (Perhaps I should add here a note about eyebrows. They were most definitely a fetish for Kyōka, who often described the beauty of both women and men by reference to this feature of the body. Traditionally, eyebrows were an important marker of marital status. Women shaved them off upon getting married. Thus, Otsuya's concealing her eyebrows and saying "Does this become me?" suggests her envy—as a geisha—of the wife's position, and especially of the incomparable beauty of the woman of the Bellflower Pond. This yearning invites tragedy, as she is ultimately mistaken for the woman she longs to become.)

Isaku's extended narrative appears within Sakai's and forms a third narrative layer, N3. But it does not simply replace N2 as a stable point of narrative authority. Just as N1 encircles N2, so too does N2 remain in the background while N3 is in progress. The result is even more instability. Consider the many narrative viewpoints represented in the following passage as we move toward the final, catastrophic moment.

"'Whenever you're ready,' I said. I came here to this room. I brought a lantern with me."

"Yes. *The one with the swirling comma pattern on it.*" *Sakai couldn't resist the comment.*

"That's right." Isaku responded darkly, seeming to swallow his words. "You seem to know a lot about it."

"Twice. In the bathhouse. I saw it."

"What? We don't keep a lantern in the bathhouse. Not unless—"

Given Isaku's response, this was hardly the time for Sakai to say he had just seen the lantern again, just now, when the cook walked across the garden. "You were saying," he urged the cook to continue his story.

"Sorry. I feel a little—. That's right. She finished her preparations. She had put on a little makeup after her second trip to the bathhouse. Her kimono was bluish-gray, but against her face it seemed more like violet. Her complexion was white beyond compare . . . there in front of the mirror."

Needless to say, Sakai turned around and looked over to the corner of his room.

"The mouthpiece of her smoking pipe was gold, and the rest was plated with an alloy of copper and gold. She had dyed her teeth, it seems. She took out some paper, held it up to her forehead, and looked at me with her oval face. 'Does this become me?'"

Sakai's words, "I see, I see, I see," seemed to turn into a chunk of ice that lodged in his throat. He was speechless.

"The edge of the room seemed to grow white with bellflower blossoms. 'It more than becomes you,' I told her."

"She took the paper from her forehead, and I could see the freshly shaved pale skin where her eyebrows had been. 'How do I compare to the Bellflower Lake woman?'

"'You're like her sister. No, I'd say you're twice as beautiful.'

Essays

"I'll be cursed for saying that, but I couldn't help it. Now listen to this."

" 'So, Otsuya, how are we going to handle this?' [Italics mine]

As Isaku continues his narrative, N3, we are reminded of Sakai's presence as the hearer of his story by the intrusions of N1: "Sakai couldn't resist the comment." "Given Isaku's response, this was hardly the time for Sakai to say he had just seen the lantern again, just now, when the cook walked across the garden," and so on. N2, Sakai's direct point of view, is not fully represented here, other than as direct speech, words bracketed in quotation marks: "Yes. The one with the swirling comma pattern on it," or "Twice. In the bathhouse. I saw it," and so on.

The directness of such comments is made possible by these punctuation marks, which are, of course, a feature widely employed in more stable narrative strategies than the one we find here. While it is also true that the inclusion of dialogue is a widely encountered feature of Edo-period fiction, quotation marks did not consistently appear in Japanese fiction until methods of stable, omniscient narration began to make themselves felt. Considered in this historical context, the quotation marks we find here in "A Quiet Obsession" indicate a compromise between direct and indirect narration, between presentational and representational discourse. They function as a bridge to interiority, as it were, though the greater point of this story, certainly, is that this bridge to self knowledge is never fully crossed. In truth, the direct access to the inner thoughts of a person that quotation marks provide is actually rendered largely ineffective, as huge portions of this and many other of Kyōka's stories are nothing but quotation—stories within stories, as we have called them. Indeed, so lengthy and extensive are these quotations that we tend to forget what is being quoted and what is not. Thus, the narrator's powerful and direct access to the character's mind, this privileged access to the truth, is consistently displaced by the less authorial method of hearsay, a feature that is reinforced by various features of Japanese grammar.

Note how Kyōka reminds us of N2, Sakai's direct point of view (which expresses his emotional state as he listens to Isaku's story) with the insertion of "Needless to say, Sakai turned around and looked over to the corner of his room." We do not actually see what he sees because we are not *told* what he sees, only that he looks to see something (which we as readers then imagine). In other words, for this brief moment, we the readers see neither from the point of view of N1 nor N2. We see from an *unnarrated* position, which can only be our own, the readers'. The brilliance of this technique lies here: we know exactly what Sakai is looking for without having to be told (or even shown) what it is. We ourselves experience the past as present. In this situation, the ellipsis or unfulfilled narrative expectation works more directly and powerfully on the reader than a description of what Sakai did or did not see. Not only does it create an awareness of possibilities, but it also begins preparing us for the jarring denouement, which is all about seeing (or not seeing?) what is (or is not?) there to see.

From this point on, the story becomes steadily more unpredictable and destabilized. As Sakai's fear steadily mounts, Isaku's narrative position begins to skip around wildly. At one moment, we see through his eyes, "She took the paper from her forehead, and I could see the freshly shaved pale skin where her eyebrows had been." At another, we hear what he (claims to have) heard Otsuya say, "'How do I compare to the Bellflower Lake woman?'"

We learn his answer, "'You're like her sister. No, I'd say you're twice as beautiful.'" We are even given a moment of comment, "I'll be cursed for that, but I couldn't help saying it." But then we are quickly recalled from this moment of distanced clarity and reflexivity with the injunction, "Now listen to this." Once again, we flounder for a moment because the direct address to us is about someone we do not even know. "'So, Otsuya, how are we going to handle this?'"

Needless to say, these narrative complexities are all tied to an equally complicated temporal scheme. As narrated by Isaku, Otsuya's death happened one year previous to Sakai's visit. Temporally speaking, the incident belongs to the perfected past. Yet, just as Kyōka is inconsistent in his use of the conventions of third-person narrative, so too does he handle time in ways that are corrosive to the necessary

Essays

distance required by the modern tendency to cast events as having occurred in the past. If, for instance, the time of N1 is the present, call it T1, where the writer is addressing the reader directly, then each additional layer of narration ought to be placed in a perfected temporal past. This convention is important, because the historicity of stable, psychologically penetrating narrative lies here: from a position in the (would be normal or stabilized) present, we recover and try to understand the (traumatic or unstable) past. Sakai's story, N2, belongs to the past, T2; just as Isaku's story, N3, belongs to a still deeper past, T3. Similarly, the stories that Isaku relates, N4, belong even further tucked away in the realm of what has happened, T4.

To reinforce an already established point, Kyōka's handling of various unstable narrative positions creates a situation where the past is reconstituted in a way that actually overwhelms the present. His technique does not simply inform the (modern) present. The assumption that the writer is telling a story about something that happened gradually breaks down to a point where time-in-the-past is no longer controlled by time-in-the-present, and (narrated) events-in-the-past become as present as events-in-the-present. Consider once again, for instance, the passage where Sakai sees the ghost. Here, as N1 and N2 melt together into one, T1, the narrator's present temporal position, becomes displaced by T2, Sakai's past position. Here is the passage once again.

> Sakai held his breath, unable to sit or stand.
>
> Her kimono was like fallen maple leaves under snow—her snowy white skin enveloping those leaves. She deftly rearranged the collar of her kimono, which had been pulled down in the back to expose the nape of her neck. Then she reached over and grabbed the tissue that was lying on the floor near her knee. She rolled it, and wiped the palm of her hand. When she dropped the paper onto the tatami, it looked like white face powder spilling down.
>
> She rustled her kimono, and he smelled the incense that had been infused in the silk, so much like the scent of human skin that he had encountered in the bathhouse. She turned halfway in his direction, and raised a smoking pipe to her lips. The mouthpiece was white, and the barrel of the pipe shiny and black.

Tōn, came the sounding of ashes being knocked out of her pipe. She suddenly turned fully toward Sakai. She looked at him with her melon-shaped face, her thick eyelids and straight nose. Her skin was frighteningly white. She covered both her eyebrows with the paper, and looked directly at him with her big eyes. "Does this become me?"

She smiled and revealed blackened teeth.

Still smiling, she pulled the skirts of her kimono together and stood. Her face rose toward the lintels of the sliding door, as she stretched upward.

From the position of N1, this incident is about something that happened to Sakai and therefore belongs to the past, or T2. But, to state the obvious, this frightening scene is presented in a way that gives it a life of its own, a monstrousness, if you will. We might think that the figure of the beautiful female specter could come to life so vividly only by way of Sakai's memory, his interiority. But the passage is not framed in a way that reminds the reader that this is a memory (and that its content is history). It is more direct than that: even if the tense of the verbs remains the same, the past somehow seems present. Here, the writer, N1, has lost his distance, completely entering into the interior of Sakai, N2, without bothering to note that penetration, either with quotation marks or by another narrative device. As a consequence, the (represented) past appears in the present as nothing but a (presented) ghostly presence. This, then, is the mechanism that makes ghost stories both frightening and necessary: the dead really do not belong to the past; they are as real as our fears about them; and as such they are present in the present. They *were* "once upon a time" at a time that supposedly has advanced beyond the traditional past, which now returns to threaten.

This tendency for the past to overwhelm the present is nowhere more evident than in the conclusion of this story. Having told Sakai about Otsuya's death and his part in her accidental murder, Isaku's psychological distance from these events collapses entirely. As a result, all things past become present, and we are left to consider Isaku's condition as nothing less than madness. Isaku as narrator sees himself, Isaku the narrated, with the past-but-now-present Otsuya by his side.

Essays

"As for me, sir, look! There I am! Coming from the bathhouse, over the bridge. Sir, that's me, coming this way. See! A madman, like me! I'm coming here! And there, at my side. That's her, Otsuya!" Sakai clenched his teeth. "Isaku-san. Don't be afraid. She doesn't blame you for what happened."
But then the electric bulb in Sakai's room became a swirling comma. It floated darkly in the air, and suddenly a paper lantern appeared above their *kotatsu*.
"Does this become me?" the beautiful one asked. And suddenly the room filled with water, and snow carpeted the tatami like bellflowers blooming whitely at the water's edge.

No doubt for some this ending comes too quickly. But to say that we have not been prepared for it is to expose our expectation for a more mediated (rigorously modern) kind of narrative that consistently keeps the past out of the present. Kyōka's ghost story, like many other ghost stories, does not lock the specter in perfected time. Consequently, there is no peace for Isaku, nor for Sakai, who must also quake with fear. Furthermore, what guarantees do we have that the same horror will not break through the narrative stratum and threaten the writer himself? And isn't the reader, too, vulnerable in this collapsing of the mediating, re-presenting Real? Here, along with those distancing, protecting, and empowering narrative conventions of past-tense third-person, with which we have now become overly familiar, past deeds have undermined and eaten away time-in-the-present. As this happens, we are left to entertain the possibility that the (modern) present is perishable and that our safety within it is the fantasy. We lose the finality of the past. We lose history as a form of truth. We lose fiction as fiction. There is no escaping what has happened. We are truly haunted.

If it is true that psychoanalysis attempts to revisit the traumatic past in order to stabilize the present, and if it is also true that history performs a similar kind of justification through redescribing the past in order to understand the present, then we must ask what is to be gained in a world where past traumas can become present in such a direct, unmediated form. At least for Kyōka, the "fantasy" of past-in-the-present assumes the ritualistic, even shamanistic, function of

Charles Shirō Inouye

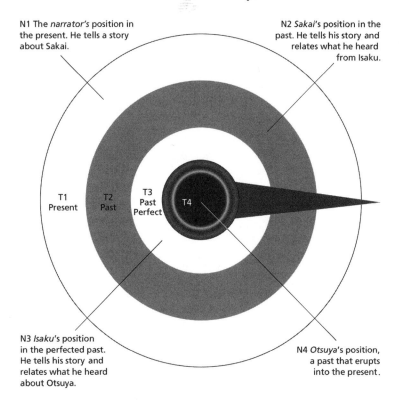

N1 The *narrator's* position in the present. He tells a story about Sakai.

N2 *Sakai's* position in the past. He tells his story and relates what he heard from Isaku.

T1 Present

T2 Past

T3 Past Perfect

T4

N3 *Isaku's* position in the perfected past. He tells his story and relates what he heard about Otsuya.

N4 *Otsuya's* position, a past that erupts into the present.

Figure 1. The Narrative Structure of a Ghost Story (Time [T]) and Narrative Position [N]). Otsuya is dead but cannot be contained in the past. In the ghost story, the supposedly perfected past erupts into the present. This tendency to destroy temporal barriers is intimated on every level of narration, appearing as hearsay and the retelling of past events.

recovering (not simply remembering) the dead. For reasons that are made clearer to us by the final story in this collection, "The Heart-vine," Kyōka was haunted by death—his mother's, his father's, his grandmother's, his younger brother's, his own—in ways that required the immediate recovery that only nonrealistic, nonpsychological literary visitation could provide.

Essays

"The Heartvine"

"The Heartvine" (Rukōshinsō, 1939) was Kyōka's last story, published just two months before his death. When he began writing the manuscript, he was already suffering from lung cancer and was probably aware that this would be his last project. I have included it in this collection both because of its strength as a story and because it is key to an evaluation of the author's lifetime contribution. My desire to translate it into English came many years ago, when I had the opportunity to study the manuscript in the treasure room of the new Keio University library. The life-and-death struggle visible on those pages —long passages blacked out and weakly yet persistently rewritten again and again—compelled me to introduce this fruit of the author's final passion to English readers. This is a story that Kyōka knew he had to get right. This is his final testament.

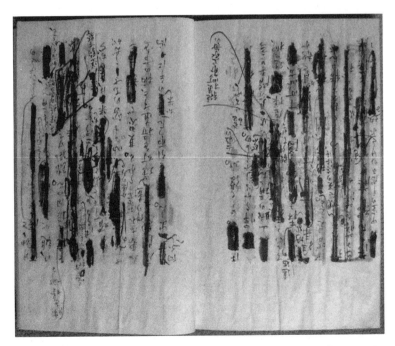

Figure 2. Blackened manuscript pages of "The Heartvine" express Kyōka's agonized desire to get the story right one last time.

The "Heartvine" is set in Kanazawa, Kyōka's hometown and a place about which he had decidedly mixed feelings. Kanazawa is a provincial capital and former castle town on the coast facing Korea. He left it in 1890, when he was seventeen, to pursue a literary career in Tokyo. His plan was to apprentice under Ozaki Kōyō, then one of two or three leading literary stars of the day; and although it took Kyōka nearly a year before he had the courage to meet Kōyō and become his student, he went on to become the master's most devoted (and eventually his most famous) protégé. Kyōka disliked the provincial snobbery of Kanazawa and never intended to live there again once he had made his escape, even though it was impossible to break the hold that the place continued to have on his imagination. When his father died in 1894 and he was forced to return to Kanazawa, he did so with great reluctance.

Kyōka was the oldest son of the Izumi household and therefore responsible for his family's welfare. Suddenly saddled with great financial responsibility, he felt crushed, as if his future as a writer had been cut short by misfortune. Despondent, even suicidal, he received encouragement from Kōyō, who was famous for the concern he extended to his students. Kyōka's dedicated mentor sensed the danger and sent him the following letter.

> because of your lack of courage, your heart is like wind-blown hemp. Because your life is difficult, you have been enticed by the allure of death, like a poppy frightened by the demons of the moat. Your heart is as weak as a reed. What does it matter that your poverty is miserable? When you came into this world, you weren't surrounded by walls of carved wood and curtains of brocade.
>
> To be born amid crumbling walls in a ramshackle house, to chew bread and drink water, is this not heaven? Enjoy that heaven! A great poet is one whose soul is like a diamond. Fire cannot burn it, water cannot drown it, no sword can pierce it, no cudgel can smash it. How much less, then, can it be damaged by hunger for a bowl of rice![14]

We do not know all the details, but Kyōka seems to have done more than just think about the possibility of suicide. He wrote about the temptation to throw himself into the Kanazawa Castle moat in a drafted story, "The Night Bell Tolls" (Shōsei yahanroku,

Essays

1895); and it was this manuscript that prompted Kōyō to write the letter partially quoted above. Many years later, long after Kōyō's death and just prior to his own demise, Kyōka revisited that difficult time in "The Heartvine."

> Before his very eyes, Tsujimachi saw a woman walking down the slope. She was only twenty years old on the night she threw herself into the Thousand Wing Abyss. . . . By gallantly leaping into the water, she died a noble death. Unlike her, he—the young man standing at the edge of the black water—was nothing but a coward. He went on living, shamelessly. And now he was an old man, the very one who had stopped to rest halfway up the stone steps at the Senshō Temple.

"The Night Bell Tolls" and "The Heartvine" address this same event: Kyōka's actual trip to the moat, where he was shocked back to life by the sight of a young woman throwing herself into the water before he could end his own life. We know that the moat surrounding the Kanazawa Castle was a famous spot for suicides. In 1894 alone, nine people took their lives there, including a young woman who might have been the model for Yoshikura Sachi in "The Night Bell Tolls" and for Hatsuji in "The Heartvine." An article from Kanazawa's *Northern Reporter (Hokkoku shinbun),* dated April 16, 1894, gives the following account.

Suicide at the Castle Moat

> Yesterday at about ten in the morning, a body was discovered floating in the Kanazawa Castle Moat. It was immediately reported to the West Kanazawa Police Headquarters, and . . . the corpse was retrieved and an autopsy performed. Pathologists determined that the woman was eighteen or nineteen years old. Although her address and name is unknown, from appearances she was either a prostitute or a serving girl at an eating establishment. To avoid unbecoming exposure, she had tied the skirts of her kimono to her legs with string. According to regulations, the corpse was buried in a temporary grave on Mount Utatsu.

A follow-up article appears in the same local newspaper:

Charles Shirō Inouye

Young Beauty Throws Herself in Moat, Family Background

The young beauty who threw herself into the Kanazawa Castle Moat was Yuki (nineteen years old), daughter of Yoshimura Matsutarō, resident of Yokoyasue-chō 84 Banchi. She was employed as a head worker at a local sewing factory, and was noted for her skillful work. . . . Recently, she was ordered by her employer to fill an order for a customer. She worked diligently to produce the work, but her employer found it unacceptable. . . . Yuki, usually reserved in all she did, felt compelled to do the work over again. Her employer did not care for the results of this second attempt either. . . . On the night of the 14th, she left her home, saying she was going to pray at the Kaji Hachiman Shrine, and killed herself.[15]

We do not know if Kyōka actually witnessed this woman's suicide. It is possible that he was there at the water's edge, ready to throw himself in; but we cannot say with perfect certainty. A second, slightly different version of what transpired on that night comes to us from Kanbara Enkō, the son of Meboso Teru, who is the model for Okyō in "The Heartvine." According to his account, Teru awoke to discover that the door was open and that Kyōka, her cousin, was not in his bed. She told her son that she immediately ran out into the night, and made her way to the castle moat, where she found Kyōka about to jump. "Had I not run after him, we would have lost him."[16]

In either case, whether it was Yoshimura Yuki or Meboso Teru (or both) who played the role of saving angel, the effect of this event had profound consequences for Kyōka's vision as a writer. Saved by a young woman, Kyōka melded the image of women like her—young, beautiful, artistic, and misunderstood by the coarse people around them who could never understand their refinement—with that of his dead mother. Desolated by her death, he went on to spend the rest of his life trying to recapture her by way of this literary creation: a woman who was eternally young and beautiful, both a temptress and a mother, a bringer of salvation. Thus, we understand this story's ties both to Omie, the suffering savior figure in *A Song by Lantern Light,* and to the mechanism of recovering the dead by bringing the past into the present, as evidenced in "A Quiet Obsession." Kyōka wanted his beautiful young mother to be alive and with him again. In memory of his mother, whose family temple was the Renshōji, the setting for this story, he memorialized Yoshimura Yuki and also Meboso Teru, who provided comfort and guidance during his crisis in Kanazawa and throughout his adult life. They were there in place of his missing mother. This final story honors them all.

As a journey toward death, this is yet another narrative of trespass. A movement away from life is expressed by the path Tsujimachi and Oyone must take to proceed upward and away from the city in order to reach the lonely graves of Okyō and Hatsuji on Mount Utatsu. As already mentioned, water is an important marker of this journey. By the beginning of the story, Tsujimachi and Oyone have already crossed over to the north bank of the Asano River, the border that demarcates the ordered and civilized space of the city from the far-bank territory of the dead, the erotic, and the dispossessed. Although not described precisely as it now exists, the Renshōji, located on Mount Utatsu not far from the Eastern Brothel, provides the setting for this encounter with dragonfly spirits. In order to do this translation, I personally visited the temple a number of times over several years. Covered over by a canopy of thick woods, the flight of steps to the graveyard behind the main temple is broken-down and difficult to climb. Today, the graves are moss-covered and largely forgotten. Worn smooth by centuries of rain and snow, they are strung with spiderwebs and are home to enormous centipedes, swarms of mosquitoes, and butterflies of startling colors and sizes. In the summer, the trees drone with the cries of cicadas. In the winter, the hillside is quiet and still.

As this shadowy world itself progresses from late afternoon to night, Oyone, "slender and graceful from head to toe," leads the elderly Tsujimachi both closer to his own death (in the present) and to that night when he nearly took his life (in the past). The erotic tension that ebbs and flows between them is indirectly expressed by the lantern he has brought—white, luminous, rounded. The lantern expresses many things: the beauty of a young woman's body; the whiteness of skin; the luminosity of the moon, an important Buddhist symbol of enlightenment. It is also a token of Tsujimachi's life, almost carelessly purchased. Without specific meaning, its whiteness, finally inscribed with dragonfly images by way of Oyone's red-dipped brush, takes on traditional significance as a sign of final offering.

The erotic tension of "The Heartvine" is similarly expressed by the naked "skin" of Hatsuji's grave, which is manhandled by the workers, and finally clothed with the unselfish offering of Oyone's coat. We are told that Oyone's mother, even more gallant, would have given all her clothing if necessary; and the possibility of her nakedness expresses a familial kind of surface that reminds us of earlier heroines. Oyone, Okyō, and Hatsuji are the last in a long line. They belong to that order of alluring yet self-sacrificing maternal women who have had to suffer in Kyōka's place. His career as a writer, indeed his very life, depended on them—on both their beauty and their willingness to suffer.

Typically, they have been beyond reach. Like the reflection of a flower in a mirror, these women have been powerfully unattainable —attractive yet sexually unavailable. For a few years before this final story, the author departed from the usual formula, giving his men an actual, carnal desire for women. As a result, the narrative patterns that had sustained him and given structure to his words for so long finally broke down. But here, as a final gesture and with his last bit of energy as an artist, he returns to the archetype one last time.

We are made aware of erotic possibilities as we are made aware of the grave. But there is an important difference that sets this story apart from those which came before. Here, with death beckoning, we encounter maturity, an appreciation that comes from Tsujimachi's awareness of his culpability as an artist.

Tsujimachi was moved by Oyone's compassion. He offered to help her put on the jacket. "Here. Turn this way."

"Tsujimachi-san. Are you sure it's all right?"

"You're here as your mother's proxy. How could there be anything wrong helping an old friend's daughter with her coat?"

"I suppose it's all right."

When she turned toward him, her hair brushed against his chest. To his surprise, he felt a chill run through his body.

Essays

"I miss my . . . mother."

Tsujimachi had had some professional dealings with the theater and the making of movies. A moment ago, he had been thinking that he could take a scene like this and exploit it for profit. It was an evil thought that secretly sprouted in his heart. But this time there was no allure, no desire. Tears came to his eyes.

Why these tears? Is Tsujimachi looking nostalgically back on a long career, or ahead to the imminent visitation of death? Are they tears of gratitude? Of disappointment? Of enlightenment? Whether teleological or terminal, the end of allure and desire is clear. The fearful Kyōka spent his life in pursuit, escaping death through art in order to live (and temporarily die) to be with that which he loved. Here in this story, we feel a somber, and even grateful, assessment of the price that has been paid. In short, "The Heartvine" is a story of a writer ready to die. That being so, what does this apology say about the ability of art to sustain life? If literature can in some real sense be sustaining, what is this narrative mechanism of desire that is compelling enough to make life continue?

The climactic glory of "The Heartvine" lies in the peaceful reality of Oyone's beauty, in the color of fall leaves, and in the remembrance of great weakness as contrasted with the unforgettable profusion of glistening wings moving across a stratum of urban sky. Kyōka's description of the vitality of dragonflies is remarkable, a worthy subject for Miyazaki Hayao's animated visions of flight.

> Everywhere I went, the city was full of them—as high as the rooftops, above and below, left and right, vertical and horizontal, like a blizzard of cherry blossoms floating in a shining pale-crimson rain, wings translucent, bodies red, a flood of dragonflies spilling over everywhere, not running into each other or dancing wildly in a maelstrom, but flying diagonally toward the sky, diagonally toward the ground, diagonally right, and diagonally left, all of them flying in unison to the north, perhaps to Asakusa, or Senju, and beyond? It was almost beyond my ability to imagine. A bioluminescence at Akashi-chō, right in the middle of the day! A reflection of the Sumida River in midair!
>
> "Once I was finished in Akashi-chō, I hurried off to Akasaka.

And there they were again, flying everywhere—masses of dragonflies. I got to my dentist's office and sat down in the seat. They were flying outside the window, seeming to thin out a bit. Even so, I'm not talking about just a thousand or two thousand. They came up to the dentist's second-floor window, about to the eaves of the house across the street, flying at about the level of the telephone wires—not much higher than that, nor much lower. Each of them filled the same layer of the sky. Passing by in countless numbers, their stratum was neither very thick nor very dense, more like a thin translucence, the fluttering wings of each insect.

"To my eyes, the low sky of Tokyo was a light crimson covered with coarsely woven silk and wrapped in a silver mist. The taller buildings and wooded hills looked like rocky islands sticking out above the white waves that were wrapped in the colors of the setting sun.

"'A lot of dragonflies out today,' I finally had to say.

"'It's been that way since early this morning,' my dentist replied.

The sexual vitality of these Odonata, strong enough to lift a taxi from the streets, is both compelling and, as Tsujimachi hopes to establish, natural. They are not flying one by one, but in mated pairs. They are unclothed and unembarrassed. Their seasonal regularity is comforting, brazen proof that life goes on.

One gift we receive from Kyōka's long and impassioned pursuit of salvation, then, especially as it is capped with this final moment of humility, is an awareness of all those things that can take life away, even as we are living it. We are envious of the talents of others. In our desire to be counted among the acceptable, we fear what a truly lived life would be. We easily forget those who have paid a price for our survival. We are quick to condemn and crassly exploit the forces that make life compelling—the desire to create, to enjoy pleasure and beauty, to appreciate and be appreciated. As a member of a war-mongering society, one that in the 1930s disastrously devolved into the truly monstrous "ten thousand hearts beating as one," Kyōka's own tortured heart declared simpler, quixotic truths. There is some worth in his world of lanterns and shadows. The pursuit of the dead is as beautiful as it is sorrowful.

Essays

Tsujimachi looked out over the darkened castle town lying below. Flickering through the willow trees, the lights of the city flowed upon the surface of the river. Stepping down the long flight of steps, he and Oyone descended into the valley of darkness. The lights of the slums on this side of the river had yet to appear.

A tofu peddler making his way home in the dark, stopped suddenly, as if to avoid a collision.

"Look. Dragonflies!"

Oyone immediately fell to her knees and pressed her hands together in prayer.

The paper lantern that Tsujimachi had hung on the handle of Hatsuji's monument, where the gravestone now rested, passed through the temple gate and slowly rose into the night sky. On a single gust of wind that blew down from the mountain, two dragonflies quietly stirred, and the images of two women appeared.

With his last bit of remaining energy, Kyōka paid homage to those who had sustained him. Without our ancestors and other noble ones who have acted on our behalf, we would not be here. Like us, they had their time to live and to sacrifice. Like them, we will soon pass on. Life is full of sorrows, beginnings that lead to endings. Yet if the dead dwell beyond us, on the far side of the river, they are made present by those like Izumi Kyōka who, in fearful transgression, dared to write about the shadows of day and the lanterns of night.

Notes

1. The earliest sustained treatment of the cinematic features of the story can be found in Izawa Atsushi, "Uta andon ni okeru eigateki hyō-gen" (Cinematic expressions in *A Song by Lantern Light*) in *Kokubungaku shiryō to kanshō*, no. 156 (May 1949): 80–82.

2. The tragic sense of this story is lost in Naruse Mikio's 1943 film adaptation. Following Kubota Mantarō's screenplay, Naruse gives us an ending that could not be happier. Kidahachi is forgiven. He performs side by side with his adoptive father as Omie dances.

Charles Shirō Inouye

3. For a discussion of love during this transitional period, see Saeki Junko, *Iro to ai no hikakubunka shi* (A comparative cultural history of lust and love) (Tokyo: Iwanami shoten, 1998).

4. Itō Sei, "Kindai Nihon bungaku ni okeru 'ai' no kyogi" (The falsehood of love in modern Japanese literature), in *Itō Sei zenshū* (Tokyo: Shinchōsha, 1973), 18:260–268.

5. For a nuanced rumination of the meaning of suicide in service to one's lord, see Mori Ōgai's famous story "The Abe Family" (Abe ichizoku), in David Dilworth and J. Thomas Rimer, eds., *The Historical Fiction of Mori Ōgai* (Honolulu: University of Hawai'i Press, 1991), 67–99.

6. Reasserting the superiority of Confucian hierarchy, Yūkoku wrote: "Unless the names of 'ruler' and 'subject' are rectified, the statuses of high and low will not be strictly adhered to. The noble will become the base and the base will become the noble, the exalted and despised will lose their respective places in society, the strong will overpower the weak, the many will oppress the few, and the day of doom will be near at hand." Bob Wakabayashi, *Anti-Foreignism and Western Learning in Early-Modern Japan: The New Thesis of 1825* (Cambridge, Mass.: Harvard University Press, 1986), 52.

7. Tanizaki Jun'ichirō, "Junsui ni 'Nihonteki' na 'Kyōka sekai'" (The purely Japanese world of Izumi Kyōka), *Tanizaki Jun'ichirō zenshū* (Tokyo: Chūō kōron sha, 1968) 22:336–338.

8. A similar sense of belonging and being certainly obtains within feudal or tribal societies as well. However, in a modern world one's territory is greatly expanded—from domain to nation, for instance—and the notion of one's independence as an agent is heightened in relationship to generalized principles that theoretically apply to all people—for example, citizenship, human rights, and so forth.

9. For the use of *manga* during the Second World War, see John Dower, *War without Mercy: Race and Power in the Pacific War* (New York: Pantheon Books, 1986).

10. Nanette Twine, trans., "The Essence of the Novel," *Occasional Papers, Department of Japanese, University of Queensland*, no. 11 (1981): 24.

11. Tayama Katai, *Kindai no shōsetsu* (The modern novel) (Tokyo: Daitō shuppansha, 1941), 96.

12. For this analysis, I am expanding a reading first put forward by Noguchi Takehiko, "Mushibamareta genzaichi" (The worm-eaten present), in *Nippon kindai hihyō no anguru* (Tokyo: Seidōsha, 1992), 95–108.

13. Shifting to third-person interiority in many Japanese novels is subtle indeed—perhaps too subtle to be marked by the first-person pronoun.

14. Reproduced in Muramatsu Sadataka, *Izumi Kyōka* (Tokyo: Bunsendō, 1966), 85–86.

15. The articles are reproduced in Takakuwa Noriko, "Ikai to gensō," *Kokubungaku kaishaku to kyōzai no kenkyū*, June 1990, 106.

16. Kobayashi Teruya, who interviewed Kanbara, has not yet written this information down. He was kind enough to relate it to me at his home in Kanazawa on February 18, 1996.

About the Translator

Charles Shirō Inouye is associate professor of Japanese at Tufts University. His *Similitude of Blossoms: A Critical Biography of Izumi Kyōka* (1998) was the first English-language monograph to be published on Kyōka, and an earlier volume of Kyōka translations appeared as *Japanese Gothic Tales* (1996). He was formerly dean of the Colleges for Undergraduate Education at Tufts.